LORD FENTON'S
FOLLY

OTHER BOOKS BY
JOSI S. KILPACK

The Sadie Hoffmiller Culinary Mystery Series:
Lemon Tart, English Trifle, Devil's Food Cake, Key Lime Pie,
Blackberry Crumble, Pumpkin Roll, Banana Split,
Tres Leches Cupcakes, Baked Alaska, Rocky Road, Fortune Cookie,
Wedding Cake, Sadie's Little Black Recipe Book

OTHER PROPER ROMANCE NOVELS

A Heart Revealed by Josi S. Kilpack

Edenbrooke by Julianne Donaldson

Blackmoore by Julianne Donaldson

Longing for Home by Sarah M. Eden

Longing for Home, vol. 2: Hope Springs by Sarah M. Eden

LORD FENTON'S FOLLY

A PROPER ROMANCE

JOSI S. KILPACK

SHADOW
MOUNTAIN

Library of Congress Cataloging-in-Publication Data

Kilpack, Josi S., author.

Lord Fenton's folly / Josi S. Kilpack.

pages cm

Summary: "Lord Fenton and Alice Stanbridge's marriage is one of convenience for him, but one of love for her. When Alice realizes the truth, she matches Fenton wit for wit until they both learn to see the truth of each other's hearts and find love beyond the folly"—Provided by publisher.

ISBN 978-1-62972-066-1 (paperbound)

I. Title.

PS3561.I412L67 2015

813'.54—dc23   2015004828

Printed in the United States of America

Publishers Printing, Salt Lake City, UT

10   9   8   7   6   5   4   3   2   1

For Linda
1948–2013

CHAPTER 1

Lord Fenton—Charles Archibald Theler—moved his adolescent arms and legs as fast as they could go toward the small shed just past the tree line, not sure if he was running more from the fire or from someone's notice of his proximity to the scene. Either source catching up with him would not bode well.

Fenton reached the doorway—the door having fallen off its hinges some years before—and grabbed hold of the aging wood frame. Graying daylight showed through the gaps in the shed walls. He spun around, pushed his sweat-damp hair from his forehead and looked first at the skies and then at the white smoke rising from the field he'd just evacuated. The dry grass had turned to flames faster than he'd expected, blackening like oil spilled from a container, until the fire had leaped up and begun running in multiple directions. It had reminded him of how an army might fan out to face the enemy on every side. A full fifteen feet had already burned before he realized he ought to make a run for it, even if it meant being unable to survey his handiwork.

Safe in the doorway of the shed, he was equal parts afraid and amazed at what he had done. If the fire kept growing, however, the fear would surely take over. It had never been his intention for more than the meadow grass to burn.

"Come on," he said, through his labored breaths. He looked at the sky in supplication. What if the entire wood caught fire? What if, despite his careful planning, someone got hurt? "Come on!" he said again, pleading this time.

A moment later his wish was granted as the skies burst open and the rain with which England was so well acquainted poured from the sky. None of the drizzly sprinkles that were often the only weather in Town—no, this was a torrent. The first significant storm Essex County had seen in almost a month.

His father and Mr. Stanbridge had talked of the unusually dry season every evening of this blasted week. It was through those conversations that sixteen-year-old Fenton, on break from Eton and bored stiff at Mr. Stanbridge's country estate, had come up with what some might call mischief but he preferred to think of as science. Scientific discovery always began with a question in need of answering. Answers like gravity and tides being linked to the phases of the moon had changed the world because someone thought to ask how a thing worked.

Fenton's question was how well a meadow—four weeks without rain—would burn. The science master might not see the merit in such a question, but as the days of the house party drew out, Fenton found himself more and more curious. Would the grass simply smolder? England was such a wet place even when it wasn't raining every day. Or would it all go up in a giant rush of fire? After coming up with what felt like a foolproof plan, he had executed the steps and what a wonder it had been!

"Did you start that fire?"

"Good grief!" Fenton said as he spun around and pressed his back against the doorway, his heart racing all over again. When he saw that the voice addressing him belonged to a girl sitting on an overturned bucket, he relaxed some. But not much. He recognized the youngest daughter of Mr. Stanbridge himself: Alice. If she reported what she'd seen to her father, Fenton would really be in the suds. Fortunately, Fenton had recently discovered he could be quite charming when he put his mind to it, especially with the ladies, and as she was a small lady he felt sure he could charm her too.

He forced a smile to cover whatever expression of surprise might have made way onto his face, and relaxed as the rain continued to pound outside the shed. Water was beginning to drip from the rafters as well, but not so profusely that he was concerned.

"What fire?" He waved toward the doorway, where the only thing to be seen was sheeting rain, and ignored the smell of wet charcoal in the air. He slipped the tinderbox he had stolen from the library mantel into the back of his waistband and immediately felt it fall to the leg of his breeches tucked into his boots. "I did, however, start the rain, if you must know."

"God made the rain," Alice said. She stared up at him with hazel eyes set into a round face. Was she eight or nine years old? She didn't often join the guests for the different activities that Fenton found so dull.

"Did He now?" Fenton said, trying to determine how to best gain her trust. "But perhaps I told Him to make it. I am a viscount you know, and one day I will be an earl. Noblemen rule the world."

Her eyes went wide, though he was unsure whether it was because of the possibility of his statement or the blasphemy of it. Was she particularly pious? That might work against him.

"Noblemen *assist* in the rule of England, but we are still a monarchy," Alice said with shaky confidence. "King Fernando rules Spain again, and a president rules America, which is a republic. No one rules the *world* except God, and no one tells Him what to do." She stood up and brushed off her skirts that ended a few inches above her ankle. She was thin and small and dressed in a blue frock, with skin too brown and spots across her nose that testified to the probability that she regularly escaped the house without a bonnet. She walked to the doorway of the shed and looked out on the scene, staying as far from him as she could. The rain was easing, but only just. She looked at the burnt portion of the meadow, then looked up at him—he was at least a foot taller than she was. "You're lucky God decided to douse your fire, otherwise you'd have burned me up and gone right to hell."

He couldn't help but laugh when she smiled at her own joke, and he felt confident this conversation was ultimately going to work in his favor. "Well, I am lucky indeed, then," Fenton said with an acknowledging nod of his head. "Only I might end up in purgatory all the same if my father learns what I did. It *was* calculated, you know. I've been watching the skies for days and this storm was sweeping to the west fast enough for me to time its arrival nearly to the minute based on the proximity of the clouds and distance of the thunder." He lifted the watch attached to his waistcoat as though to prove his diligence.

She looked at the watch then back at the rain-soaked field. Without the fire and smoke the black space was not so impressive. "You still could have burned me up."

"Or you could have run away. What are you doing in this shed so far from the house anyway?"

Her expression fell into a pouty frown. "Everyone's leaving for London except me. I hate it when they go."

Fenton searched for something frivolous to say but it was not so long ago he had been in this girl's same position, and he could not ignore the empathy. "I used to hate it when they left me too," he said, remembering how he would stand at the nursery window and watch his parents' carriage disappear down the lane. Father was stoic at the parting, maybe even eager, but his mother always cried when she left him, fairly smothering him with hugs and kisses and apologies before Father insisted they get on their way. "I always wondered why she left at all when she seemed to feel bad for doing so."

"Who is 'she'? Your sister?"

Fenton hadn't realized he'd said the last part out loud and shook himself back to the present. "I meant my mother." Sharing made him uncomfortable. Perhaps because it was so personal—not anything like what he had ever said to anyone else. Lady Chariton had insisted her son be educated at home until three years ago when Fenton's father had demanded he go to Eton. Fenton did not like school, but he would never admit that the biggest reason for his dislike was because he missed his mother so much.

"I have two sisters and a father to leave me," Alice said, looking out the doorway again. "But no mother."

Fenton wondered if he should point out the coy glances he'd noticed being shared between her father and the widowed Lady Foust but decided not to. He had not forgotten what he'd seen when he returned from school last week, a day earlier than expected, and wished he could forget altogether the exchange he'd witnessed between his father and a housemaid. Wished he could forget the additional clarity it brought to mind of other incidents of women being where they ought not be, of his father's attention to women that seemed kinder than was his nature. More than that, however, Fenton wished he could forget his mother's face when he'd told her of what he'd seen. It had seemed the obvious thing to do—ask for his mother's help in understanding what he'd witnessed—but it had hurt her. He'd seen his words cut through her like a blade and hated himself for it.

Alice took a deep breath and let it out, saving Fenton from his thoughts. "Everyone will go to London next week. I've never been left at Warren House without anyone at all." She paused and let out a huff of breath. "Everyone treats me like a baby only because I'm the youngest. I'll be eleven just after Guy Fawkes, you know."

"Which makes you ten and a half."

She narrowed her eyes, and he smiled at the honesty of her reaction.

"What you need is to think of something you can do while they are gone. If you keep your mind occupied, you shan't find yourself in the doldrums."

"Like starting fires?"

Fenton laughed again. It was proving difficult to find the upper hand in this conversation. "I would not recommend that, like I said it was a scientific experiment based on unique circumstance and not one to try again. Do you like to read?"

"They only let me read baby books."

"Factor numbers?"

"No."

"Ride ponies?"

"Horses make me sneeze and itch."

Fenton searched his mind for what other pursuits a young girl might occupy herself with while wondering why he was having this ridiculous conversation. And yet he needed to gain her friendship so she wouldn't give him away regarding the fire. "Do you like to sew?"

Alice's eyes narrowed even more. "I do not like to sew or sing or play the pianoforte. I don't like to draw or play with blocks or write my letters."

"Well, then, what *do* you like to do?"

She considered for a moment, her eyebrows pulled together. Then her expression relaxed. "I like to dig."

"Dig? You mean dig in the earth?"

She nodded. "And swim."

"Swim?" Fenton repeated. Whoever heard of a girl swimming?

"And run," she said finally, a smile tugging at the corner of her mouth. "Maybe I will run after the carriage all the way to London."

"You are a peculiar girl." Fenton looked over the trees to the upper floor of Warren House in the distance. He needed to return to his room soon if he hoped to keep the ruse that he'd been taking a nap when the fire had started.

"I know," she said with a sigh. "That's what everyone says. Sometimes I'm too silly, sometimes I'm too harsh. I can never seem to get it right."

"There's nothing *wrong* with being peculiar," Fenton said. He had his own peculiarities and he quite liked them—more and more with time. Playing out a role of one kind or another made him feel more secure somehow. Protected, though he was unsure what he felt he needed protection from exactly. "I'd like to make you a deal, Miss Alice."

"What kind of deal?" Alice asked with suspicion as she turned her attention to him.

"Well, even though God and I worked it out for the rain to

remedy my fire experiment—" She narrowed her eyes and he hurried forward so as not to be chastised again. "It would put me quite in the suds with my father if he knew I'd been a part of it. You're not a tattler, are you?"

"You're only saying that so that I'll be so ashamed to be one that I'll keep your secret."

Fenton was trying to find another approach when she spoke. "What do I get if I keep your secret?"

"What do you *get*?"

"You're trying to bargain with me—I have two older sisters. I know what a bargain is, and I know how to keep a secret. What would I get for my part?"

"Um, a sweet?"

Those eyes narrowed again.

"A new pair of slippers. My mother's cobbler could . . ."

She wrinkled her nose.

"Okay, then, what do you suggest?"

She pondered for a short while, then looked at him with a continued doubting expression that spurred him to want very much to fulfill whatever wish she had if only to be worthy of a better regard in the future. "I want my very own garden."

"What?"

Suddenly Alice was quite animated. "I want my own garden where I can dig and plant whatever I want and my governess cannot get angry at me. I want it all my own—no cook, no gardener, no one to tell me what to do with it or what to grow in it. Can you give me that?"

How on earth could I give her such a thing? Fenton wondered, but then he thought a little more and wondered if it would be that difficult. "You'll keep my secret?"

She nodded and he believed her.

"Has anyone told you that you can't have a garden? It would be unfair to send me on a fool's errand."

"Cook doesn't let me in her garden after what I did to the rosemary. Father said he would see to a spot of my own, but that was months ago and now he is leaving for London and told me not to pester him anymore." She dropped her chin in a way very similar to a professor Fenton once had and gave him a stern look. "There is much work to be done in a garden, you know. It would keep my mind occupied, just as you recommended."

"Then I shall see that you get a garden."

She smiled. A real smile that showed a slight gap between her large front teeth and lit up her face to the degree that he thought—just for a moment—perhaps she would grow up pretty one day. He put out his hand. "We have to shake hands, that's giving our word to one another—gentleman to lady."

Alice took his hand and gave it one good shake before pulling it away and wiping it on the side of her dress as though eager to be free of his touch.

"And now I must make a run for it," Fenton said. "I'm afraid I haven't time to continue this discussion."

"But you'll see that I get my garden?"

"And you'll see that my father doesn't flog me for having set that perfectly planned fire?"

She nodded. He gave a sharp nod in return and then dashed out of the shed. There was a path skirting the trees to the north that he could use to approach the house, then it was simply the matter of

climbing the trellis, slipping back inside the bedroom window, stash-
ing his wet clothes, and pretending to have slept the afternoon away
until this raging storm quite woke him from his nap. Oh, and figure
out how to get this girl a garden all her own.

CHAPTER 2

Alice Stanbridge had, until that Tuesday, March 11—she wrote it in her diary to make sure she didn't forget—only known Lord Fenton as the funny young man with straw-colored hair who visited the family estate each spring prior to her family leaving for London. Papa always had a big house party—he called it the first event of the season, but Alice knew the season counted only if you were in London, Bath, or Brighton. Lord Fenton was always included in this house party along with his parents, Lord and Lady Chariton. Alice was deemed too young for the events that catered to their guests, and was too nervous to sing or perform as an excuse to be among them, so her interactions with Lord Fenton were reserved for a few picnics and . . . one grass fire.

After her exchange with Lord Fenton, however, she found every excuse she could think of to make herself seen. She insisted on taking breakfast with their guests, even though she usually ate in the nursery. She volunteered to turn Chloe's sheet music in order to be in the drawing room in the evening, when usually she was content with her own company. She even agreed to sing with her sisters, though she kept her voice small so as not to throw them off—she'd been told by Rebecca that she had horrible pitch and mixed the rest of them up.

Each time she concocted a new opportunity to be in the midst of company with Lord Fenton, she watched him like a hawk. Sometimes he would catch her eye and smile, other times he looked uncomfortable beneath her attention. She didn't care that her focus made him shifty. In her experience, most grown-ups forgot promises they made to children. But Lord Fenton wasn't really a grown-up; he was only one year older than Chloe. Maybe he still remembered what it felt like to be at the mercy of adults. She dearly wanted a garden and though not having one would not leave her any worse than she was already, her hope kept her quite focused on its procurement. If anyone could arrange a garden for her, Lord Fenton could. That was what she kept telling herself; that was why she kept her eye on him every chance possible.

As the days of the party continued and no garden arrived, Alice began considering her options for reminding Lord Fenton of his promise. Unfortunately she had very few possibilities to pursue. She was only ten-and-a-half years old, she was kept apart from the guests, and although she knew she could tell on him regarding the fire, she didn't want to. He was nice and he'd talked to her in the shed that day as though she mattered.

Finally, on Tuesday, there was a knock at the nursery door. The governess got up from the table where she had been coaching Alice through a letter to her grandmother and opened the door.

"Oh, hello, Lord Fenton," Miss Granger said in that same giggly kind of voice Chloe used when she talked to young men.

Alice was standing beside Miss Granger before Fenton responded.

"Good afternoon, Miss Granger." He bowed slightly at the waist, then winked at Alice as he straightened. She felt a smile stretch across her face and could scarcely keep her feet in place. Fenton addressed the governess. "I wonder if I might borrow Miss Alice for an hour or so."

"Oh, well, I'll have to talk with Mr. Stanbr—"

Alice burst forward like a ball from one of her father's guns. She grabbed Lord Fenton's hand and ran down the hall while calling over her shoulder, "It is fine, Miss Granger. Didn't Papa tell you Lord Fenton was coming for me?" She ran as fast as she could, grateful that Lord Fenton didn't try to stop her. Somehow, she'd known he wouldn't.

Only when they reached the stairs did Lord Fenton tug on her arm, pulling her to a stop. She looked at him in frustration. "You have my garden, don't you?"

For a moment his face was thoughtful, but then a wide smile popped his cheeks out and made his blue eyes twinkle. "I do, but we must leave with a bit more decorum or they shall think we are up to something."

Aren't we up to something? Alice thought. But she nodded and took the stairs at a much more proper pace. A footman was waiting at the back entrance and when Lord Fenton nodded toward the man, Alice realized he'd been asked to chaperone. It wasn't until they were a few yards from the house—the footman keeping a discreet distance—that Lord Fenton spoke again.

"I want you to know this was not an easy task you set for me," he said, looking at her pointedly and lifting an eyebrow. "I had to speak with any number of servants and then your father and then the servants again."

"But they didn't say no to you, did they, Lord Fenton?" Alice broke in, unable to contain her excitement. "That's because you're going to be an earl one day and Chloe will be a countess and so they want you to be *real* comfortable during your stay and make sure that if ever there's a carriage ride, Chloe is seated as close to you as can be considered proper. I knew they would let you give me a garden. I knew it!"

She stopped jabbering when she realized Lord Fenton wasn't walking beside her any longer. He was several paces behind her and with a huff of frustration she went back to him, grabbed his arm with both hands, and dragged him forward. She thought he looked a little shocked, but she couldn't imagine why. He'd surely seen this garden. She was the one who had yet to lay eyes on it.

"Chloe is fifteen years old," Lord Fenton said in a dry tone.

Alice looked up at him. "So?"

"I am only sixteen years old!"

"Soon to be seventeen," Alice corrected.

Lord Fenton stopped again, forcing her to stop as well, and looked down at her. "How do you know that?"

"Do you honestly think my sisters talk of anything else? Never mind Papa." She rolled her eyes, knowing her anticipation of the garden was causing her to be terribly informal with Lord Fenton. But she couldn't help it. She was ten, no matter how hard she tried to act like her older sisters sometimes, and she had a present waiting for her if she could only get Lord Fenton to move.

"Am I expected to make a . . . a match with Chloe?"

"Of course," Alice said, throwing up her hands. How could he be so ignorant of something that seemed to be her sisters' only topic of conversation? "Where's my garden?"

14

"Just one minute more," Lord Fenton said, looking serious. "How can I make a match at sixteen?"

"Almost seven—"

"Almost seventeen, whatever you wish it to be," he snapped, then calmed himself. "Forgive my tone, Miss Alice, but I am far too young to make a match."

"Well, yes, right now you are. But you are the heir to an earldom, which means you'll be highly sought after once you turn, oh, twenty-one or something, and if you've already set your cap for Chloe, it's not unheard of for a gentlemen of your rank to marry that young. You'll be finished with University by then."

"I have never known a man of noble birth to marry at twenty-one."

"It's the modern age," Alice said in a husky voice that didn't sound nearly as much like her father as she'd thought it would. She cleared her throat and tried again to mimic her father's words and tone. "'And there are only so many earls out there. I mean to join our houses, mark my word.'"

Lord Fenton looked past her to the trees. She knew that look—he was thinking about something else—and that was the last thing she wanted. She grabbed his hand and held it tight with both of her own. "*Please* show me my garden."

He met her eyes and a moment later his expression softened. "That is why we came out here, was it not?"

She nodded and, thankfully, he started walking again. As he did so he explained that she could go to the gardener to request starts, but was not to take them from his plants herself, and that, if she wanted, Mr. Jefferies would clear part of the greenhouse for her use as well. The cook would not meddle with her plot, but if Alice ever had herbs or vegetables—assuming she grew any of those things—that she wanted the cook to use, she could take them to the kitchens herself. Papa wanted her to choose one dress she would use for her gardening, and her governess would now teach her botany and horticulture—something Alice had begged for on numerous occasions. It was to be understood that if her garden became a nuisance, it could be taken from her, but if she obeyed the rules, acted well her part, and did not let it detract from her training to become a lady of society, this garden was hers and hers alone.

Alice absorbed every word. They came around a portion of a stone wall and there it was: a large open patch of ground, brown and frothy looking, cut into the weeds and grasses of a forgotten part of the Stanbridge estate.

"It's four yards by four yards," Lord Fenton explained. "You can put stones around the edges if you want to as a border. You may use the gardener's tools on Tuesdays and Fridays only, and they must go back where you found them when you finish."

Alice began walking the perimeter of her own piece of ground, amazed that Lord Fenton had found a way to secure her request. Maybe noblemen really did rule the world. She fell to her knees at the edge of her new garden and pushed her hands into the damp, cool soil. Her soil.

"One last thing."

She looked up, her hands still in the earth. Lord Fenton reached inside his coat and pulled out two brown leather gloves. "Mr. Stanbridge does not want his daughter going about with soil under her fingernails, so you must wear gloves and wash with a brush when you come in."

"Working gloves!" Alice exclaimed, then jumped to her feet and raced to take the gloves from Lord Fenton. She put them on and, though they were a little big, they were wonderful: thick and heavy and begging for earth. After inspecting the gloves closely, Alice looked at Lord Fenton, who seemed quite pleased with her reaction. She had the strangest inclination to hug him, but instead gave a quick curtsy. "Thank you so much, Lord Fenton."

He bowed so low it looked like he might fall over, twirling his hand through the air as he did so and making her laugh. "It was my pleasure," he said in a funny voice, almost like a girl. He then straightened and offered her his elbow like gentlemen did for ladies when they walked together. "Now, if you will allow me to attend with you to the gardener's shed, it being Tuesday, I shall assist you in choosing your implements for today's work, though I shall not dig myself. I shouldn't want to ruin my new breeches." He shuddered dramatically.

Alice smiled broadly and took his arm in order to be led to the gardener's shed—the footman still following at a distance. Alice had never felt so grown-up or carefree as she did at that moment. London was no longer of any consequence at all.

Two days later, the house party broke up—some families returning to their homes while others went directly to London where they would enjoy the events of the early season and take advantage of the tailors, mantua makers, and seamstresses of Town. Alice stood by the window of the nursery at the top of the house and watched the traveling coach with Lord Fenton's family's coat of arms disappear down the drive. Her new garden gloves—already used to plant some snapdragons and lavender—were clasped in her hands. No one had ever made her feel as important as Lord Fenton had when he'd presented her the garden. He was so handsome, so funny, and so very kind to her. And although she knew that everyone would say she was far too young to be in love, Alice was.

With her whole ten-and-a-half-year-old heart she knew it.

CHAPTER 3

March 1818

Alice looked through the carriage window at the impressive house rising four stories above the ground and took a breath. "It is so big," she said in awe.

"Please don't say such things once we are inside," her stepmother, Maryanne—the former Lady Foust—said, eyeing Alice with trepidation from across the carriage.

Alice sat back against the cushions. "I won't, but it *is* an impressive house."

"Of course," Maryanne said, waving away Alice's appreciation. "But you cannot seem to have noticed or you will be deemed a rustic."

Alice gave Maryanne a teasing grin. "I *am* a rustic."

This flustered Maryanne. "No one will know if you hold yourself as you've been taught. So many people have invested in your season. We expect you will not show us foolish to have done it."

Alice's humor faded as she regarded the woman who had been married to her father for almost ten years. After a moment, Alice let the initial irritation of her stepmother's comment pass. Alice *did* appreciate the sacrifices made for her and did not want to increase anyone's anxiety. "I know what is expected of me," she said with a slight nod. "And I shall conduct myself well, I promise."

Maryanne nodded, but let out a deep breath, revealing her continued nervousness. While her fears were a bit offensive—Alice had worked hard to learn all she needed to know—now that Alice was in London she better understood the difference between country society and the *ton*. There was such grandness to the events here, such fine fashion and manners.

In recent years her father's financial situation had changed when some investments turned sour. Chloe and Rebecca had already had their London seasons and made good matches. Unable to turn Alice out as he had her sisters, however, Alice's father had begged off her season until he could do it properly. But the family's circumstances did not improve, and so Alice had not had a season the last two years either. It had not looked as though she would be able to come even this year, despite the fact that she was now twenty years old, but Rebecca had secured the use of her in-law's London house and Chloe had taken responsibility for a modest—but acceptable—wardrobe.

And so they were here, and Alice was determined to make the most of it. But Alice *was* a rustic. Except for the few years she attended school in Bath, she had lived her entire life in a small hamlet in northern Essex, and she found London very intimidating despite her attempts to appear confident of her place.

To make things even more discomfiting, Maryanne had agreed to come to London for just one month's time; that's how long she was willing to be away from her sons, Alice's half-brothers, who were nine and seven years old. When the month was up, Alice's sister Rebecca would take over as her sponsor in London, but Rebecca was married to an attorney, putting her connections below those that Maryanne could provide thanks to her first marriage to the younger son of a viscount. They were therefore trying to take in as many of the higher *ton* events as possible while Maryanne was in Town, giving an air of franticness to everything they did and increasing the pressure Alice felt to make a good match.

The handing over of sponsorship from Maryanne to Rebecca was yet one more way in which Alice felt like a complication within her family, something to be dealt with. Not that she wasn't loved—she knew she was—but Alice often felt stretched between her older sisters who were so polished and accomplished with families of their own, and her younger brothers who were so cherished and accommodated; Maryanne doted on her sons.

Alice had learned to expect little consideration, as it was somehow always a complication when she did, and managed herself quite independently at Warren House. She could not manage herself in London though, and the continual reminders of everyone's sacrifices in accommodating her was uncomfortable to say the least. Yet there was no course but to make the best of it; be gracious and polished and give no reason for anyone to regret their part. How she hoped to make a match that would satisfy her family and secure her future.

The carriage came to a stop and the two women were helped down to the cobbled drive by the coachman. A grand staircase was lit with torches and, as they made their way to the front doors of the house, Maryanne spoke of the last time she had attended a ball at the Duke of Stoddard's estate in Wimbledon. It had been during Rebecca's season—the sister closest to Alice in age though there were nearly four years between them—and the night had been so unusually warm that several women had fainted. One of the fainting women hit a chair on her way to the floor, that hit a candle, that lit a curtain on fire. It was doused quickly, of course, but the evening became quite memorable due to such unexpected events.

"We shall hope for no fires tonight," Maryanne said.

Alice could not help but think of another fire—not so much of an accident—that had introduced her to a boy who was now a man who might be in London too. Thinking of Lord Fenton made her stomach bubble. Her sisters had told her of the silliness and pranks he was famous for amid society, to say nothing of his flirting, but in Alice's mind he was dashing and handsome: the kind of man heroes in novels were based upon. He might very well be here tonight, and her insides shivered with giddiness at the possibility.

Maryanne looked about them nervously once they reached the top of the stairs. In hopes of relieving her stepmother's anxiety, Alice leaned in to be sure she was not overheard. "I hope that what you truly mean is that there are no fires other than those I shall spark in the hearts of eligible men."

Maryanne choked back the laugh, and then reprimanded Alice with a tap on the arm with her fan. But her humor was restored and by the time they were announced, her chin was up and no one would have expected she had had any concern at all. For Alice's part, her nerves were just beginning, but she held tight to her training and moved about the room at Maryanne's side, carrying herself properly, being introduced to other attendees, and ignoring the way other girls sized her up while she measured herself against them.

Eventually they found a piece of ground to root themselves in alongside Maryanne's cousin who had a daughter coming out this season as well, though Alice was twenty and Harriet only sixteen. Alice had met Harriet on one other occasion and was glad for a level of familiarity among such an intimidating crowd. Harriet's brother—who could not be any older than Alice—asked Alice to dance, and she was happy to take the floor. Her first dance in London! How many would follow? What if he were the only gentleman to ask her to dance tonight?

Despite her fears, Alice was asked to dance often enough to feel quite equal to the other debutantes, easing her nerves and making her feel light on her feet. She made fine conversation with her partners and kept a continual smile on her lips—her sisters said her smile was her finest feature.

Two hours in, she and Maryanne decided to take some refreshment. On the way to the tables, Alice involuntarily tightened her grip on Maryanne's arm.

"What is it?" Maryanne asked, looking around.

"Lady Chariton." Alice nodded in the direction of the elegant matron sitting with a few other women on the far side of the refreshment tables.

"So it is," Maryanne said, sounding pleased. She looked around a bit more. "I wonder if Lord Fenton is here."

The sound of his name sent Alice's heart racing, and she wished for the hundredth time that her ten-year-old self had kept her affections to herself.

They did not see Lord Fenton in the crowd as they made their way toward his mother. It had been several years since Alice's father had hosted the annual house party that Lord and Lady Chariton always attended, but Alice thought the countess looked as though she had aged dramatically since they had last visited. She was very thin, and her skin seemed stretched out somehow—loose on her bones— but she was regal and pleased to see them when they gained her attention and introduced themselves.

After standing and pressing cheeks with both of them, Lady Chariton turned her attention to Alice quite pointedly. "What a lovely young woman you have become, Miss Stanbridge."

"Thank you, Lady Chariton," Alice said with a gracious bow of her head. "You look very well this evening."

"Thank you, my dear. It is a shame Charles is not here. I would have so liked for him to have seen you all grown up."

Alice's blush surely said too much, and she looked down at the floor in hopes of hiding the flush of her cheeks. Her reaction to Lord Fenton—both inward and outward—was such a contrast to her usual character that it left her quite at odds with herself.

"Where *is* Lord Fenton this evening?" Maryanne asked, a bit boldly, Alice thought. Still, she was curious for the answer.

"I'm afraid we don't often attend the same events in Town. I shall see him on Sunday, however, and tell him that I saw the both of you. How is Mr. Stanbridge, and the rest of your family?"

Maryanne began updating Lady Chariton on their family when a woman appeared from the crowd and placed a hand on Maryanne's arm. Maryanne looked at the woman, her eyebrows lifting in abject surprise. "Diane?" she said, interrupting the account she was giving to Lady Chariton. Maryanne and this new arrival embraced. "Oh, it has been an age and yet you have not changed a whit."

"You mean to say I looked like an old crow when we saw each other last?" Diane said as they pulled apart but kept hold of one another's hands. Both women laughed before Diane spoke again. "You on the other hand look just as you did when last we parted. Why, I'd have known you in a moment, anywhere at all."

"Oh, go on," Maryanne said with a shake of her head. "When did you come to London? Why did you not tell me you would be here? I'd have sought you out first thing."

Alice cleared her throat as a signal to Maryanne of where she was and who she was with. After all her worry regarding Alice acting properly, it was somewhat humorous to have Maryanne be the one to show ill manners. Alice was careful to hide her smile, however, when Maryanne swiftly turned back to Lady Chariton.

"Oh, I am so sorry," she said, her neck pink with embarrassment. "This is my dear friend, Mrs. Diane Hughes. Mrs. Hughes, this is Lady Chariton, an old friend of Mr. Stanbridge's family, and this is my stepdaughter, Alice Stanbridge, the youngest of Harold's girls." The women nodded to one another before Maryanne turned to Lady Chariton with an apologetic expression. "Please forgive me for my lack of manners, Lady Chariton. Diane has been in India for . . ." She turned to Mrs. Hughes. "Has it been twelve years?"

"Nearly thirteen," Mrs. Hughes said with a nod. "We came back so the boys could go to school. I had not expected you would be in London from your last letter. Of course, that letter was posted in November and only just found us before we left Bombay."

"We did not think we would be able to afford to give Alice a—" Maryanne stopped herself, then turned to Lady Chariton as her entire face reddened at yet another faux pas, this one proclaiming their financial situation. Alice, equally embarrassed but hoping to diffuse the discomfort, hurried to offer a solution before anyone needed to make more apologies.

"Maryanne, why don't you and Mrs. Hughes find a corner where you can catch up with one another? I shall have some refreshment and join you later."

"She shall of course stay with me until you return," Lady

Chariton offered, surprising everyone and causing Alice to swallow nervously. Had her offer to give Maryanne time to converse with her old friend put Lady Chariton in the position of needing to serve as her chaperone? Alice had only meant to assert her independence.

Lady Chariton continued, "I should ever so much like to catch up with Alice."

Alice's hands were instantly clammy. *Catch up with Alice?* Why, the two of them had never *conversed* even when Lady Chariton had come to Warren House, except for those simple exchanges of etiquette that were expected between a child of the house and a titled guest. But Alice was certainly not going to argue at the woman's attention. It could only do her reputation credit to receive it, and she might learn a bit more of Lord Fenton during the exchange.

"That would be lovely," Alice said, giving Maryanne a reassuring look.

"Are you certain?" Maryanne asked, her eyebrows knit together.

Lady Chariton assured her that she was happy to attend Alice and then waved the two women off. Maryanne looked over her shoulder only once before Mrs. Hughes quite dominated her attention.

Lady Chariton smiled at Alice. "Come, dear, let us sit down, if you would. I am not one for standing long."

They found an empty pair of chairs set back from the crowd, and Alice perched on the edge of the satin cushion, unsure what to say or how to act with this woman who was so far above her station. Alice licked her lips and wished she'd been able to get a glass of punch so her mouth would not be so dry.

"I hope you do not mind my saying so," Lady Chariton said, looking intently into Alice's face, "but you look so very much like your mother."

Alice was startled by the comment to the point that her nerves were forgotten. "You knew my mother?" In all the years Lady Chariton had been coming to Warren House, Alice had assumed it was her father and Lord Chariton who had shared an acquaintance.

"We were girls together, didn't you know?"

Alice shook her head.

"I was older than she was by four years," Lady Chariton said, "and I married before she was even out to society, but I have many fond memories of your mother." Her eyes became sad, and she reached for Alice's hand. She did not need to say it out loud for Alice to know that Lady Chariton was mindful that Alice had no memories of her mother. Rachel Stanbridge had died from complications of Alice's birth—another aspect that often made her conspicuous within her family. Had her mother had only two daughters, she would have lived to raise them.

Alice did not say such things out loud, however, not to anyone, and because she didn't want to make Lady Chariton uncomfortable she brightened her smile. "I daresay it makes me feel as though I did know her when people tell me of her." Lady Chariton seemed relieved, prompting Alice to continue. "And, of course, other people have commented on how closely I resemble her, which is another connection I feel blessed to share."

"It is quite remarkable." Lady Chariton seemed to realize she was staring and so she looked away for a moment and changed her position so she wasn't facing Alice quite so directly. "I wonder if it would bore you to hear an old woman reminisce."

"Not at all," Alice said, feeling a rush of eagerness. She wished the people who had known her mother spoke of her more; but once her father had married Maryanne, speaking of the first wife had become a rare occurrence at Warren House. "I love to hear of my mother's life. How did you know her? Did you grow up in West Essex?"

Lady Chariton nodded. "In the same parish as Rachel's family. Our mothers were close friends, and both Rachel and I were the youngest daughters." Her features softened as her memories moved a far way off. "Rachel and I would play together when our mothers visited each other, something that happened at least once a week— more when the weather was fine. One of my favorite memories of Rachel was when I was, oh, ten or eleven years old. She'd have been only six or seven then, but she was usually the leader of our mischief. We girls had been shooed out to the garden that day and though I don't know how she did it, somehow Rachel had taken hold of a knife and hidden it in her stocking."

Lady Chariton laughed at the memory and shook her head before continuing the story of how relieved she'd been when Rachel had explained that the knife was for the purpose of making squash boats rather than something more sinister. The girls had stolen the squash from the cook's garden, sliced and hollowed them out, and then floated the boats down a brook.

"We ran from one spot to the next, cheering on our ships until we had run so far we didn't recognize the place. Without that brook to follow back, we'd never have found our way home, and then when we did make our way back, our mothers were set to paddle us for wandering off." Lady Chariton put a hand on Alice's arm. "I immediately fell to tears and apologies, but not Rachel." She shook her head. "No, Rachel lifted her chin and said that we had done no wrong, only played as any boy would be allowed to play, and therefore we should not be punished for simply using our heads for a bit of fun." Lady Chariton laughed heartily then, covering her mouth until she could control herself. "Your mother was a scamp indeed, Alice, but, oh, what a will she had about her—I admired it so; I never had such gumption."

Lady Chariton paused, her smile fading for a moment before she looked back into Alice's face and began another story about a time the two girls had talked their mothers into having matching dresses made for them so they could pretend they were sisters when they went to church. Alice listened closely and felt as though she were seeing Lady Chariton grow younger through the telling of these girlhood tales. At the same time, her mother's presence began to loom more solidly in her mind: hazel eyes, hair the color of walnuts, and a quick mind with the willingness to speak it. Alice was so much the same, though she'd learned to keep her thoughts to herself as few people wanted to hear them.

By the time Maryanne returned, Alice was laughing behind her own hand over a story that included her mother hiding in a wine barrel in hopes of frightening her older brother, but her brother never came and Rachel was left with a horrible headache from the wine fumes.

Alice was sorry to see the conference come to an end, but she had occupied the woman's attention for nearly half an hour and knew it would be impolite to request it continue even longer.

Lady Chariton took Alice's hand in both of hers and looked directly into her eyes. "You are a dear girl to let me prattle so, Alice. What a joy it was to return to days of such happy memories."

"The pleasure has most certainly been mine," Alice said as though they were old friends. "You are a grand woman to be so generous in your stories to me. I shall cherish them. Thank you."

After Alice and Maryanne quit Lady Chariton's company,

Maryanne lifted her eyebrows and turned her head to catch Alice's eye. "My, my, but she was attentive to you. Twice I came to return, but the two of you looked so thick I dared not interrupt."

"She is a lovely woman," Alice said, equally surprised and gratified by the woman's attention. It had not seemed to bother Lady Chariton that Alice was not dressed to the height of fashion, that her family's situation had come under difficulty in recent years, or that Alice was decades younger than the matron. Lady Chariton had acted as though none of those things mattered and for the space of the conversation, they had not.

"It is a shame Lord Fenton wasn't here," Maryanne said as they returned to their place on the edge of the dance floor. She gave Alice a teasing grin. "Perhaps he would have fawned over you as his mother did."

"I'm sure he would not." But Alice could not help but wonder if his mother's kindness might be a good omen. She wondered how long it would be until she saw Lord Fenton in Town. Perhaps he would be as happy to see Alice as his mother had been. One could only hope.

CHAPTER 4

"Are you ready to face your fate, Fenton?" David Burbidge asked, his eyes fairly dancing with anticipation.

Fenton regarded him with a bored expression and, without moving his head, shifted his glance to the other man sitting across from him in the carriage, Oscar Newtonhouser, though his friends called him Newt. "You have approved of this scrap?" Fenton asked. Newt was usually the more levelheaded of the two, though thinking there was any amount of levelheadedness between them gave far more credit than they deserved.

"I find it quite charming. It shall be the very thing to bring out the color of your eyes." He blinked quickly and clasped his hands under his chin for effect.

"Surely there are not two sillier men in all of England than the pair of you," Fenton said.

Burbidge and Newt looked at each other and burst out laughing. Once they could contain themselves—twenty-two seconds by Fenton's pocket watch; he timed it so as to look sufficiently bored with their ridiculousness—Burbidge spoke again. "For the next hour, I feel sure *you* will wear the title of the silliest Englishman *very well*."

Fenton let out an overly dramatic sigh and raised his head so he was staring at the carriage ceiling. "Let's get this over with," he said with the foppish elocution appropriate to his London persona.

He looked at his companions, grinning like cats, and then at the hatbox between them on the carriage floor. Burbidge glanced quickly at Newt, then reached forward and pulled off the lid of the box. Newt wasted no time lifting the horrid thing out and turning it slowly so Fenton could see the hideous hat from every angle. Truly he needed to give up drinking. The wagers he entered into when he was too far into his cups were getting out of hand, even with his tolerance for the ridiculous being higher than that of most men.

Fenton peered through the feathers—there were artificial hummingbirds attached to a few of them—and gave his most brilliant smile. The exuberant expressions on his friends' faces changed to confusion. "Wherever did you get this *amazing* confection? I shall order three more in every color."

"It used to belong to Newt's mother."

"But we built it up a bit."

"Well," Fenton said, lifting an eyebrow and noting the extra ribbons added to the back and curled like locks of hair, "if either of your inheritances run dry, you have a future as milliners."

That the men were unsure whether he was completely quizzing them caused Fenton to reconsider keeping their friendships at all, but of course he did not show his annoyance. Instead he took the hat from Newt's hands and placed it on his head. There were two long purple ribbons, which he tied under his chin in a pretty bow.

"Do I have it right?" he asked, turning his head this way and that, causing the multicolored ostrich plumes to float and dance above him. He could not see the movements himself due to the wide brim, but he watched Newt and Burbidge's eyes as they followed the frothy feathers. "If I put it on backwards I shall never be able to show myself in this company again."

"I think it is on right," Burbidge said, still uncertain of Fenton's disposition. The carriage began to slow, signaling they had arrived at their destination.

"I don't think it matters all that much," Newt said. A green feather fell in front of Fenton's face. "It's monstrous no matter how you tie it on."

"Monstrous?" Fenton pulled back and put one hand to his chest as though affronted. With his other hand he batted away the wayward plume. "A pox on you for such rudeness." He turned and pushed open the door just as the carriage came to a full stop.

Once out on the cobbles, he straightened his gold-trimmed black tailcoat and made a display of brushing off his golden pantaloons tucked into his shiny black Hessian boots complete with gold tassels like those Prinny himself was known to wear. Fenton had dressed more conservatively than usual tonight in anticipation of this joke his friends were concocting but had not expected something quite so flamboyant as the hat to accompany his evening dress. "You can blame no one but yourself," he muttered when he knew his friends wouldn't overhear him. He turned to the open carriage door through which his friends watched him, lifted his chin, and put his hands on his hips. "Well, are you coming or aren't you?"

Burbidge and Newt fairly fell over each other to get out of the carriage, but he didn't wait for them. Instead, he spun on the heel of his right boot, pulled back his shoulders, and walked with confidence to the front door of the card party unfortunate enough to be the stage for tonight's presentation. Might the Whitbys find it funny? Gads he hoped so.

The reaction to his entry was equal parts mirth and derision—both of which he pretended not to notice. He greeted friends and acquaintances who had already arrived—avoided the hosts for fear they would ask him to remove the hat—and checked his watch rather slyly so as not to alert Burbidge and Newt to his discomfort. He asked himself more than once why he was doing this and if the role of larger-than-life ne'er-do-well was worth all the aggravation. He was used to being the center of attention and knew that many invitations were sent to his rooms in hopes he would be entertaining to the other guests—he was a dandy, after all—but this was a relatively conservative crowd for such a display and his invitation had come due to his family's connections rather than his own merit.

"No brandy tonight," he charged his reflection in a hallway mirror. "Spare yourself tomorrow's misery at least by avoiding an equally humiliating wager as this one."

He entered the next room, struck a pose, and bowed in gratitude for the laughter that greeted him and his ridiculous hat. As he rose, he caught the narrowed eyes of the one man whom he did not mind discomfiting, and in an instant Fenton no longer regretted this joke or this company. Instead, he felt the invigoration of the upcoming sparring match.

Fenton straightened and crossed the room. "What a surprise!" he said, putting his hand on the back of the man's chair and giving it a shake. "How do you do, Father mine? It has been an *age* since we have found ourselves sharing an evening's entertainment, has it not?"

"Stop your ridiculous pandering." Fenton's father, the Right

Honorable William Theler, Earl of Chariton, looked at the hand of cards he held as he spoke. The whiteness of his thumb holding the cards gave further credence to the tone of his voice, kept low so as to be heard only by the men closest to the two of them.

"Pandering?" Fenton placed his hand to his chest once again. "Why Father, I am *deeply* hurt. Do you not like my hat?" He preened and posed, but his father would not look up from his cards. The rest of the room, however, was evenly divided between those who were entertained and those who were uncomfortable, giving Fenton a stab of conscience. Focusing on his father again helped him keep his confidence. He had no shame in causing his *father* embarrassment. "Newt says it brings out the color of my eyes. Would you agree?"

Lord Chariton slammed his cards onto the table, and the entire room went quiet. He stood slowly, every eye, including Fenton's, glued to the man who was likely the highest-ranking guest at this party. Father and son were nearly the same height so when Lord Chariton turned to face Fenton they were eye level.

"Have you no dignity?" his father said softly enough for only Fenton to hear, except they were in a completely silent room. Everyone present could hear the disgust and disappointment in the earl's tone.

Despite himself, Fenton felt heat creep up his neck.

Lord Chariton turned to one of the men at the table and inclined his head. "I offer you my most sincere apologies, Whitby, for my son's poor character and this display. I shall like to meet with you tomorrow to see how I might rectify this situation and continue our discussion. For this evening's part, I fear that my remaining will only draw greater discomfort to all of us. Unlike my son, I have no desire to show such disrespect." With a parting glare at Fenton, he strode from the room, leaving an air of awkwardness behind him.

Like the rest of the room, Fenton was unsure what to do. Granted he had never targeted his father so directly before; at other events they ignored one another and seemed equally content with the arrangement. Perhaps Fenton's discomfort with the hat made him that much more susceptible to the temptation of taunting his father so as to avoid his self-recriminations. Whispered conversations began to grow amid the guests, and Fenton tried to think of a resolution. His pride could not afford to concede to his father's reprimand, but neither did he want to pour salt on the wound. If only he could choose against either one.

He pasted a smile on his face and turned back to the table, looking directly at Mr. Whitby. "Do *you* like my hat, sir?" he asked, lifting his eyebrows. "Surely you are not so stodgy as that old man." He pointed a thumb toward the doorway through which his father had exited.

Mr. Whitby glared at him—the reaction he had expected but not hoped for—and Fenton laughed again. He caught the eye of a debutante trying to hide her smile. He winked, her cheeks flamed, and then he exited the room as though in search of better company.

In the hall he consulted his watch; there were seventeen minutes left for the wager. He would need brandy to get through it, certainly. One glass would shore up his confidence until he could make some excuse and remove himself from this dratted event where he had managed to make everyone uncomfortable. He wanted people to laugh with him and think him extreme but not regret his attendance. He attempted to find validation in having succeeded at making his father uncomfortable, but it was little balm at the moment.

"One glass," he told himself as he headed for the sideboard set up with drink for the evening and batted away another blasted feather that fell onto his face. "Maybe two."

CHAPTER 5

Fenton knew from the quality of light seeping in around the heavy drapes of his bedroom window that it was past noon. He lifted his pounding head from the pillow and attempted to sit upright, only to fall back against the pillows once more, which did not remedy his discomfort. He had a vague memory of having tried to limit his drinks the night before, but his current state was so familiar he felt certain he had not restrained himself. The longer he lay there—stretched between the choppy memories of the night before and the misery of this moment—the more the two parts combined to remind him why he had not kept himself to any limits. That horrid hat. His father's derision. Mr. Whitby.

Fenton pulled a pillow over his face and raged over the entire incident, irritated that the confrontation with his father had not at least given him some feeling of relief. Rather, it had increased his aggravation and frustration and . . . exhaustion. Perhaps that was the best word to describe his life right now; he was exhausted. Tired of London. Tired of society. Tired of everyone and everything he had built around himself. What was it all for? To irritate his father?

To gain some kind of acknowledgment from the man? He feared that playing the role of a fool so well had turned him into that very thing.

There was a familiar knock at the door. "Come in, Barker," Fenton said to his valet.

Fenton stayed abed as Barker opened the drapes just enough to light the room. The valet then went about setting the room into some kind of order. Fenton might have been embarrassed to be rising so late and in such a state if not for the fact that it was becoming more and more common; Barker was surely not surprised by the circumstance. It was not a credit to Fenton that he was on his way to being labeled a drunk, and yet he was not sure he even cared anymore. Perhaps life was better when one was unconscious for most of the waking hours. At the moment Fenton found it difficult to argue otherwise.

After a few silent minutes, through which Fenton's head continued to pound, Barker cleared his throat in the way of requesting a conversation.

"Yes?" Fenton asked.

"A message has come from your father, my lord."

Fenton could think of half a dozen ways to justify not reading what was surely a scolding, but it had been years since his father had bothered to issue a reprimand and some infantile part of Fenton was glad for the attention. He held out his hand for the note, and Barker pulled it from the front pocket of his coat.

Fenton sat up while fingering the indentation of the seal, then nodded toward the window so Barker would pull the drapes wider. The flood of light made him wince, but he took a breath, kept his eyes closed for a few moments, and then blinked until they adjusted to the brightened room. He broke the wax wafer and unfolded the paper. The earl had kept it short.

London House at 2:00

He hadn't even bothered to sign it.

Fenton tossed the letter to the other side of the bed and threw an arm over his eyes. His skull throbbed. "Barker, I shall need you to return a message to my father that I cannot be to the house until four o'clock. Then I shall need a bath and be readied with dress appropriate to an execution—the pink-and-red striped waistcoat with the pink coat and white pantaloons should be sufficient. Set out the red boots with the gold buckles. I'm sure they are the earl's favorite."

Fenton might be worn-out by the role of fop he played in society, but he refused to give his father the satisfaction of subduing it now.

At ten minutes past four, Fenton knocked at his parents' London townhouse and greeted Handleby when he opened the door. The butler had always liked Fenton—most people *did* like his light manner and good humor—and they spoke while Handleby took Fenton's hat and cloak. "Your father awaits you in his study, my lord."

Just outside the door, Fenton rolled his shoulders and lifted his chin—it was time to perform.

Handleby opened the door and announced Fenton before standing to the side and allowing him entry.

"Good luck, my lord," he whispered as Fenton strode past him, deepening Fenton's fears regarding this meeting. If the servants knew of what lay in store, Fenton had reason to be worried.

The door closed and Fenton stepped close to the front of his father's desk. Lord Chariton didn't look up. Fenton put one foot forward, pointed at a slight angle that kept his knee bent. "Good afternoon, Father. How are you this fine day? Is not the sunshine refreshing?" He lifted one hand toward the window and propped the other on his hip.

"Enough, Charles. Sit."

Undeterred, Fenton put a thumb and finger on either side of his chin and regarded the two brown leather chairs facing the desk. "But which chair shall I sit in, Father? It is *such* a decision. Shall I choose the one to your right, or is the lighting better for my complexion if I sit in the one on the left?" He clucked his tongue while sitting in one of the chairs. He wriggled around a bit then moved to the other. After wriggling around on that one too he stood again, turned to look at both chairs, and then sat in the first. "Yes, this one is it," he said, grinning widely. He crossed one leg over the other then threaded his fingers together and rested them on his thigh, keeping his spine straight. "Proceed with your scolding, Father. Now that I am comfortable I am prepared to withstand it as best I can while showing appropriate repentance."

His father stared at him, cold and angry. Fenton stared back, a silent, unblinking duel. Finally, the earl leaned back in his chair. "I am cutting you off, Charles."

The initial rush of fear that moved through Fenton's chest was immediately extinguished by basic reason. "You can't cut me off, Father. I am your heir. It's written in the stars and in the heraldry." He smiled a bit wider. "I'm afraid you have no choice but to tolerate my"—he waved his hand through the air as though searching for the word—"extravagant manner."

"I have been considering this for some time and recently sat down with another member of Parliament to further discuss the possibilities. There is a process of legally disinheriting an heir, and I have reached the point of humiliation that convinces me it is my only solution."

Fenton laughed and then shook his head, though his heart was beginning to race. Could the earl do it? Was there truly a process for such a thing? "You're bluffing," he said. "But I can play along. What would you like me to change? Shall I not wear hats to parties? Shall I promise to wear only black boots?" Fenton lifted one foot to be sure his father saw the shiny red leather. "I can ease up a bit, I suppose, if for the sake of your sensibilities."

"I am not bluffing, nor am I negotiating. Your behavior is atrocious and embarrassing not only to me but to all of our society as a whole. Last night was beyond all respectability and manners. Whitby is an important man in the government and you made a fool of him in his own home. I owe it to him, and to every other respectable person of my acquaintance, to remedy this situation once and for all. I shall leave you with an income since you have no basis to earn a living, and you shall then be free to pursue your life as you see fit. I shall no longer have to share in the burden of shame you bring upon our family name, my friends will not feel obligated to include you in their circles, and I will no longer worry over the state of my holdings should they one day fall into your very incapable hands."

"I don't believe you," Fenton replied in a low tone, having dropped his façade. His chest was getting hot and his head began to swirl with the possibility this might not be a joke after all. "It is a larger discredit for you to cut off your only son than it is to bear out my choice of entertainments."

"For many years, the situation has been exactly that," his father agreed, looking at Fenton with cold eyes. "I have withstood the whispered disparagement of my friends and acquaintances and told myself that any number of respectable men have put up with the same until their sons traded the bacon in their heads for brains and settled down to do their duty. Last night convinced me that my patience was misplaced and that you were a man without respect or dignity. I should have done this sooner, but I shan't let regret at my delay prevent this course another minute."

Fenton clenched his jaw and took a breath, trying to maintain his composure. "I'm sorry, but did you just refer to yourself as a *respectable* man? I'm afraid whatever followed that misrepresentation was lost. Perhaps you could repeat yourself."

His father's gaze darkened even as his voice rose in volume. "Your judgments toward me are juvenile and only further show how ridiculous you are." He leaned an elbow on the desk and stared down the barrel of his finger. "You are an infant and an idiot, and I have quite worn out my use for you."

Rage rolled through Fenton like a thundercloud, but he kept his jaw clenched. He would not give into the man's goading. Let the earl be the only one to lose his patience. *Respectability, my eye.* "So," Fenton said when he felt able to speak, keeping his tone as light as possible. "You shall cut me off with a few yellow dogs to see me through and then, what, the next earl of Chariton shall be your cousin's son—the very boy whom you have often referred to as cotton-headed? You would prefer to have him carry your *sacred* family name that is so *respectable*? Has the man ever even been in London? Is he not commissioned in the navy or some such thing?"

His father did not rise to anger again and instead relaxed into his chair. The look of pleasure on his face was maddening. "I have just this morning sent a letter to Frederick, requesting he come to London. By the time he is able to arrange it, all should be in place—I need but to prove to Parliament that my holdings are in jeopardy should you inherit. As you have taken no responsibility in anything and your antics are well-known in town, I believe Parliament will be eager to confirm my request. You shall then be Charles Theler and nothing more. You shall have full control of the funds I leave to you—two thousand pounds a year for the term of your natural life—and you will become responsible for your own debts and expenses. I will no longer offer apologies on your behalf to my friends and associates. I will no longer pay your gambling debts or cover your foibles. You will have *no* access to the family estates unless you are invited, as would be any other guest, and you shall be stricken from the book of heraldry completely. Your children—should you ever have any—will be cut off from all inheritance and title. Forever."

Each threat hit Fenton like a lightning bolt. Though he and his father had stood off against each other for years, there had never been anything like this. And the earl had already sent a letter to his cousin's son? He had a plan in place for going to Parliament? Fenton wanted to doubt him, but there was a frightening amount of sincerity and relief in his father's words and he feared he truly had pushed the man too far.

"And my mother?" Fenton asked, though he could not keep his voice calm any longer. "She has agreed to this?"

The pause was all the answer Fenton needed.

"You haven't told her," he pronounced before his father formed a response. "You are intent to consign me to poverty—her only son— and haven't even *told* her. Oh, you are the very model of honor, aren't you, Father? *So* good. *So* wise."

"She has no legal say in this, and you know it," his father spat. "*I* am the head. *I* am the one who makes the decisions for this family. Without her lily-handed ways perhaps you would have become a son a man could take pride in."

Fenton stood, his hand forming a fist. "You will not insult my mother," he said slowly and with great restraint as he glared down at the man he wished he dared to strike.

"But *you* will?" Lord Chariton also rose to his feet. "You humiliate and insult her every day of your life. It is as much for her good as it is my own that I am making a public and legal separation between us. You have made your mother a laughingstock; she can barely hold up her head in society for the embarrassment you have caused her."

"That is not true!" Fenton yelled, the raging fire in his chest igniting. "She would tell me if she felt as you do, but she has not. *She* is not so worried of what people think that she would do this to her own flesh and blood. She is not—"

"Get out of my house!" the earl shouted in a voice that shook the windows. He pointed to the door, his face red and eyes bulging. "I have seen the last of you I ever want to see. I shall have the constable upon you if you remain here another minute! You are a worthless windbag without a mote of intellect or grace, and I will no longer be burdened by your useless and ridiculous carcass! From this day forward you are not my son!"

Fenton could not breathe as every word crashed into him. Lord Chariton's cruelty brought a strange sense of validation. For almost a decade, Fenton had believed that the honorable Lord Chariton could not love anyone, that all he cared for was his own satisfaction and pleasure and the people in his life mattered only for the benefit they could be for him. Which is why Fenton had taken great pains to be of as little benefit as he possibly could, a veritable thorn in the man's side. His father's vile words confirmed how right Fenton was.

But there was little satisfaction in proving his point. His father was cutting him off. His father would no longer claim him as his son. Fenton would not become the Earl of Chariton one day, in fact he would not be Lord Fenton anymore—Frederick would. There truly was no love between them at all. Perhaps—as he had long suspected—there never had been.

For a brief moment Fenton thought of his brother, who would have been older than Fenton by four years had he lived past his third birthday. Adam was not a topic Fenton's parents spoke of, and Fenton wondered if one reason he was always at odds with his father was because he was *not* the firstborn. Did his father resent Fenton for who he was not? Had Fenton always been a poor substitute for the rightful heir lost to illness at an age when children were easy to love?

Such resentment, if it existed, did not explain his father's appetite for women, however, which is what had truly come between father and son, or the pain and humiliation Lord Chariton inflicted on his wife by indulging such desires. For an instant, Fenton wondered how different they all might have been if Adam had lived. Adam could have measured up, and Fenton could have lived without such hatred toward the man he wanted so very much not to be.

Struck by such unexpected thoughts and shaken by his father's determination, Fenton turned on his heel without another word and left the room. In the foyer, he grabbed his hat and coat, ignoring

Handleby's anxious look, and marched out the door, down the street, and through the square. He walked and walked and walked until he found himself in one of the gaming hells in a less savory part of town. He slid into a chair in the stuffy room and ordered rum. If he had ever needed a drink in his life, it was today.

CHAPTER 6

Fenton woke up on Friday much as he had on Thursday—thick-headed and sick. He could not keep drinking like this. Once Barker left him, Fenton paced and raged then paced and raged some more, trying to determine what, if anything, he could do. Perhaps apologizing to his father would save him, but not only would an apology taste so very bitter, he did not think it would be enough. The earl had been resolute.

What if Fenton appealed to his mother? Considering the idea brought back the words his father had said and stabbed him afresh: *"You humiliate and insult her every day of your life."* Fenton's mother had always filled him with all the love and admiration many aristocratic parents held back from their children. She had been his playmate as a child and a friend and support for everything he had done since. As difficulties had increased between Fenton and his father, Fenton's connection with his mother had deepened. Could she really feel this humiliated and insulted by Fenton's behavior? Had she expressed her disappointment to Fenton's father, spurring him toward this course?

By four o'clock Fenton was drinking again.

He awoke Saturday to another headache.

"Have I received any messages from my father, Barker?" he asked, sipping a cup of strong tea that did little for his head. He sat on the edge of his bed, hunched over like a beggar and afraid to stand. He'd had three days of hard drinking and his stomach ached for want of food, though the sight of the breakfast tray made him feel even more ill.

"No, my lord. Should you want to look over the stack of correspondence that has come these last days? There is any number of invitations and requests after your health. Mr. Burbidge sent you a posy."

Fenton waved him away. "I want to see none of that, only something from my parents."

"Very good, my lord," Barker said. "I shall prepare a bath."

Fenton bathed and dressed and then went outside for fresh air, though the London sky was blocked by clouds and smog. He sat on a bench outside his boardinghouse with his head in his hands for nearly half an hour before he was fit to walk. He still felt half drunk, and yet wished for another drink so badly that his mouth went dry just thinking about it.

Eventually he knew that the only course that might work would be to present himself to his mother and ask for her help. Lord Chariton had little consideration for his wife in any respect, but she *was* Lady Chariton. She *was* Fenton's mother. If anyone could have influence it would be she.

Fenton soon found himself at the door to his parents' London house, fear driving him to the very humility he'd refused to acknowledge two days before.

Handleby answered his knock and let him into the house.

"Is my father here?" Fenton asked, raising a hand to his head that continued to ache.

"At the club, sir."

Thank the heavens, Fenton thought. "And my mother?"

"In her bedchamber."

At two o'clock in the afternoon? Fenton wondered, but only for a moment. "Will you tell her that I need to speak to her if possible?"

"Yes, my lord. You may remove to the drawing room to wait."

Fenton went to the drawing room, but was there only a few minutes before Handleby informed him that his mother would see him in her bedchamber.

Lady Chariton was still in her dressing gown and seated in one of the chairs before her fireplace. The past two years had beset her with one illness after another until she was looking far older than her fifty-one years. Though she had been a young bride, Fenton had not been born until she was twenty-and-five years old and no more children had followed. She often said that she'd prayed him to life and she'd dared not seem ungrateful to want for another child. He had always believed her when she said such sweet things. Yet she had not sent for him after his father's pronouncement. Was that because she didn't know of Lord Chariton's threats or because Fenton really had worn out her patience?

Lady Chariton reached a thin hand towards him and he crossed to her, kissed her soft cheek, and then sat. He took her hand and held it in both of his own.

Feeling her compassionate touch now, when he felt so wretched, brought tears to his eyes and returned him to that small boy who ran to her for comfort. "Mama," he said quietly, dropping his head and trying not to fall into tears. He blamed the drinking for his lack of control as much as he blamed his father's threat, but he knew it was mostly being in her company. His mother was the only person from whom he felt genuine love and acceptance. In recent years, with him staying in his own rooms and enjoying his own society, they had not seen one another as often as they once did, but they maintained a connection he did not see between his friends and their mothers.

"I know," she said, reaching her other hand to smooth his hair.

He looked up at her. "You know?"

"Not until it was decided. The letter to Frederick had already been sent."

Fenton waited for her to say she had dissuaded his father from his threatened course, but she did not.

"He is quite set upon this, Charles."

"Surely there is something you can do?" Fenton said, shocked at her seeming acceptance. Though he knew his father was right in that she had no legal power, he expected she would still object to it. Yet she sounded so resigned. Did she agree to this course?

"He is the earl," Lady Chariton said, her own eyes glassy with unshed tears. "I am here only in name, as ever I have been."

"But he will listen to you," Fenton said. "Surely you can plead my case."

"And what case shall I plead?" Her tone was not cold or harsh, but her words left Fenton speechless. "You have made a spectacle of yourself for years, Charles, and you show no interest in the responsibilities of your position. Perhaps a simpler life will help you to find your way."

"Mama," Fenton said in shock. "Do you hear what you are saying?"

She put a cool hand along his cheek and the sadness of her smile caused his throat to tighten. She *was* embarrassed by him. He *had* hurt her with his antics. "You will always be my son, Charles. My love for you will never change no matter what Parliament might decide, but it is difficult to argue that you are equal to the responsibilities that are yours through birthright when you do nothing to fulfill them. Because Foxcroft belongs to me, it shall transfer to you as part of the entailment, so you shall have a holding in that estate. But your father is determined to protect his own holdings and secure the continuation of what seven generations have built."

Fenton stared at his mother for several seconds without knowing what to say. Foxcroft was little balm for the losses. "You believe I am incapable of the responsibility of the earldom?"

"I think you are *quite* capable," his mother clarified. "You are smart and able and passionate about many things, but you have shown yourself unwilling to apply yourself to the family holdings. You make a mockery of our position in society. You gamble and spend money with abandon and have done nothing to show aptitude or inclination toward any other course but continued dissipation."

"Have I not lived as many young noblemen do? Is it not a rite of passage to enjoy the pleasures of the city in our youth?"

"Perhaps," Lady Chariton said. "But that does not change the fact that your father can control who inherits his title, and his mind is set against you." She sighed and took Fenton's hand in both of her own. "It breaks my heart to see this turn, Charles, truly it does. But I have no more argument to make. Had it not been for my continual insistence that you will one day rise to your level, this would have happened before now. I can offer him no continued assurance when you show me nothing to base it on. Mrs. Whitby is a dear friend of mine, but she was deeply embarrassed by your display and would not let me call on her to offer an apology. I am heartsick for the discomfort you have caused so many people. I know not what to do to amend it any longer."

The emotion Fenton had tried to hold back was becoming too strong, and he blinked quickly. "I am sorry, Mama. I never meant to cause you pain." But he *had* meant to cause his father pain. What a child he was to have let that goal overtake every bit of his person to the degree that his own mother could not see his worth.

"Of course you didn't," she said, touching his cheek again. She looked into his face and paused, as though carefully considering her words. "I also do not believe you are happy with the life you live, Charles. Perhaps this change of circumstance will bring about a better future. I so long to see you settled, with children you can love as I have loved you. You are my greatest joy and always shall be, but if you remain upon your current course, I worry you shall never know that kind of joy for yourself."

Fenton only half listened to her words—it was not the first time she had shared her wishes for his future—but he was not ready for such things. The idea of being a husband and father was as difficult to ponder upon as to captain a naval ship or work in a factory. "I can curtail my behavior," he said. "The scene at Whitbys' was extreme, I know that. I have been drinking too much and it has gotten the better of me. I shall improve on that wise and keep better control of my actions and finances. I can promise never to make such a spectacle again and shall apologize to the Whitbys personally."

"Every time you leave your rooms you are a spectacle," his mother said, nodding toward the turquoise coat and bright yellow waistcoat with embroidered hummingbirds he had worn today.

Though he belonged to the dandy set—known for their fashion

and wit—he did tend to fall to the Macaroni side of such things, taking his colors and trims to the extreme. It was all part of his attempt to vex his father, or at least it had begun that way.

Lady Chariton continued. "There are not apologies enough that can change what has been done. You already know that Oxford only kept you for your father's restitution and continual pleadings on your behalf. Whitby is so angry about what happened Wednesday evening he will not even speak with your father at the club. And the expenses you incur have become a matter of concern, should they continue to rise as they have these last years. It has altogether become simply too much."

"I can dress more conservatively," Fenton said, feeling the desperation rise as the picture his mother painted became so very stark to him. Was it any wonder that neither of his parents had any hope of him rising? "I shall take over my duties to the matters of my responsibility. I shall even move back to this house if you would prefer I didn't have my independence for a time. I shall learn the way of things, be more circumspect in my spending, and prove to you both that I am capable of this. I shall rise to my privilege, Mother. I shall make you proud." Even as he said it, he felt a surge of longing in his chest for that very thing—purpose, responsibility. She was right that he was not happy on his current course, it was wearing him out and he was ready for change. This could be his chance to prove to everyone, himself included, what he was capable of.

Her expression did not change as he would have liked. "Charles," she said, an apology laced between her words, "I fear such a promise would not turn your father's mind."

"Surely there is something," he pleaded. "Some way I can restore this." He could be humble and obedient and responsible. "Mother, please, help me find a way."

She regarded him for several moments, her considerate expression giving him the barest hope that perhaps there was a solution. "I could appeal to him for a larger settlement so that your lifestyle is not so changed."

"It is not the money," Fenton said, though of course it was in part. "I *do* want to be a better man. I want to take on this responsibility and carry on the heritage of our family. For some time I have felt . . . dissatisfied, and with this turn, I am eager to embrace a life of greater purpose. I can be the man to make you proud, Mother. I can." It would not resolve his desire to punish his father, but at the moment, upsetting his father was a thing to be sniffed at and reprimanded for having brought him to this point. Fenton had thought he was punishing his father with his behavior, not himself.

Lady Chariton regarded him for a moment longer, then let out a breath. "I shall talk to him again and share your humility, but honestly, Charles, I would not dare hope too much. He is a stubborn man and does not give me much ear."

Fenton had no other course *but* to hope. Upon returning to his room, he added up the bills he had yet to turn over to his father's secretary: two hundred pounds for a new greatcoat—burgundy with six capes—and three hundred pounds' worth of pantaloons in a variety of shades and half a dozen cravats. He was particularly hard on his cravats and refused to wear them if they were not snow-white and perfectly starched.

In addition to his wardrobe expenses, he owed nearly four hundred pounds to Waiters for the last two weeks he'd spent at their tables, and rent on his rooms on St. James Street was due soon.

There were membership fees, Barker's services, upkeep of his curricle and horses—they could not be supported by a mere two thousand pounds a year. To imagine the changes in his lifestyle was unthinkable. And humiliating. His heritage had always been a matter of pride and security, and he expected to take responsibility one day, serve in Parliament, and manage the family holdings. He had done nothing to prepare for that course, however, and could see with his unveiled eyes that he had pushed his boundaries too far. There was no wondering why everyone felt him incapable.

He sent notes of apology to the night's entertainment he had previously agreed to attend and then waited. Waited for word from his mother. Waited to learn of his fate.

Though the liquor on the sideboard called to him, he refused to give in to the temptation. He needed to keep a clear head. He needed to remain in possession of his faculties. Certainly his unchecked drinking had played a role in the unraveling of his life. He had promised his mother he would be a better man and he would start today in hopes his determination would invite redemption.

It wasn't until the next morning that Barker handed him a note. Because Fenton had not drunk himself into oblivion the night before, he was not soggy-headed and was grateful for the clarity. Relieved to see his mother's precise hand, he swung his legs over the side of the bed and fumbled to open the letter. He scanned the words, too anxious to read them one by one until he could surmise that her appeal to the earl seemed to have worked. Lord Chariton had taken her counsel; Fenton was preserved! Only when he knew his fate had been spared was he able to read the letter in its entirety:

Dearest Charles,

I have had quite a conference with your father and defended your position as eloquently as I possibly could. I have never rallied for anything in the whole of my life as much as I have for this. Your father is not of a mind to give me much ear, but I did not relent. The negotiation that came of my zealousness required that I make great promises on your behalf, but your father has agreed to stay his hand if, and only if, you agree to fulfill the following expectations:

- *Assume the management of the estate associated with your current title.*
- *Employ a capable secretary who will help you organize yourself and move you forward to the running of your holding and management of your lifestyle and funds. Your father will approve this choice before it is fully determined.*
- *Conduct yourself with greater decorum amid society, presenting yourself as befitting your station.*
- *Make an adequate match with a woman of respectability before the season ends and marry her by Michaelmas, in six months' time.*

If you can agree to these provisions, your father is willing to forgo his decision to disinherit you. I cannot impress upon you enough that you must rise to this, Charles. You must be committed to this course. Should you fail to meet these expectations, both you and I will pay a heavy price.

My dear boy, it is the greatest wish of my mother's

heart that you shall embrace this as an opportunity to find joy and comfort. I beg of you to make the amends necessary with your father to make this course work. Become a man your parents can be proud of. I beg you to do it.

Your Loving Mother,

Lady Chariton

CHAPTER 7

Rebecca nudged Alice and nodded toward the doorway. "There he is."

Alice turned her head and felt a shiver down her spine in response to seeing the man of her childhood fantasy—Lord Fenton himself.

"Is he as handsome as you imagined?" Rebecca whispered.

"Indeed," Alice said, but she frowned slightly. His knee breeches were emerald green and his silver coat was embroidered with a floral pattern. "Goodness, he really has become a dandy."

"But a handsome one," Rebecca said, tapping her sister on the arm with her fan. "And rich as Croesus."

Alice did not care about Lord Fenton's fortune, though it certainly didn't hurt her opinion of him. The more powerful effect of seeing him was the reaction she had to his presence. For years she had thought what a silly girl she was to let her fancy run so amok. And yet here he was, and her knees were *truly* weak—it was fortunate she was already seated. When he caught sight of her, he paused and she wondered if he were trying to place her in his memory. Surely she did not look the same as she had when he had last seen her; she'd been twelve years old the last time he'd come to one of her father's house parties. Finally he smiled, warming her as though he were the very sun.

A gentleman took Lord Fenton's attention, and not long after that dinner was announced. Lady Chariton had invited the entire Stanbridge family to the dinner party at her London home. Alice's father, Maryanne, Rebecca, and Alice had made this evening a priority, though Rebecca's husband had been unable to attend.

This dinner was the event Alice had looked forward to the most since her arrival in town nearly a fortnight ago. At each *ton* event she attended, she had hoped to see Lord Fenton, but not once had they been at the same party at the same time. On two occasions he had been there earlier but had already taken his leave before she arrived; at another he had cancelled at the last minute. But she had known he would be here tonight and had been in the grip of a continual case of butterflies all day in anticipation. Now that she had seen him, those butterflies seemed satisfied and her emotions transitioned into those of eager expectations rather than anxious ones.

Lord Fenton was seated almost as far away from her as he could be at the twenty-six-place table. She watched him engaging with the young women on either side of him—both of them beautiful and well dressed—and tried to talk herself out of feeling jealous. The blonde on his right blushed when he leaned in and whispered something in her ear, and Alice felt her own cheeks warm with envy of the shared intimacy.

Alice was soon engaged in conversation with the gentleman on her left. He was kind and attentive but he was not Lord Fenton, her childhood hero and fantasy brought to life. Outside of this infatuation, few people would accuse Alice of being a romantic, and she had all but been convinced that her affections for Lord Fenton were nothing more than the remnants of a childhood fancy; but being in the same room as him was invigorating.

And, oh, but he *was* handsome. His hair had darkened to a golden color, and he wore it combed forward in the latest fashion, held in place with some type of wax or oil that made his hair shine under the candlelight. His eyes were a rich blue, like the wings of a bluebird, and his brow and jaw were firm and strong. The gangly days of his youth had given way to broad shoulders and powerful legs. He was taller than most men in the room, and between his physique and his flair for style he commanded attention seemingly without any effort. Even his movements were perfect, a casual toss of his head when he laughed, the languid way he raised an eyebrow in question, and now and again the exaggerated movements of his hand making graceful circles in the air as he emphasized some point.

It was while Alice was caught up in such thoughts that Lord Fenton caught her watching him across the table. Alice ducked her head, embarrassed to have been found staring, but when she looked up again, he was smiling in her direction and gave her a quick wink. Her stomach erupted in butterflies again, and it was all she could do to keep her hand from shaking as she lifted her glass and took a drink in an attempt to cover her reaction. She tried not to look at him for the rest of dinner, but between courses and conversations she kept finding her gaze drifting toward him again and again.

The women removed to the drawing room after dinner was complete, but it was not long before the gentlemen joined them. Alice's heart was near to racing when Lord Fenton appeared before her with his mother, who gave them a proper introduction. Lady Chariton referred to Alice as a dear friend, such as her mother had been before her. Lord Fenton bent over her hand ceremoniously and then straightened, causing Alice to look up into his face as he was some inches taller than she.

"My, but it has been an age, Miss Stanbridge."

Alice found herself spellbound by his proximity. Lady Chariton excused herself while Lord Fenton sat down on the chair closest to the settee Alice occupied with Rebecca. He exchanged small talk with Rebecca, as they were acquainted previously, before turning those beautiful blue eyes to Alice. Every thought in her head skittered away.

"I daresay you have grown into quite a remarkable woman in the years since I saw you last, Miss Stanbridge." Alice's cheeks caught fire, and his lips spread into a smile. He leaned in slightly and emphasized his compliment. "Quite remarkable."

Alice could think of absolutely nothing to say. It was a few more seconds until he spoke again. "Though you were much more talkative back then."

"I am sorry, my lord," she stammered, trying to get ahold of herself and fearing she never would until he removed himself, which would defeat her hopes for this evening entirely. "You've grown up as well—so much I hardly recognized you."

"I shall take that as a grand compliment," he said, shaking his head dramatically. "I was rather pathetic as a child, I'm afraid, and quite glad to know that you consider me improved."

She nodded, overcome with how truly improved he was. He even smelled divine, like menthol and sage.

"And how is your garden from those years past?" he asked when she said nothing to spur the conversation forward.

Alice could only manage a nod, and Rebecca, seated beside her, cleared her throat to draw Lord Fenton's attention. "She has a much larger garden at Warren House now, walled in by a trellis that runs over with all number of climbing vines. She manages the cook's herb garden as well. I hope it is not all that shocking for you to hear, Lord Fenton, but that little plot you arranged for our Alice all those years ago quite set her on a course."

Lord Fenton smiled even wider, but more with the left side of his mouth than the right. Alice felt sure she was melting, only it was too slow for anyone else to notice. And she did not mind a bit. If the last sight of Lord Fenton she ever saw was him smiling at her, she would be happy through the eternities.

"Is that so?" Lord Fenton asked Alice. "Pray, tell me what do you grow in this trellised garden of yours?"

"Roses," Alice blurted. "Potatoes too."

Lord Fenton raised an eyebrow as his smile widened. "You don't say?"

She nodded even though his eyes were laughing at her. "And snapdragons—they are my favorite, you know—and columbine and hydrangeas and thyme along the walkways."

Rebecca nudged her with her elbow, alerting Alice to the cake she was making of herself. She reigned in her babbling. "I love to grow things." All these years she had been waiting to see Lord Fenton again and she said she loved to grow things? If she could melt a bit faster she could save all of them this embarrassment! She cleared her throat, took a breath to calm herself, and tried again. "How are you, Lord Fenton? How is your family?"

His expression stilled, but then he seemed to push his smile a bit bigger. "All is well with my family and myself. And yours?" He included Rebecca in the question. "Is your father in good health? Your sister?"

Rebecca gave an update regarding their father—who was playing cards in another room—and the rest of their family, in response to which Lord Fenton offered his compliments. They spoke of the weather and the elegance of the drawing room. When the conversation died out, he turned back to Alice and fixed her with those eyes that were surely the most amazing shade of blue as ever she'd seen.

"I must know, Miss Stanbridge. Did you ever take up sewing?"

Alice's heart soared at his remembrance of such a thing from a childhood conversation, but she tried not to nod too effusively while also committing to not sounding like an idiot again when she spoke to him this time. "I had no choice but to take it up at some point, my lord. I believe it is what drawing rooms were made for—so that women would have a place to sew. Therefore, if I wanted to be in a drawing room during daylight hours, I had to stitch."

He chuckled, increasing Alice's confidence enough that she continued. "And I learned to play the pianoforte, though not well I'm afraid."

"Do you ride now, too? Or read more than, what did you call them, baby books?"

Her cheeks colored. What a precocious child she'd been, and yet he'd remembered so many details. "I'm afraid horses still make me itch and sneeze, but I do quite enjoy reading."

"And what do you read?" Lord Fenton asked. He waved a hand in the direction of the young women he'd been seated between at dinner. They were trying to get his attention with flips of their head and emphasizing their bosom while appearing not to. "Those girls claim to read only histories."

"Well," Alice said, adjusting her position as she tried to decipher the intent behind his question. She felt sure that "those girls" had somehow disappointed him with their answer. If she didn't know better, she might think he was interviewing the lot of them. "I like a history now and again," she said. "But I must admit that most of my reading is confined to books regarding botany and herbs. I've been known to read a romance from time to time, but did you know those books are mostly about girls who like to sew?"

Lord Fenton laughed at that, and she smiled a bit wider, especially when those two history-reading girls looked her way with narrowed eyes. Lord Fenton was by far the most eligible and well-connected man in the room—perhaps in all of London—and was giving *her* his full attention. Her pride in such a thing was warranted; no one would argue the point.

"So you are not entertained by romance, then?" Lord Fenton asked.

Another odd question, but she felt sure of the answer he was requesting and against her own character gave it to him. "I believe romances are for silly girls or homely ones. I choose to think that I am neither." She could scarce believe she'd said such a thing, and judging by the way Rebecca gasped and coughed, she'd taken her sister quite by surprise as well.

Lord Fenton, however, merely lifted his eyebrows in an appraising way as he continued to regard her.

"Shall you be attending the balloon ascension in Hyde Park tomorrow morning, my lord?" Rebecca asked, a poorly concealed attempt at rescue. "As this is Alice's first time to London we are taking in a variety of activities."

"Certainly not," Lord Fenton said, his voice suddenly lyrical as he made an exaggerated frown and put his hand to his chest dramatically. "Far too early in the morning for me. Why, I don't think I have ever attended a single ascension in all my years. Are they truly worth waking up before the sun? Seems awfully uncomfortable."

The three of them chatted for some time about the entertainments of London, until Lord Fenton was cajoled into playing a round of cards in another room. He gave an elaborate bow that reminded Alice of the one he'd given her on the day she received the garden. She felt cocooned within a cloud of sweet nostalgia. "I hope to see you ladies again," he said, giving Alice's hand a squeeze before releasing it.

They agreed likewise, and Alice sighed as she watched him retreat from the room.

"Alice," her sister said, leaning in so as not to be overheard. "What on earth were you thinking? 'Silly or homely girls, and I don't believe I am either'?" She shook her head. "That was the most outrageous flirting I have ever heard from you—very bold indeed."

"I truly can't say what possessed me," Alice said, feeling a bit lightheaded. "Other than the fact that I fear my childhood fancy was not so specific to my youth as I had once convinced myself."

Rebecca's eyes grew wide at such a confession. "Alice," she finally said, her voice even, "Lord Fenton shall have his pick of women once he decides to marry. While I agree you are neither silly nor homely, you came off as one of the dozens of girls who have set their cap for an earl and mean to get him through any manner of outrageous behavior."

"I shan't get him," Alice said, feeling the regret of the truth and embarrassment for believing—just for a moment—that perhaps she could. "Not with Father's situation. I know that."

Alice understood that her future had been greatly affected by her father's change in circumstance. Furthermore, she expected everyone in London knew her family's situation. She'd heard plenty of gossip about the situation of other girls making presentation and knew her story was circulating as well. At best, she was seen as a pretty enough debutante with little settled upon her—four hundred pounds was all—and only moderate connections. At worst she could be deemed a fortune hunter hoping to improve her father's position.

For a man with his pick of women, Alice Stanbridge would not make the grade—unless Lord Fenton was the type of man to be affected by nostalgia and romance. To hope for such a thing was as invigorating as it was ill-fated.

"It was wonderful to see him again," Alice said, trying to keep the realization of her inadequacies out of her tone. "I shall content myself with his kind reception tonight. It was very good of him to be so welcoming."

"I'm sorry, Alice," Rebecca said with such pity that Alice looked away. It was one thing to feel the lack of hope within your own mind, quite another to feel the pity of others because of it.

Rebecca took Alice's hand. "I don't know that it will make you feel any better, but along with being eligible, Lord Fenton is the greatest flirt I have ever known. I do not think his attention to any female is directed toward matrimony, and any time I have heard of him forming an attachment to a particular woman, he suddenly leaves town, breaking ties completely, not to mention the hearts that have been set upon him."

"Attachments?" Alice asked. Surely he did not break *engagements*—no one would let their daughters near him if he had a history of breaking even one engagement, let alone several. She could not imagine Rebecca was insinuating anything immoral, however; he would be equally cut out of society if he were taking advantage of his position and damaging the reputation of young women in society. "Is his be-havior unchaste?"

Rebecca shook her head. "I have never heard more than him stealing a kiss or two, and that is no less than any young buck will do when given the chance. What I mean is that he seems the kind of man with whom women fall in love quite easily, but it seems to be all a game to him."

Alice's heart tightened hearing Rebecca justify Lord Fenton's at-tention to her this evening. "I have no expectation," she assured her sister, patting Rebecca's hand. "You may rest easy knowing that my heart is quite safe."

If only that were true.

CHAPTER 8

"Is there anything else, then?" Lord Chariton's solicitor asked, looking between the two men sitting on opposite sides of Lord Chariton's desk. Fenton had just signed the paperwork—a contract his father had drawn up reflecting the terms of their arrangement. It was insulting and degrading, and yet Fenton had signed. In the two and a half weeks since receiving his mother's letter that outlined the responsibilities he was to rise to, he had resigned himself to his fate, and each aspect of the requirements had moved forward, some faster than others.

"No, Mr. Benson," Lord Chariton said, not looking at his solicitor standing beside the desk. "Please see that the agreement is properly filed."

"Very good," Mr. Benson said, keeping his attention directed to the earl. "I shall proceed with Lord Fenton's education for the remainder of the afternoon in the library, then. The candidates for the position of his secretary shall begin to arrive in half an hour's time for their interviews."

"Very good," Lord Chariton said as he stood and stepped back from the desk, allowing Mr. Benson to gather the papers. Fenton stood as well and straightened his coat—a claret color which looked very well against the dark woods of his father's office—not that either of these two men would notice such a thing. "Mr. Benson, might my son and I have a word before he joins you in the library?".

Mr. Benson nodded and quickly left the room, pulling the door shut behind him. It was all Fenton could do to contain his irritation. Though he'd agreed to the plan and had begun adjusting to his commitments regarding it, his feelings toward his father had not softened one whit. The man was a tyrant, and despite the fact that they were now working together in some respects, their time in one another's company had been limited.

Fenton was in no mood for a private conference. To return to his seat would allow his father to look down on him, which Fenton did not like as it made his father seem authoritative, but to remain standing would show more respect than he felt toward the man. He returned to his chair and lounged back, resting one ankle upon the opposite knee. There had been nothing in the contract he'd just signed about standing to attention. Not specifically anyway.

"It goes without saying that all of this was your mother's idea," Lord Chariton said, waving his hand through the air. "I am quite willing to let you go."

"Yes," Fenton said evenly. "I am aware of that." He still had yet to determine why his father had gone along with it; the earl had taken every opportunity to express how much he detested the arrangement.

"But I am glad to avoid the scandal of it." Lord Chariton took a breath and leaned back in his chair. For the first time he met Fenton's eyes. "With the contract signed, I shall no longer be tolerant of your dandyism. You look ridiculous."

"Mother said that I did not have to dispose of my wardrobe." Fenton had considered that a win, but agreed to favor his more conservative pieces when in appropriate company. The claret-colored suit with the green-and-red striped waistcoat seemed appropriate for today's meeting—it was not bright nor was it silk or even satin.

"When you are transacting business, you will dress the part—conservative and in keeping with the company you shall be in."

"Black and gray, then?" Fenton said with disgust. "As though I am in mourning?"

"As though you are a respectable man who knows his place," his father said. "Tell your mother to help you find some suits that will reflect your responsibility—save your peacocking for your friends."

"Very well," Fenton said, waving his hand in the air and keeping his tone flippant even though he knew he was pressing his luck. He couldn't quite make himself act fully the part he'd agreed to play, even as he worried his father would change his mind because of it.

"It will do no good to make such agreements as we have made only to have you disgracing us both in public now that I am showing confidence in your ability to rise above the man you've been," Lord Chariton snapped. "I want to be sure you are taking this seriously and not seeing it as yet one more game to play until you tire of it."

Oh, how Fenton wanted to argue, but what good would that do? He had agreed to all of his father's requests, and his mother had allowed him to keep his fashions for social events with his peers. To poke at the agreement now by continuing his untowardness would do him no good at all and could, instead, push his father's patience to its limit. Rather than say as much, Fenton just nodded.

"You will show me respect, or I shall end this now," his father said. "Take it seriously."

Fenton took a breath to calm himself, then straightened and held his father's glare. "Yes, my lord." The words burned on his tongue, but he hoped that in time they would not taste so acidic. "I signed your contract. I assure you I am quite serious in this endeavor."

His father harrumphed, as though dissatisfied. Fenton clenched his teeth but kept his expression free of his true feelings.

"I shall try to keep our time in one another's company to a minimum, Charles. I do not know that either of us can be expected to play such roles of accommodation often, but I expect better than I have seen thus far."

"I should add my hearty agreement to such limitations of one another's company," Fenton said.

Lord Chariton scowled and shook his head. "You are still an embarrassment of a son."

"And you are still a cad of a father."

His father narrowed his eyes, and Fenton hurried to add, "But I shall keep such thoughts to myself and behave as I have agreed to. Perhaps if both of us ease off from baiting one another we shall find more accord."

His father watched him a moment before nodding in agreement. Then he waved Fenton out of the room without another word.

Mr. Benson was waiting in the library, and Fenton joined him at the small table set by the window. The polite smile Mr. Benson gave Fenton was strained, and Fenton considered that the claret-colored suit was not doing him any favors with this man either.

"I do thank you for your help, Mr. Benson," Fenton said with sincerity. "I very much want to do well."

Mr. Benson regarded him with some doubt, but then nodded. "I shall do all I can to enhance your success. I believe it best to begin with an overview of the Chariton holdings before focusing on those items in which you will be personally involved. Is that acceptable?"

Fenton was surprised by the wave of eagerness he felt, surprised that he could truly want such responsibility and understanding. And yet he did. It felt good to have the opportunity to expand himself for a purpose. It was his greatest hope to show both of his parents how well he could fill the shoes laid out for him, and in this way he welcomed all the new expectations he faced. He would succeed. He would prove himself capable of being the man he was born to be.

When all was finished at the London house regarding the hiring of his secretary—a man named Mr. Webb—and Fenton's education, Fenton walked with Mr. Benson to the door and thanked him again for his time. Then he checked his watch and hurried upstairs to his mother's sitting room for tea. He was a few minutes later than he'd planned but hoped she had waited.

Lady Chariton had indeed waited for him, and he kissed her cheek when he arrived. He settled into a chair and relayed the details of the day. The pride in her face muted his continued irritation with his father until he could look back on the afternoon and feel nothing but contentment and even excitement about all that was taking place.

"I would not have guessed it to be so interesting," he said, taking another cinnamon scone when she offered it to him. They had always been his favorite, and she made sure they were included when he came for tea. "Mr. Webb and I shall be leaving for Fentonview on Tuesday and spend the rest of the week becoming familiar with it. I haven't been there in years."

In truth he had spent most of his years since Oxford in London, only now and again visiting the home of a friend or going to whichever one of the family estates his mother was staying in at any given time but never remaining for more than a few weeks. It would be strange to live in the country, but Mr. Benson had encouraged Fenton to winter at Fentonview so as to position himself correctly with the staff and better oversee the management of the estate.

Fenton wondered what the society was like in Hampshire and chose to be optimistic that he would enjoy the adventure of new company—heaven knew the old company was wearing increasingly thin now that he was attempting to be a responsible man. He could barely stand Newt's antics these days, for instance, to say nothing of Burbidge, who had taken to poking feathers in Fenton's hair whenever they met.

"Fentonview is a lovely estate," his mother said. "Small, and with a fair amount of unusable land, but beautiful, especially this time of year."

"Excellent. As I shall be wintering there, you will have to come visit and see what you think of me in the role of lord of the manor." He struck a pose, inclining his chin and lowering his eyelids, gratified when his mother laughed.

"And who will winter there with you?" his mother asked as he reached for yet another scone.

Fenton opened his mouth to say that he did not think many of his friends would find it all that interesting when he realized what she meant. He let out a dramatic, but sincere, breath. "I keep forgetting about this wife business. I have until Michaelmas—surely I can wait a bit longer before I make my choice."

"From a man who hasn't the faintest idea of what goes into a courtship and a wedding, I should not be surprised by such a comment. But let me assure you that time is of the essence. Especially if you plan to go to Fentonview after the season is finished in June. Having a match in place will make the transition easier, and it is not necessary to have a long courtship."

Fenton frowned. "A wife feels like an awful lot of work, Mama. Is not managing the estate enough for me to worry about right now?"

Lady Chariton laughed and shook her head. "You have made an effort to meet a number of young women these last weeks—I've watched you make the rounds—surely one of them has risen in your esteem. If you cannot yet make a choice, at least be intent on furthering your connection to the women that catch your attention. You have not taken a one of them on a carriage ride, or even sent round a posy to declare your admiration. A wife is not something you pick as if choosing a waistcoat to wear to a party."

Fenton considered that statement with an exaggerated scowl for several ticks of the clock on the mantel, then shook his head. "I can't say that any debutante has caught my eye, Mama, and the thing of it is, I am not *interested* in having a wife." In fact, the whole idea of it made his palms sweat. Not with eager anticipation, but with pure anxiety. How could he be responsible for a wife when he was only just becoming responsible for himself? "Does it not seem unfair for me to ensnare some young woman when I am unsure of my interests? I have not even decided if I prefer blue eyes to brown, and as a wife will accompany me for the rest of my life, I feel quite anxious about rushing my decision."

"Her eye color will not matter nearly as much as her disposition," Lady Chariton assured him. "And that you feel no particular affection can work in your favor as it will keep your mind clear enough to make a *wise* choice rather than an infatuated one. Make a decision on wisdom and then get to know a woman well enough to know if she would be a good match for you. You have your pick, Charles, and any number of suitable women are *very* attentive to you."

Fenton was silent a moment as he considered his mother's words. He knew that when his parents had married, his mother had fancied herself in love. He also knew that over time that love had faded into merely a legal connection, and that was all. His parents had little to do with one another—not even living at the same estate most of the year—and treated one another with polite indifference. Their negotiation of his responsibilities was perhaps the most interaction they had shared in years.

Fenton would be a fair husband, a kind one, and one day a good father to his children. Only he was not ready for such things. The very idea of being a husband was unsettling, the idea that his marriage could produce a child and make him a father . . . unreal.

His mother interrupted his thoughts—thank goodness—but he did not hear what she said. "Excuse me, Mama. I was woolgathering."

"I asked you what you thought of Alice Stanbridge."

"Miss Stanbridge?" he repeated. His mind returned to the conversation he'd had with her a few nights earlier at his mother's dinner party. She was a good conversationalist and had turned out pretty after all, with a wide smile he quite liked. But her dress had been outdated and a dusty color of green. There wasn't anything, truly, that set her apart from anyone else except for the shared connection from their youth. But of what import was that? Some silly interaction from years ago could not weigh in her favor all that much. "I can't say I've thought much of her at all. We have only spoken the one time."

"I was able to speak with her at length some weeks ago, when she first arrived in Town, and I found her *very* pleasant. Respectful, bright, and pretty too. I was friends with her mother when we were girls, you know, and we used to go to the house parties her father threw in Essex. Do you remember?"

"Of course," Fenton said. "I thought her a peculiar girl back then." She had certainly grown up, however, and as Fenton thought back to her at the dinner party and looked past the drab gown, the more unconscious details of his notice slipped into his mind: the shapeliness of her figure, the smoothness of her skin, and the modest confidence in which she held herself.

"She seems a very good sort of girl," Lady Chariton continued. "Do you not find her attractive? She has a beautiful smile, and lovely eyes. Why, everything about her is feminine and fine, I think."

Pondering on the attractiveness of Alice Stanbridge in regard to the type of wife she could be was not necessarily something Fenton liked to give way too. Years ago, he had determined not to fall victim to such notice. He was a flirt to be sure, and unopposed to making women blush and simper through compliments; however, he did not allow his thoughts to run wild. Not ever. It seemed to him that the relations between men and women posed a great threat to one's self-control, and he knew too well the damage that could be done. His father's words to him all those years ago that men would be men and their nature could not be changed was rather frightening to Fenton. As though men could not control that part of their character—as though fidelity was impossible. Fenton had determined *not* to be such a man.

Yet he was to be married? How would he square that with his determination not to let appetite control him? Would his father's words be proven correct after all? Would he find it impossible to be faithful and therefore bring the same pain to the woman he married that his father had brought to Fenton's mother for all these years?

"Charles?"

"Yes, sorry, Mama," Fenton said, coming back to the present yet again and glad she did not know his thoughts. "I can't say I have a particular opinion of Miss Stanbridge, but it seems you do."

Lady Chariton turned her cup on her saucer, watching it instead of meeting Fenton's eye when she spoke. "I wouldn't ask you to rely solely on my judgment, of course, but she seems to be a steady girl, and I felt from the first time I met her here in London that she would make a fine wife."

"For *me*?" Fenton pressed. His mother's opinion meant more to him than he wanted her to know for fear she might manipulate it somehow if she realized how insecure he was with his own ability to choose. But he did not feel as though he could make this choice, not with any confidence.

Lady Chariton gave a shrug of one shoulder. "Perhaps you could spend a bit more time with her and see if you don't find her pleasing too."

Fenton put his saucer back on the tray, making an instantaneous decision that eased his mind quite a lot. To look at every woman he met as a potential wife was irritating, and after only two weeks he was quite tired of it. Perhaps the solution was to orchestrate a match that would not lay all aspects of matrimony at his feet at once. Perhaps treating it as a business arrangement would help it to be exactly that, thereby freeing him from the discomfiting realities he was not yet prepared to face.

"I leave for Fentonview on Tuesday and shan't be back for a week. Courting is such a boring prospect, and you yourself said that to become infatuated with anyone might become a complication." He paused, considered one last time what he was going to say next, and decided he felt as good about it as could be expected. "You like Alice Stanbridge and feel she would make a good wife for me?"

Lady Chariton looked confused and perhaps a bit concerned. "I do, but—"

"Then that is good enough for me," Fenton said, rising to his feet and smiling broadly at his mother, who stared back at him in surprise. "I do find her appealing, and what's more, she is not a silly little thing without a practical thought in her head." He struck a pose, his thumb and forefinger on his chin as he looked out the window a moment, then nodded crisply and turned to his mother, who looked shocked by his pronouncement. "Yes, I think Alice Stanbridge is *exactly* what I should like in a wife, and so I shall see to it before I leave for Hampshire. I see no reason to wait until Michaelmas." He leaned in and kissed his mother's hand. "Thank you for your help, Mama. I shall let you know how she responds to my proposal."

CHAPTER 9

Rebecca and Alice were attending to breakfast Monday morning— it had been five days since the dinner party at the home of Lord and Lady Chariton—when the butler told them that their parents requested their presence in the drawing room. The sisters exchanged curious glances, but stood and made their way to the drawing room. A message for their father had been delivered as they were coming to breakfast, and now Alice worried it was bad news.

When they entered the drawing room, both their father and Maryanne turned from where they had been whispering to one another by the fireplace and looked directly at Alice.

Alice wiped at her face, worried that perhaps she had some jam about her mouth or something to explain their intent looks.

"Papa?" Rebecca asked.

Mr. Stanbridge lifted the letter he held in his hand but though his mouth opened and shut he did not speak.

"What is it?" Alice said, as her alarm deepened. "What has happened?"

"Lord Fenton . . ." Maryanne began. She paused and licked her lips before she spoke again. "Lord Fenton has . . . asked for Alice's hand."

For an instant, the room froze.

"What?" Rebecca said.

Mr. Stanbridge held out the letter, and Alice crossed the room quickly. She grabbed the paper and scanned the words as shock and joy and excitement bubbled up from her very toes. "I don't believe it," she whispered, committing the words of the letter to memory.

It is my desire to request your daughter's hand in marriage. . . . I shall be attending to matters of business out of Town for the next week but request an audience with you upon my return . . . look forward to working out the details.

Marriage. In a letter? Did people do such things?

"I cannot believe it," Rebecca said, having read the letter over Alice's shoulder. "How could this be?"

"The letter came just a few minutes ago," her father said. "Lord Chariton is an old friend, of course, but . . ."

"Lady Chariton has been quite particular in her attention to Alice here in London, has she not?" Maryanne added.

Alice nodded in agreement about Lady Chariton's solicitude and read the letter again, her mind hazy from shock. "I have spoken with Lord Fenton only once here in Town." But they had shared a connection years ago. Warmth spread from her toes upward through her entire body as she realized that the regard must not have been hers alone all these years. This was fate. It was God's hand!

"Lord Fenton *is* of marriageable age and situation," Rebecca said as though trying to justify this unexpected circumstance. "I understand he has been taking over a degree of responsibility of late—but I just . . . I do not know what to think of this."

"To propose in a letter?" Papa asked. He turned to look at Maryanne, who shrugged, equally confused.

"It is very strange," she said.

"Very strange," Rebecca repeated as the three of them exchanged worried looks that Alice found rather offensive. Why was it so hard to believe that Lord Fenton could be in love with her? Was her position within their family so overlooked that they could not even consider that someone *could* see her? *Want* her?

"As he says, he is busy with his work and leaving Town," Alice said, anxious to have their support. "And as we are all acquainted with one another he knew we would not look down on such a unique presentation. Besides, I told him I am a practical girl. This is simply a practical proposal." Surely he would make up for the lack of romance at a later date. The idea made her heart flip over in her chest and her smile widened. Lord Fenton—the most eligible bachelor in all of England!

Rebecca and Maryanne shared another look but did not comment, causing Alice's heart to tighten and her ire to rise.

"Are you not happy?" she asked sharply.

Did they not realize this connection would benefit all of them? What it could do for their father's situation alone seemed worthy of their celebration, and what it did for Alice's confidence, future, and security was beyond explanation. Rebecca had said Lord Fenton could have his choice of women, and his choice had been Alice—the one so often set apart, the one so often overlooked. But not any longer. From this day forward her entire life was different; she was different. She could command respect and notice, distinction and position. She would be above her sisters in station and wealth; *she* would be the admired one, the one finally chosen above anyone else.

Even though she realized how arrogant and selfish her thoughts were, she could not help it—finally, she had arrived in a place where no one could ever ignore her again. She would be *Lady Fenton*. One day she would be a *countess*!

She looked at her family still processing the proposal and felt her chest tighten even more. "You all act as though it is impossible for Lord Fenton to want me for a wife. Is my merit so very low?"

"We *are* happy for you, of course," Maryanne said, placing a hand on Alice's arm and smiling, though it was somewhat forced. "And Lord Fenton shall be the luckiest of men to have a wife such as yourself, it's just that . . ."

"What?" Alice asked, raising her eyebrows in challenge. Did they not realize how rude their reactions were? "It is just that *what*?"

"We're just so confused," Papa finally said, his forehead creasing.

Alice looked from one to the next and made a decision. Let them be confused and befuddled and so certain of her insignificance. She would not be affected by it. For once she would proclaim herself and allow the fullness of her feelings to be seen.

"Think what you will, but for my part, this is worthy of celebration!" She clapped her hands together and felt as though she were in a dream as she twirled toward the windows for a better view of what was surely the most beautiful day London had ever known.

Of all the women in London, Lord Fenton had chosen her. She would bask in the joy of such a thing and feel every ounce of happiness it could bring to her. In the course of mere minutes her entire world had changed, and she was fit to burst because of it!

CHAPTER 10

Alice accepted Lord Fenton's proposal through a letter her father delivered the same morning. She wanted to be sure he received it before he left London. By the time he returned a week later, her family had overcome their shock and joined in her celebration—every one of them would be affected by this rise in station and was therefore excited about the prospect.

On the second night after Lord Fenton's return to Town, Alice and Rebecca waited eagerly for his carriage to arrive. It would be the first event that Alice and Fenton would attend as an engaged couple, and she could hardly contain herself as she paced back and forth in the foyer.

"Are you nervous or excited?" Rebecca asked, watching her sister with an indulgent smile.

"I certainly can't choose one over the other so I must proclaim myself equally both." Alice reached the doorway to the drawing room and turned on her heel to pace the other direction. *Lady Fenton*, she said in her mind, trying to get used to the title. A title! Her title! She turned to face her sister. "Should I have another feather in my hair, do you think?" She waved to the two white plumes attached to the back of her elaborate hairdo. Chloe had lent Alice her own lady's maid to help her ready herself for the evening, and though Alice loved the presentation, she was unused to such finery. In addition to the feathers, she wore a triple strand of pearls about her neck—lent by Maryanne—and six thin silver bracelets on her left wrist—lent by Rebecca. "Is it out of sorts to have an even number? It seems most ladies wear one or three feathers at a time."

"You count the feathers women wear in their hair?" Rebecca asked, tilting her head. "I honestly do not believe it matters."

Alice nodded and tried to feel better, but she was terrified of not presenting herself as she should. What if Lord Fenton was displeased with her? What if people whispered behind their hands that she was not quite the thing? She had never before cared what other people thought, which only made it more difficult to process her fears now. There was a knock at the door, and Alice spun to face it.

"You're going to be wonderful," Rebecca whispered from behind her. "Just relax, have a good time, remember who you are and who you are with."

A footman opened the door, and Lord Fenton stood at the threshold. He bowed elaborately, apologized profusely for being tardy on account of his shoes being in need of a second polish, and then put out an arm for each woman in order to escort them to the carriage.

Alice caught his eye as he handed her up and smiled rather coyly, but he seemed to have looked away before he could see it. She and Rebecca settled on one side of the carriage, while Lord Fenton and Lady Chariton sat on the other side. If it were not such a large coach perhaps her knees would have touched Lord Fenton's, but as it was there was a great deal of space between them. The journey to the ball was filled with Lord Fenton's account of the estate he had just returned from, and Alice took pride in his obvious attentiveness to it.

Alice felt a shiver through her entire body as she entered the ball on Lord Fenton's arm. It was impossible not to notice the eyes that turned their way and the admiring whisper that rose from the crowd. She unconsciously tightened her grip on Lord Fenton's arm, and he answered by patting her fingers and leaning toward her. "I suspect we are the talk of the town," he said, but the levity she expected for such a comment—especially from a man so easily amused—was not there. Rather it sounded heavy, almost disappointed.

She looked up at him but only caught his glance for a moment before he looked away and moved forward. "We shall both need to do the pretty, I'm afraid, and accept all these congratulations with graciousness."

"How else would we accept them?" Alice asked, but there was no time for him to answer before they were officially announced. There was even less time to reflect on the exchange as they were indeed descended upon by any number of Lord Fenton's acquaintances. It was some time later that her intended led her to the floor for a quadrille. Lifted on the breath of so many well-wishes and envying looks, Alice let go of her inhibitions in order to match him in elegance and manner throughout the dance. Had she ever felt like such a princess in her entire life?

"You are an excellent dancer, Miss Stanbridge," Lord Fenton said as he led her off the floor when the dance came to an end.

"As are you, Lord Fenton," she said, feeling shy all of a sudden. "I hope we might dance again this evening."

"I shouldn't want to deny the other young men your company."

They reached his mother at the edge of the crowd and he bowed to the women, then excused himself for a game of whist in another room.

Alice watched him go, unsure how to interpret the unease she felt by his departure. She had never spent much time in any man's company, so it was likely her inexperience that had her feeling unsettled, but he did not seem particularly interested in her company tonight. Not as she had expected he would. Had she done something wrong?

"Alice?" Rebecca said softly. "Are you all right?"

Alice immediately repaired any negativity that might be showing on her face and turned to her sister. "Of course I am all right," she said with a bit of a laugh so as to make Rebecca's inquiry seem ridiculous. "It's all just so heady."

"To be sure," Rebecca said, seemingly appeased.

A young man was suddenly before Alice, bowing and asking her to dance. He'd no sooner formed the question when another young man stepped up and said that he would be "absolutely destroyed" if she did not agree to dance the next set with him.

"You see, I am David Burbidge—Lord Fenton's closest friend," the second man said. "And I am absolutely agog with curiosity about the woman who saved poor Fenton from bachelorhood. You must be quite a lady to have won such a heart as his." He grinned, and Alice was trying to form a response to his brazen commentary when the first man elbowed Mr. Burbidge in the ribs and pushed him aside.

"*I* am Lord Fenton's closest friend," he insisted. "But I must admit to equal curiosity as this bit of baggage," he jabbed his thumb in Mr. Burbidge's direction. "My name is Oscar Newtonhouser." He bowed elaborately, much like Lord Fenton sometimes did, and rose with a grin equal to Mr. Burbidge's. He put out his hand and lifted his eyebrows, which she thought might have some color added to them to make them match his purple coat. "Shall we take the floor, Miss Stanbridge? You will soon find that I am not only Lord Fenton's closest friend, but I am also a far better dancer than Mr. Burbidge here. My, but the man has two left feet."

Mr. Burbidge stood with his arms crossed and rolled his eyes while Mr. Newtonhouser made his proclamations. Alice did not know what to make of either one of them.

"I shall await you with bated breath," Mr. Burbidge said, taking Alice's other hand and bending over it. He released it dramatically and then placed his hand against his heart. Alice allowed herself to be led to the floor by Mr. Newtonhouser and cast a questioning look toward Rebecca. That her sister was merely amused and not irritated helped put Alice's mind at ease.

It did not take long for Alice to realize that Mr. Newtonhouser was a complete tease. He laid on such thick compliments that by the end of the dance it was all she could do not to laugh out loud. Mr. Burbidge turned out to be almost the same, save that he counted the steps he executed with the precision of someone who did not take naturally to the dance. Neither man could be taken seriously, and Alice did not even try. Instead, she simply enjoyed their silly attention—at least for those first two dances.

An hour later they lined up to dance with her again—she suddenly was in high demand—but made the same silly exchanges with one another that were not quite so amusing as they had been the first time. By the third time they came for her, she had been dancing for hours, and her ability to endure their antics was drowned out by weariness. She could not refuse them but was grateful when Mr. Newtonhouser returned her from the floor and she found Lord Fenton waiting, his expression polite but not amused.

"You are harassing my fiancée," he said to both men when they scurried over to tell him what a fine dancer Alice was.

"Harassing?" Mr. Burbidge said, turning to Mr. Newtonhouser. "Did you hear that, Newt? He thinks we're harassing his beloved."

His beloved. Alice liked the sound of that and moved to stand beside Lord Fenton, though she sensed him stiffen somewhat by her proximity. He bantered with his friends for some time, ignoring Alice completely until she was about to take offense. Then he looked at her, and as always, she felt a bit wobbly beneath his attention. "They did not try to get you drunk or steal your slippers, did they?"

Alice lifted her eyebrows while the other two men protested such accusations. "No," she said, shocked she could be at risk for such things. "They were perfect gentlemen." Mr. Burbidge and Mr. Newtonhouser grinned proudly, prompting her to add, "Albeit silly gentlemen."

The proud smiles quickly dissolved and Lord Fenton finally shooed the men away like a couple of cats. Then he sighed. "I'm afraid my friends do not always reflect well on me," he said, watching them go.

His tone was somewhat severe, making Alice feel defensive toward the men who, while silly, were certainly kind. But she did not know what to say to this man who would be her husband. She did not want to start an argument.

Lord Fenton led her to the floor for only their second dance of the night, but as soon as they were finished, he was whisked away by some other acquaintance. He'd encouraged Alice to visit with his mother, who was sitting away from the crowds. Alice did as he'd suggested, but as she made her way to Lady Chariton's side, she had a most unwelcome thought: Lord Fenton did not want to be in her company. No sooner had she thought it, however, than she cast it aside. What a silly thought. He was simply newly back in Town, likely worn out by his trip, and becoming reacquainted with his friends.

"Are you all right, Alice?"

Alice turned to Lady Chariton, the second person to ask her that question this evening.

And for the second time, Alice altered her expression. "Of course," she said. "Why, I daresay I'm the belle of the ball tonight."

Lady Chariton smiled widely and took Alice's hand. "Oh, I cannot tell you how pleased I am in Charles's choice in you." She spoke with such sincerity that Alice's concerns dwindled until they didn't seem to exist at all. "You will be such a blessing for him."

Alice clasped the woman's hand in both of her own. "I do hope so, Lady Chariton. It is the greatest wish of my heart to make him happy."

CHAPTER 11

Two nights after that first ball, Alice and Lord Fenton attended a dinner party where Lord Fenton was as charming and gracious and kind as she could ever want him to be. But he was not seated beside her at dinner, and he did not seek her out in the drawing room after the men had enjoyed their port. In fact, he continued to enjoy more port over cards, and then some brandy, and then another glass of brandy until he was so far into his cups that Alice found herself embarrassed to the point of attempting to help the situation.

"Lady Chariton," Alice said quietly after she'd found her soon-to-be mother-in-law in another room and asked to speak with her. They stepped away from the group of women, and Alice kept her voice low so as not to be overheard. "I do not mean to overstep my bounds, but do you think perhaps we might leave early? I'm afraid I have a bit of a headache."

"Oh, my poor dear," Lady Chariton said, placing a cool hand on Alice's cheek. "Have you made mention of it to Lord Fenton?"

Alice looked over her shoulder toward the card room just as a rather loud version of a drinking song burst forth in her fiancé's near-perfect tenor voice. The truth was she had not spoken much at all to Lord Fenton. He had been engaging with everyone at this party except for her, it seemed, though she did not like to think of it so pointedly. She looked back at Lady Chariton and said nothing. She did not need to.

Lady Chariton gave a quick nod and told her to ask a footman to ready their carriage. She also took the responsibility of extracting her son from the card room and seeing him through the house rather than risk his making a display before more of the guests.

Lord Fenton was drunk and therefore quite ridiculous for the first few minutes of the carriage ride. Finally he slung his head back against the cushions and began to snore. Alice kept her attention on the window, humiliated for both herself and Lady Chariton. Being engaged to the most eligible man in London was not turning out to be as rosy as she had thought it would be, and her troubled thoughts were getting harder to still in her mind.

"He is under a great deal of pressure," Lady Chariton said. "He has taken on a lot of responsibility these last months."

"Yes," Alice said, smiling reassuringly at the older woman. "I am not passing judgment." Or at least she was trying very, *very* hard not to. This man was to be her husband. He was beautiful and charming and everything a girl could want. It was reasonable for her to expect a few flaws in his character—everyone had them—and yet the idea of marrying a drunkard was distinctly unappealing and worrisome. The idea that he avoided her company was even more so.

Lord Fenton led out another snore and his head lolled to one side.

"I shall have a word with him in the morning," Lady Chariton said, pointedly ignoring her son. "And I shall ask you to not think of this for another moment. Everything will be all right."

"Of course," Alice said, determined to take such advice to heart.

The next day, Lord Fenton sent her a note of apology for his "indulgence" and a large bouquet of roses, which brought a smile to her face. She put the bouquet on a small table framed by the drawing room window that faced the street, boldly wanting it to be seen by any passersby. If there was lingering discomfort from the night, it quickly scampered off each time she looked at the flowers. Everything would be all right, Lady Chariton had said, and so it would be. Of course it would.

The legalities of the match were soon decided and agreed to without Alice's presence being necessary; it was between the men to make such an agreement. The wedding date was decided—May ninth—and then Lord Fenton was gone to another family estate. The house of Chariton had five!

Alice immersed herself in purchasing wedding clothes, planning what dishes they would serve at the luncheon, and attending to the seemingly infinite details of the wedding, often with help from Lady Chariton, who was nothing short of wonderful. Did Alice want lilies or delphinium in her bouquet? Should they marry in a church or get a special license that would allow them to be married at the principal Chariton estate in Berkshire? Who should make the guest list? Would they return to London immediately or take a short bridal trip, perhaps to one of the other family estates?

Alice felt so far below the status of Lord Fenton's family that she often deferred to Lady Chariton's decisions. She did not care for a great deal of pomp and frippery, and as the banns were already being read in their respective parish churches, she was quite satisfied with whatever arrangements Lady Chariton would want for her only son.

Alice did not see Lord Fenton again until he returned to Town two weeks before the wedding. By that time a special license had been granted for them to marry in the drawing room of the Berkshire estate, from which she and Lord Fenton would travel to East Sussex for a short bridal trip—something only the very wealthy and prominent could afford to do. The wedding clothes had been ordered, and Alice had finished the last of the handwritten invitations just the day before Lord Fenton returned.

The first time they saw each other again was to attend a luncheon at the home of an acquaintance of Lady Chariton, who fairly gushed over "little Charles" and his bride. As always, Alice loved being in Lord Fenton's company, but her awareness that they did not seem to know one another as she felt an engaged couple should, and that he had never, not even once, attempted to show his affection for her, could not be pushed away as it had in the past. The moments of concern and discomfort, which she had previously attempted to talk herself out of, could not be quieted at the house of his aunt, where she watched her intended be effusive and charming to everyone except, it seemed, herself. In fact he all but ignored her, and his inattention began to feel like avoidance.

In all the events they had attended together, which she could count on one hand, none had given them opportunity to be alone—not even in the carriage ride to or from. Though he was complimentary to her, he rarely met her eye, and in fact the most interested he'd ever been in talking with her had happened at his mother's dinner party where they had first become reacquainted. He had never asked her on a ride, just the two of them, or stayed by her side at an event.

Such thoughts were heavy in her mind when she returned home from the luncheon. She lay on her bed with a cloth over her eyes as she sorted through her thoughts and made the decision to take matters into her own hands. Perhaps, like her, he simply did not know how to act like an engaged couple. Perhaps he was afraid of offending her or making her uncomfortable. If that were the case, then she needed to be more inviting. Instead of waiting for him to turn his affections more completely toward her, she would need to draw such attention from him. Perhaps the problem was that she had not been inviting enough, and he was simply being a gentleman, unwilling to cross a line she had not intended to draw between them.

That night they attended a fete at Vauxhall Gardens—arriving by boat, no less—and Alice saw the perfect opportunity to have some time alone with her intended. As the guests began to spread out from the pavilion, she coaxed Lord Fenton to show her the meandering footpaths and coves the outdoor park was known for. She had never been to Vauxhall before, and she loved the splendor of it at night, all lit up with gas lights so recently introduced to the city. To fill the time until they reached the anticipated privacy, Alice pointed out the names of the trees and flowers and shrubs they passed. She knew most of them and reciting the information helped make her feel comfortable. She felt she was holding his attention until she looked up to see his expression rather pinched.

"Lord Fenton?" she asked. "Is something amiss?"

He looked over his shoulder, and she followed suit, realizing they were quite alone—just as she'd hoped. "Perhaps we should join the rest of the party," Lord Fenton said, already turning her back the way they'd come. "They shall wonder where we've gone."

"As we are an engaged couple, I do not think they shall wonder all that much." She had her hand at his elbow and stepped around to face him, looking up into those eyes that were but one part of what made him so attractive. She smiled as coyly as she knew how and lifted her chin in a way she felt would best invite his affection. "I must admit I had hoped we might have some time alone. We are to be married in two weeks and have had precious little opportunity to be together just the two of us, don't you agree?"

He looked at her a moment. She saw his eyes travel to her mouth and knew he had rightfully interpreted her forwardness, but then he took a step back. "We should join the other guests." He moved far enough away that her hand dropped from his arm.

She stood in the center of the path, confused at his behavior and embarrassed by his withdrawal. "Lord Fenton, have I offended you somehow? Are you upset with me?"

His expression was quite discomfited, something she had never seen before. He was always so confident and secure. "Of course you have not offended me. I-I only prefer to adhere to the expectations of propriety, and I should very much like another glass of champagne."

"Propriety?" she said, pulling her eyebrows together and feeling her concerns expand in her chest, making her bold. "What is improper about us being alone in a public place? We can only get to know one another so well in a crowd, and it seems there are always people around us." Beyond that, she had heard many retellings these past weeks of his pranks and absolute disregard for propriety. It seemed everyone she met had a funny story of something outrageous he'd done in the past. Surely being alone with his fiancée was less improper than outfitting a friend in harnesses and galloping behind him through Hyde Park, or dressing in all black at another friend's wedding.

"Yes, well." Lord Fenton shifted his weight from one foot to the other and straightened his waistcoat—blue, with silver birds that matched his coat and knee breeches. "I am better suited for a crowd." He attempted a smile, but it appeared disingenuous, and Alice knew through a prickling in her chest that something was not right. An engaged couple was expected to share affection and yet he seemed determined to avoid it even when a perfect opportunity was presented.

"There shall be a decided lack of crowds once we are married, Lord Fenton," Alice said.

"Which is not to take place for two more weeks, so why not enjoy such entertainments as this while there is time and opportunity?" He began walking, then paused and came back to her, putting out his arm rather stiffly and avoiding her eye. "It would not do for me to return alone, of course."

She glanced at him before controlling her expression so as not to show him how his dismissal had affected her. Had she not so often felt as though she were a complication in the lives of her family, perhaps she would not have jumped to the conclusion that the same thing was the cause for his reaction. Those times when her father said "What shall we do with Alice?" or Maryanne pointed out that "Alice's situation must be considered" had felt exactly like this. That she was not so much wanted as she was . . . there. Necessary. It was a feeling she had thought she would never feel again after Lord Fenton's proposal and her acceptance of it. He had chosen her above all others and yet she felt certain in this moment that he did not really want her at all.

If they were not at Vauxhall, perhaps she would push for an

explanation. But now was not the time or place. "Yes, my lord," she said submissively. He let out a relieved breath, pasted a polite smile on his face, and held out his arm, which she took as she was expected to.

Once they heard the voices of other guests Lord Fenton relaxed, then began chattering on about the new coat he had fitted at Weston's that afternoon and about a wager he'd made with a friend at Brooks regarding how many hunting dogs would fit into his father's traveling coach. Alice listened politely and managed to contain her feelings through the rest of the evening, but she knew she could not move forward without knowing what it was she did not understand. She was far too practical a girl to pretend this away, but oh how she wished she could.

CHAPTER 12

Alice didn't speak of her fears to anyone though she puzzled over them that night and the next day, which was Sunday—a good day for reflection. It was bad enough *she* was uncomfortable, what good would it do to have others uncomfortable too? To say nothing of her fear of pity. The idea of her family feeling sorry for her made her stomach tight. She had become used to feeling small and yet, with her engagement to Lord Fenton, she was at the top—finally. She was admired for simply having made such an advantageous match. Had she ever been admired for anything at all before this?

Alice reminded herself that she did not know Lord Fenton's mind nor had she ever seen an engagement up close enough to know if anything were *truly* out of place. But her attempts at justification never quite eliminated her unease. Instead, the worries lurked on the edges of her every thought until she finally sent a note to Lord Fenton on Monday morning and asked him to call on her that afternoon. It was not wholly acceptable for her to ask for such a thing, but the pinch in her stomach needed resolution. Alice was used to being overlooked, but she was equally used to finding solutions to her own struggles. Knowing his mind was the first step toward finding resolution.

Lord Fenton arrived promptly at two o'clock and was shown into the drawing room where Alice waited. He was dressed in sea green breeches and a matching coat with cuffs the same green-and-pink stripe as his waistcoat. A large emerald was pinned in the center of his cravat, and he swung an elaborate golden cane as he walked.

For the first time, Alice found his extreme dress off-putting, as though it were meant to be some kind of distraction, but she felt bad for making that judgment as soon as she thought it. She did not want to enter this meeting with prejudice. He seemed disappointed when he realized she was the only one awaiting him.

"Tea, please," Alice said to the footman as he bowed out of the room. "And close the door." He did as she requested, leaving Alice and Fenton standing about six feet apart. It might as well have been a mile for all the connection it afforded. Alice realized only when the silence became awkward that having been the one to invite him here, she had assumed he would arrive with some alarm and therefore press her for her reasons. She now tried to think of the right way to introduce the topic of this meeting.

"Thirteen," Lord Fenton said, taking her off guard.

"Pardon?"

Lord Fenton grinned widely and waved his cane through the air. "We were able to fit thirteen hunting dogs in Newt's father's carriage. I had thought we could get fifteen and so I suppose I lost, but if they had not been so blasted nippy with each other I'm sure I could have fit two more in." He shrugged as though it were no matter.

Having only recently pondered on how little she knew him, Alice chose to push for additional insight into what kind of man that gangly boy of sixteen had become in the last ten years. "And what, exactly, did you lose?" She thought maybe he had to buy a round of drinks or something equally trivial, commensurate with the topic of the wager.

"Two hundred pounds," he said flippantly, swinging his cane as he crossed the room to peek through the drapes at the street outside the window. He must not have seen Alice's eyes go wide, otherwise he surely would have remarked on it. Two hundred pounds on a wager of hunting dogs in carriages? That was not quite what her family had spent to have her outfitted for London—and he had wagered that same amount so flippantly? Realizing she had overestimated this man strengthened her resolve to get to the heart of the matter.

"Lord Fenton," Alice said, as he turned away from the window. He raised his eyebrows expectantly and continued to swing his cane as though he hadn't a care in the world. The hand holding the cane was tight, however, and the look of congeniality was forced. *A mask*, she thought to herself. He was pretending not to feel nervous about whatever she'd called him to discuss, and she wondered what she could say or do to earn his trust. She would not earn it with accusations. She had to be open and optimistic and yet careful too.

Taking a breath she hoped would keep her tone level, she began. "I asked the other night if I had offended you and you said I had not, but I feel a level of . . . distance, I suppose, perhaps even dissatisfaction from you regarding . . . me." She hated the heat that rose to her cheeks and hurried on before she lost her nerve. "If there is something I can do to repair your opinion of me, my lord, I would be happy to do it."

"As I said, you have not offended me," he said with a wave of his hand. His gaze strayed to the door as if hoping the discussion were over. Or perhaps he was hoping the tea tray would arrive and distract them.

"Then why do you seek out everyone's attention but mine when we are together? Why are you uncomfortable when we are alone?" Laying bare her emotions made her stomach squirm, and she had to turn away from him.

Lord Fenton did not respond right away, further disheartening her. If his answer were reassuring, he would have said so immediately.

"Please tell me the truth," she said, still not meeting his eyes for fear he would see too much within her own. "Why did you ask me to marry you if you do not want to be in my company?"

He paused again and tapped lightly at something on the floor with his cane.

Alice turned back to him, lifting her chin as though she would be satisfied with whatever he might tell her. He'd lost his flippancy and, without his mask to protect them both, she braced herself for his answer.

"I am in need of a wife," he said simply, looking at the rug.

Need, not want, Alice noted as the words turned her throat thick with emotion she would not show. She took a breath and let it go slowly, regaining her composure by the time he looked up. She could not let him see how affected she was or he would not be honest. "Why?" she asked evenly. "Why do you *need* a wife?"

He looked at the rug again, or, rather, at his buckled green shoe, which he turned from side to side as though inspecting it. "I am of an age and—"

Alice could not bear to be patronized. Not after what he'd already revealed. "You are only twenty and seven years, your father is in good health, and you have only just begun to rise to your responsibility. Why do you *need* a wife? Why do you need a wife *now?*"

When he looked up at her, she kept her expression completely neutral. "Have I not convinced you of my practical nature before now? I am not a girl of romantic fancy." She paused so as to recover from the lie—oh why had she allowed her fantasy to grow into such a weed as this? Why had she not cut it back when first it took hold of her? What kind of *practical girl* would ever allow herself to be in such a situation as this? "I should like to fulfill what is expected of me, Lord Fenton. I cannot do that if I am kept unaware of what those expectations are."

Her lack of emotion seemed to convince him to tell the truth— the painful and horrible truth. "I suppose it *is* better for you to know the whole of it, then." He paused. "My father has demanded that I rise to my responsibility and as part of our arrangement I am required to marry." He gave her a smile that would have melted her even a few days ago. However, she could see the mask for what it was now and knew there was no substance behind his charm. He spread his arms and shrugged.

Alice remained perfectly still. "Your father demanded you marry *me?*"

"No, I was allowed to choose my bride," he said, lowering his arms when she did not react to the dramatics.

"Why am I the one you chose, then?"

Within her heart something tight and hard that had become tighter and harder these last minutes released a little. It opened and stretched like the mouth of a baby bird waiting to be fed. If he could say the right words she would be filled. If he told her he *did* care for her she could still have hope. The maw of this hope opened wider and wider, and in her mind she pleaded for him to say something that could give her reason to expect some portion of the happiness and comfort she had envisioned during the weeks since his proposal. *Please say I matter to you!*

"If I am to be entirely honest—and I suspect that is what you want from me—my mother was taken with you, and you were the least objectionable female I had met."

The maw snapped closed and retreated into her heart, as still as though it had never awakened. She felt the blood drain from her face at the confirmation of her worst fear, and she turned away so he would not see it.

He does not care for me, she thought. *Not even a little.* That was why Rebecca had said he was so different at the dinner party his parents had thrown. He had been interviewing her, and every other young woman there, in order to find the *least* objectionable among them. And, perhaps, the most foolish as well.

Lord Fenton seemed to interpret her speechlessness as an invitation for more details. "My father is a controlling, cruel man and he found a way to force me to do as he wished. He was going to disinherit me, pull my title completely, and leave me with next to nothing if I did not step up to his requirements."

I am not only an unwanted bride, I am a demanded one. A necessary complication to ensure Lord Fenton kept the comfort he was used to.

He continued his explanation with an air of relief, as though he'd been holding it in and could now purge all the ugliness upon her too. "That my parents approved and your father was in need of salvation from his impending financial ruin added to the reasonableness of the transaction between us."

Her father was on the verge of ruin? She had been a card to bargain with for his salvation? She thought back to her family's reaction the day the proposal had arrived. They'd been confused and concerned, and yet she had prattled on like a child without a modicum of sense in her head. She'd thought the whole of it had a practical romance about it. After the initial reactions, her family had become excited about the match; was that because they realized how well their situations would improve? Had everyone known this marriage was nothing more than a business transaction except herself? Of course she knew many marriages, perhaps even most, were arranged for any number of reasons—only *she* had thought Lord Fenton cared for her. What did it matter to her that so many other marriages were formed on other reasons when she believed hers to be a love match?

The numbness that had replaced her hope began to change into anger, which made it easier to keep her stoic expression in place. "So, ours is to be a marriage of convenience, then," Alice said slowly, unable to keep the bite from her words as she proclaimed the truth out loud. "For everyone's good but mine."

Lord Fenton pulled his eyebrows together. "You shall be *Lady* Fenton," he said slowly.

"Ah," she said with thick sarcasm as she built another layer of protection around herself and narrowed her eyes. "How fortunate for me." She made no effort to hide her feelings in hopes he would feel some measure of the pain he'd delivered so carelessly to her.

He pulled back in surprise. "I do not understand your derision," he said defensively. "You have asked me questions that I have answered honestly. You said that is what you desired."

"Yes, you have answered honestly," she said, walking to the fireplace. He did not want her. He never had. Her family had known it and yet pleased themselves with the marriage arrangement without helping her understand the whole of it. They knew of her fancy for him—they knew *her* heart was involved—and yet not one of them felt to let her in on the reality of her arrangement. She did not feel betrayed by Lord Fenton alone, rather she felt betrayed by everyone. Set apart. Discarded.

"You may go," she said without turning. "I am now quite aware of the situation and will not discomfit either of us by prolonging this discussion."

He did not answer for a few moments, but then spoke in a hesitant voice. "Perhaps this is a good time to explain one other aspect of our arrangement."

Her fingers curled into her palms but she did not move nor speak, certain he would continue without her invitation while equally unsure that she could tolerate hearing whatever else he was to say.

"Though my father insisted I marry, he has said nothing about my . . . setting up a nursery right away. I would therefore like to wait on that aspect of our union until a time when we are perhaps in greater comfort with one another."

Alice turned in shock and confusion as her mind spun to make sense of this pronouncement. What seemed to be the only reason he would say this came to her mind, and she felt the blood drain out of her face a second time. "You have a mistress," she blurted before she could stop herself, then nearly choked on her own tongue to have said the word no woman of society would ever say out loud.

Lord Fenton's face turned red. "No, I am not a rake, Alice. I . . . I simply do not want to take on so much responsibility all at once. It has been quite enough already and . . ."

She closed her eyes and dropped her chin, praying for strength to hold herself together a few minutes longer. She should be relieved he denied having another woman—and she was—but she was also dreadfully embarrassed to realize how very unwanted she truly was.

Unable to keep her composure, Alice sat upon one of the chairs facing the cold fireplace and stared at the grate. "You should have told me the whole of this before I accepted your proposal. I should have known the terms of my agreement." She'd have never agreed if she'd known Lord Fenton's heart was not engaged. Perhaps then she could have found a man who did want her, who wanted a family, a partner, a . . . friend. She could have been a wife in more ways than just her name, with someone equally interested in building a life together. As it was, she could now see, plain as the grate in the fireplace, that she was the fulfillment of a requirement. *Nothing* more.

"I am sorry if I have . . . upset you," Lord Fenton said in a tone that sounded sincere though her heart was closed to it. "Perhaps it is of little remedy, but two months ago I had not considered marrying for some time, until I felt ready for the whole of such responsibility. I *do* have high regard for you, Alice, and I believe that, in time, we shall find good accord with one another."

Her temper snapped. How dare he try to reassure her now with such kindness and explanation! "If you had any regard for me at all you would have made sure I knew I was simply a convenient wife. Then I would not have behaved like such a silly girl."

She thought of the giddy conversations she had shared with her sister and Lady Chariton and felt ten times the fool. She had hung on Lord Fenton's arm amid the *ton* events they had attended with such arrogance, such pride at being the woman to turn the head of a man who turned so many others. She had laid her heart bare for *this*? Even now she was revealing herself through her emotion and further risking her heart. Once he pondered upon this exchange he would realize that she'd thought he loved her, and then he would pity her. She could not stand his pity—anyone's pity—and was attempting to find a way to prevent him from realizing such a thing when he spoke instead.

"Will you break the engagement?"

Alice considered that. She could tell her father that he had been cruel to use her this way, she could tell Lord Fenton she would not have him, and she could humiliate him by revealing his unwillingness to consummate the marriage as the reason for her rejection. He had made himself vulnerable by divulging such a personal thing, and she could exploit it for some manner of revenge upon him.

But her family's position in society could not withstand such a scandal, while Lord Fenton would quite surely rise above it given time. Much as she wished she could turn back the clock and reconsider with a full understanding what her acceptance of his proposal really meant, that was not an option. Not really. And so she would make him pay for it. She was obligated and would stay the course, but she would not let him forget that he was as saddled with her as she was with him.

She stood and looked Lord Fenton squarely in the face. "Why on earth would I break the engagement?" she said sweetly, enjoying the initial confusion that showed in his expression. "I am to marry one of the richest men in England, one day I shall be a countess, and, in the meantime, my family's situation could not be more improved—as you have so *graciously* explained to me." She kept her eyes cold and her heart locked. "What's more, I do not even need to make room for a man as idiotic as you in my bed. What woman in the world wouldn't want to be me, *my lord*?" She filled the last two words with as much derision as she could, wanting to make sure he knew she was not a simpering female who would beg for his attention and cry for his sympathy.

His eyes snapped, but he too lifted his chin and cocked his head. "Well then, I think we shall get on just fine, so long as we both understand that we are to look and act the part of a married couple amiably connected."

"I need only to look to your *excellent* example of falseness to know my way of it," she said, forcing a polite smile she hoped felt like ice to him. "Perhaps you could draw up a list for me with the rules you expect me to follow. As I am to act the part, I shall need instruction on how to do so."

Lord Fenton's eyes went wide, then narrowed. But as he opened his mouth to respond, there was a tapping at the door.

Maryanne entered with a bright smile. "Lord Fenton," she said, nodding to him and waving in the footman who had followed her with the tea tray. "I did not know you had called until I encountered Lewis with the tray. I sent him back for greater refreshment so that we might all enjoy it together."

"I arrived just now, Mrs. Stanbridge," Lord Fenton said, bowing over her hand in his elaborate fashion, which now annoyed Alice as much as it had once charmed her. She was careful to have the proper expression by the time Maryanne looked to her again. Maryanne must have sensed the lingering tension, however, because she looked back and forth between them.

"Is everything all right?" she asked.

"Quite," Alice said, still smiling and willing herself to appear more relaxed than she felt. "We were just discussing the wedding. I must say the role of Lady Fenton *does* seem to be a daunting one. I do not know how I shall rise to all the expectation of it." She was glad to see Lord Fenton's jaw tighten in her peripheral vision, assuring her that the thrust of her sword had hit its mark.

Maryanne crossed to her and patted her arm. "It can be overwhelming to be sure, but you have been well prepared for such a role." She turned to Fenton and began to talk of the tutors and training Alice had endured these last years, all focused on her being the proper hostess and socialite. It embarrassed Alice to hear of such things detailed as though she had to rise up to his level. But that was precisely what she had to do. She needed to match him in manners, address, practicality, and, perhaps most important, in quickness of mind. He had pulled her into this farce, but she would not be bested by him.

Lord Fenton stayed for half an hour, entertaining Maryanne with one story after another. He was truly a master at charming people. When Maryanne was not looking, Alice scowled, and when Lord Fenton requested more tea she purposely spilled it on the cuff of his sleeve, then simpered an apology only he would know was exaggerated. Maryanne was too pleased by the splendid arrangement of the match to note Alice's irritation.

Finally, Lord Fenton rose, claiming an appointment he needed to attend to before the night's entertainment. The women stood as well so he could make his good-byes. He bowed over Alice's hand with all his pomp and style, but she withdrew her hand as soon as she could, wishing her body would not respond to his touch with tingling and warmth. She used to see such a reaction as a sign of their regard for one another; now it was simply one more betrayal. He finally quit the room, and Maryanne turned to Alice and took her hands with a look of pleasure and joy.

"Oh Alice, what a lucky girl you are to have secured such a man. What a joyous life I see ahead for you."

Alice, however, could see nothing ahead of her. She could not see how she and Lord Fenton would get on. She could not see how they would cross the divide between them no matter how many years passed. One day he would want an heir; would she be anything more than that child's mother? The anger she had felt toward her family just minutes ago had grown tepid until only a heavy sorrow remained. Everything she had wanted was gone. The fairy tale she thought she had found for herself had been a ruse all along.

But Maryanne was staring at her, her expression concerned. "Alice? Is something wrong?"

Everything is wrong, she thought but of course she did not say so. "I fear I have a headache."

Maryanne's expression softened. "Well, then you must go lie down until we need to dress for the Partridge party tonight. I do hope you'll be well enough to attend." Lord Partridge was among the most respected in the House of Lords, a great politician and orator who would never have put the names of Mr. and Mrs. Stanbridge on his guest list if not for the connection their daughter was making to the house of Chariton.

"If I am not well enough, I insist you attend without me," Alice said, glad that her inability to school her expression would be blamed on her nonexistent headache.

Maryanne looked as though she might protest, prompting Alice to repeat the sentiment that the rest of the family simply must attend. "It would look poorly for all of us to skip the evening," she insisted, acting as she believed the grand Lady Fenton would—unflappable, concerned only for others. "But I *shall* retire to my bed in hopes I will feel much more the thing in a few hours' time."

When the hour to get ready for the evening came and Alice's state of mind had not improved, she once again encouraged her family to attend without her.

"Is there a message you would like me to give to Lord Fenton on your behalf?" Maryanne asked.

Alice shook her head. There were many things she would like to say to Lord Fenton, none of which could be sent through anyone else.

Maryanne made sure there was nothing else Alice needed, then kissed her lightly on the forehead and wished her well before leaving.

Alice, in her dark solitude, rolled onto her side and closed her eyes when the tears rose up. Beginning tomorrow she would act her part and behave as she ought, but tonight she would mourn all the beautiful things she had believed awaited her. She would lament the fantasy and bury the hopes and dreams she had taken for granted. In the shadow of all she had learned this afternoon she wondered why she had ever thought it different. It all seemed so obvious now, so apparent and certain that she felt ten times the fool for having dared believed anything different. What a joke. What a game. What misery.

CHAPTER 13

Alice would have complained of a headache all the way to the wedding day if she could, but she was expected to attend a garden party at the home of one of Lord Fenton's family members the day after their *tête-à-tête* in the drawing room and she would not take the chance of Lord Fenton believing that her heart was broken. Tuesday morning she awoke and gave herself a stern talking to, splashed her face with lavender water to reduce the puffiness left by her tears, and then readied herself for the event—the first she would attend with a full understanding of her situation.

The Chariton carriage came for her at precisely one o'clock, and she stepped inside expecting to see Lord Fenton and his mother; Lady Chariton had attended every other event with them. However, Lord Fenton was alone. He was dressed in a baby blue satin tailcoat and hat, with gray breeches and a pink, blue, and gray patterned waistcoat to tie it all together.

Alice refused to note how well the blue looked with his eyes and instead sighed as she settled onto the bench across from him. Showing her irritation was the only way to mask the lingering pain, and she was determined he never know how truly hurt she was. She waited for the footman to close the door before she spoke. "If I had known your mother was not attending with us I'd have pressed Maryanne or Rebecca to come—seeing as how you are better suited for crowds."

"I'm afraid Mama was not feeling well today," Lord Fenton said with enough sincerity to make Alice regret beginning their conversation with an insult.

Her feelings of betrayal had not overshadowed the kindness and attention Lady Chariton had given her. In fact, Lady Chariton was nearly the only part of this arrangement that Alice had found peace with after she'd lamented the whole of it last night and then tried to look for the positive aspects. By becoming Lord Fenton's wife, she would become Lady Chariton's daughter, and that was something she very much looked forward to.

"I insisted she stay at home," Lord Fenton added.

"I hope she feels better soon, then," Alice said, her defenses lowered quite unexpectedly. She wondered if Lord Fenton felt bad for what had happened yesterday; perhaps he wanted to make amends. She was unsure if she were prepared to be vulnerable again, but neither did she want to reject an honest offering.

"As do I," Lord Fenton agreed. "She has difficulty with the London air, I think. By the end of the season she is usually quite wrung out."

Alice felt her defenses lowering even more—until he spoke again. "Besides, I thought you wanted more time alone together." He raised an eyebrow at her, and her wall went right back up, with mortar between the stones to be sure she did not take it down so easily again.

"I have quite changed my mind on that score, *my lord*, and shall likely fake a headache again so as to leave early today."

"Oh, *please* do," Lord Fenton said with dramatic flair. "The last time I had to fake a headache turned out quite embarrassing for everyone. Ladies are much better suited for such ailments, and I should so like to play the part of the attentive fiancé squiring you away from what promises to be a tedious party. Did I tell you my aunt is a teetotaler? She allows only sherry to be served at her afternoon parties. I shall need to drink all of it myself in order to even attempt enjoyment of the event."

Alice thought of the bouquet of roses he'd sent last week as an apology for his last bout of drunkenness. "Based on past experience, I'm sure you have begun already."

He did nothing but smile and shrug. "I had to prepare myself for your *charming* company one way or another."

"If only I had considered a similar course," she said, tilting her head. "I imagine *your* company is far more appealing if one is drunk."

"Quite likely," Lord Fenton said without missing a beat. "And for some people, a little drink improves their personality. I shall very much look forward to seeing how it affects yours."

Alice shook her head before turning toward the window. They remained silent for a few minutes until Lord Fenton spoke again.

"You said you wanted to know what was expected of you as Lady Fenton." He withdrew a paper from the inside pocket of his satin coat and handed it across the carriage. "I made you a list, as requested."

Alice took the paper and scanned it, seeing the expected things: managing the servants of Lord Fenton's estate in Hampshire, answering invitations, making social calls, and hostessing events. Every task filled her with trepidation—could she do it? Though she had been taught and trained, she had never managed an actual household herself. And she couldn't ask for Lord Fenton's advice, even if he had it to give. She couldn't admit in any way that she did not feel up to the task. After all, that was the reason he chose her, so she would be Lady Fenton.

She took a breath to hide her nervousness and said, "I see nowhere on this list where it says I am to laugh at your jokes or compliment your clothing. *That* is a relief."

"I was careful not to put anything on there that would be too taxing for you," Lord Fenton said, crossing one foot over the other knee. "But if you will look toward the bottom of the list, you will see that I *am* to approve *your* wardrobe." He leaned in and lifted up the quizzing glass tied to his waistcoat. He made a show of looking over the pale yellow dress she wore. "If you don't mind my saying so, you are greatly in need of some consultation, as yellow does nothing for your complexion."

Her thoughts stumbled for a moment. She had not found the color complementary, either, but since the dressmaker and Chloe had both liked it, she had trusted their judgment over her own. She did not allow her thoughts to be lost for long, however. She could not let him think she agreed with him.

"I felt it best not to make a spectacle of myself when my intended husband insists on being a peacock." Alice scanned the list until she found the item regarding her wardrobe. "I shall refuse such things as bright orange dresses with purple bows, however, so I hope you are not expecting such ridiculous things as that."

"And risk you taking all the attention when we attend an event together? I think not." Lord Fenton smiled from across the carriage, and she realized he was quite enjoying this banter. That she was enjoying it somewhat as well did not take away from the fact that she did not want *him* to. She looked back to the last few items on the list.

"You are to purchase my *stationery*?" she asked, glancing up with a look of boredom. What a silly detail for a man to concern himself about.

Lord Fenton grinned. "I have decided your signature color will be pink."

"I do not care for pink," Alice said, suddenly seeing herself in any number of ridiculous pink gowns while she wrote letters on pink paper. "White is sufficient, or ivory, if a Macaroni like yourself cannot abide such plainness."

Lord Fenton shook his head even before she finished speaking. "My color for correspondence has of late been a lovely shade of robin's-egg blue—it lends me great distinction—and I insist my wife follow the same course, as it unifies our position. I could likely be persuaded for your color to be lavender, however, *if* you asked nicely."

"If robin's egg-blue is such a lovely shade, then I shall use it as well."

"'Pon my word, I won't stand for it," he said in that effeminate voice she had once found so humorous. He put a hand to his chest. "Blue is *my* color."

Alice dropped the list to her lap and rolled her eyes. "If you should want my stationery to give me distinction, is it not reasonable for me to choose the color that best represents me? That I am willing to have a color at all shows my attempt to cooperate with this excessively trivial detail."

"Trivial, my eye!" He exaggerated his foppish demeanor even more by throwing his hands in the air and making a squeaking squeal that made her want to slap him. "Oh, don't ever say such things!" he proclaimed, crumpling into the corner of the carriage and covering his ears with his hands.

"You are ridiculous," she said as he recovered, brushing off his coat for good measure and adjusting his hat.

"Yes, well, we all have our gifts," he said with a grin.

"And yours is acting the fool and choosing stationery."

"And your new wardrobe."

"I have no need for a new wardrobe. I was just fitted with an array of dresses that is more than sufficient."

"Lady Fenton will not wear such things as this," he said, leaning forward to flick the skirt of her yellow dress. He leaned a little closer so his head was even with hers and added, "And she shall correspond on *pink* paper."

Alice leaned forward so their noses were only a matter of inches apart. When she spoke it was almost a hiss. "She will not."

"Oh, yes, she will."

The argument might have been focused on stationery, but it was of far greater importance to Alice. She could not let him think he would have such control, that she would give way to him on things like this when she knew he was only pressing in order to establish domination. She held his eyes while ignoring the scent of his cologne. The heat of him was distracting in and of itself, and she hurried to parry an insult before she became intoxicated by her infernal attraction to this man. "I would consider very carefully the hills you choose to die upon, *my lord*, and ask yourself if stationery is truly the battle you want to engage."

"I could very well say the same to you, *my dear*," he said with equal weight. "Is stationery of such importance to you?"

She continued to hold his eyes despite their charged aggression and close proximity. "I am not the one who put it on the list."

"I am not the one who asked for the list."

"I will not use pink paper."

"Lavender, then."

She paused, not minding lavender so much but unwilling to concede because, while the topic might be the color of stationery, the implication was much more than that. If she let him control such minute details, how would she keep him from orchestrating all aspects of her life? How would she keep from becoming swallowed up in him completely? "I will use blue or white or ivory."

"Lavender."

"Lavender is for little girls and debutantes. I shall be a married woman of title. Blue or white or ivory."

"Yellow."

"You just told me it did nothing for my complexion." She paused for breath, wondering if there were any way he was as affected by their proximity as she was. When she spoke again she enunciated each word, "Blue or white or ivory."

"You are simply being stubborn," his voice rose, revealing his true irritation.

She matched him in volume and tone. "*You* are simply being a brute. Blue or white or—"

"This is ridiculous!"

She curled her fingers around the edge of the cushioned seat she was perched upon. "Blue or white or—"

"You're making this far more—"

"Blue or white or—" She was yelling now.

"Blast it all! Will you just—"

"Blue or white or—"

Lord Fenton finally threw up his hands and fell back against his seat. "By all that is holy, let's put an end to this! Your paper shall be blue!" he screamed.

"Which is precisely what I asked for!"

Lord Fenton huffed and turned away.

Satisfied, and yet not really, Alice leaned back against her own seat and crossed her arms. She looked out the window at the houses and shops sliding past her view. Oh, but this man was vexing to the extreme. How on earth should she abide it? And yet, there was something about this engagement—this back-and-forth investment, never mind that it was an argument—that was rather invigorating. As pathetic as it sounded, at least he cared enough to fight with her. And she'd won. The color of her stationery was not much, but it *was* something.

CHAPTER 14

Fenton woke up late and had to hurry on foot to the London house. There was no time for his curricle to be made ready, despite the fact that he would far prefer to arrive in it, even though the house was not far enough from his rooms to warrant the effort. When he arrived at the front door, he paused only long enough to take a breath before knocking on the door and waiting for Handleby to let him in.

"They are in your mother's bedchamber, my lord," Handleby said while Fenton handed over his hat and gloves and cane.

"Very good, thank you," Fenton said, then took the stairs two at a time. At his mother's bedchamber—the largest room in the house—he again took a breath and stood up straight before knocking on the door.

A lanky woman opened the door for him—the dressmaker, he presumed. "Good morning," she said, giving him a curtsy. "You must be Lord Fenton."

He put a hand to his chest and bowed elegantly to her with one leg pointed forward. "Please forgive me for my tardiness, madam."

"Not at all," the woman said with bright eyes, obviously wanting to make him happy. He was the one paying the bill after all, or rather, his father was.

After the fight about the stationery, he had not wanted Alice to think that choosing her wardrobe was an empty threat. He found a wicked kind of satisfaction in having followed through on this particular requirement of that blasted list she'd demanded and then resented.

"Please come in," the woman said, as though gentlemen attended such things on a regular basis.

Fenton stepped past the dressmaker into the room. Alice stood upon a slightly raised pedestal wearing a plain, basic dress while Fenton's mother and Mrs. Stanbridge sat in the fireplace chairs that had been moved to the side for a better view. A three-paneled mirror stood between Alice and the windows—something the dressmaker brought, no doubt.

In the corner of the room a dressing screen had been set up while half a dozen trunks waited near the bed, certainly filled with the fabrics, trims, and dress plates. Two of the dressmaker's attendants stood silently to the side, one of them likely the seamstress who would consult with the dressmaker as the designs were determined.

This was an unusual meeting, to be sure, but Fenton needed to make a point, and therefore a production. He had orchestrated the perfect situation and promised generous compensation for his every whim to be attended. Fenton took in the details of the situation as he crossed the room, going to his mother first.

"Mama," Lord Fenton said effusively while bowing over her hand. "Forgive me for being late. I am ever so sorry." Before she could reply, he turned to Mrs. Stanbridge and bowed over her hand as well. "And

I beg your pardon as well, Mrs. Stanbridge. I am embarrassed beyond *belief* to have kept you waiting."

"It is no bother at all," Mrs. Stanbridge said, her cheeks pink from his attention. She was always particularly responsive to his charms, which made him increase them all the more in her presence. "We were just discussing the items we hope to order today. It is very generous of you to give such a gift as this, Lord Fenton. We are indebted to you, aren't we, Alice?"

As though he hadn't noticed her before, Fenton spun around and put his hands to his chest in mock surprise. He knew she could not drop her smile without alerting their mothers to the tensions between them, but she did narrow her eyes enough for him to notice. He winked at her, knowing full well it would tighten that prissy smile. Which it did.

"My dear," he said grandly, taking two dramatic steps toward her. "Why, you are a vision in the morning, are you not?"

"Thank you, Lord Fenton," she said tightly, then faced the mirror again where she seemed to make a display of smoothing out the skirts of her dress so as to avoid meeting his eye. "Seeing as you have delayed this appointment a quarter of the hour, perhaps we should get started."

"Alice," Mrs. Stanbridge breathed, causing Alice to turn back to her.

Since Lord Fenton was between the women with his back to his mother and Mrs. Stanbridge, he was able to grin for Alice's benefit alone as she faced her stepmother over his shoulder. He wagged his eyebrows and then lifted only one while waiting to see how she would compensate for her rudeness.

Alice's jaw tightened, and Lord Fenton smiled even wider as he anticipated her dilemma. If they had been alone he felt sure she'd have harangued him until he was bloody. But they were not alone.

After a moment, Alice lifted her chin and acted her part. "I'm sorry," she said, then looked at Fenton's mother. "I suppose it is wedding jitters." Only because she had to, she looked at Fenton and curtsied an apology.

Fenton had not been so entertained in all the months he'd been in Town, and if he felt a pang of regret, it was quickly snuffed by the reminders of how sharp her tongue could be when there was no one but him to be flayed by it.

He moved toward her and lifted her hand to his lips. She clenched her teeth behind her smile; he could see how her jaw muscles tightened beneath that remarkably smooth skin. Would her skin feel as soft as it looked? Despite himself, his eye was drawn from her face to her neck, collarbone, and . . . He looked back at her face while pushing the errant thoughts away. Then he planted a particularly wet kiss on the back of her hand before wrinkling his nose at her. "All is forgiven, dearest."

"Thank you, *my lord*." She pulled her hand back, subtly wiped it on her skirt, and faced the mirrors again. That was when Fenton saw his mother's reflection. He had not realized her position afforded her a view of his face in the angled mirror. She had seen the snide expressions and taunting meant for Alice alone. Blast. He would have some explaining to do later.

"We were discussing the number of articles you expected to purchase, Lord Fenton," the dressmaker said. "We thought perhaps a ball gown, two day dresses, a garden dress, and three morning gowns."

Fenton was happy to look away from his mother's questioning and none-too-happy gaze. "Oh, we shall double that," he said quickly.

He stepped away from Alice before his eyes were tempted to notice such discomfiting details of her person again. "And it should be four ball gowns at least—we shall entertain a great deal."

He added two traveling gowns, a cloak, three shawls, six pairs of stockings, and three full sets of underclothing—as well as the necessary stays and slips to support the whole of it.

The dressmaker's eyes widened with each new pronouncement.

"Lord Fenton," Alice said when he began talking about pelisses and sleeves. "It is far too dear. I do not need half so many things."

"Nonsense." Fenton waved away her objection, though he did like the sincerity of it. He had not thought his extravagant gift would offend her sense of practicality but it only sweetened the whole of the experience to know that it did. "I want you to look the part of Lady Fenton—as we have discussed—and to do so you need a generous wardrobe and all the necessary accessories. I won't stand for any objection."

"But it is so . . . expensive."

"No such thing," Fenton said, turning back to the dressmaker and ignoring his mother's watchful gaze. Now that he had come this far, he could not hold back and therefore simply pushed forward. "But I have the final say on the styles and colors."

The dressmaker began to nod, but then looked to Alice. "Is that acceptable to you, madam?"

"Of course it is," Fenton said before Alice could argue. "Bring out your muslins, and none of that drab stuff. I want the Indian silks you keep for your best-heeled clients and an array of taffetas and velvets to look over as well. I shall make my bride into a woman of style."

For the next three hours the dressmaker, seamstress, and the assistant held up fabric after fabric to Alice's face—which became increasingly scrunched in irritation—while Fenton walked slowly around her, rubbing his chin in appraisal. That he was more attentive to her figure than the fabric was something he kept very much to himself.

At one point he was helping to drape a length of silk beneath her chin and brushed his hand across her shoulder. The energy of the touch, so casual and yet intimate, made him shiver, and he looked at Alice in time to see her cheeks turn pink before her eyes moved to the floor. He did not hold up fabrics after that, taken aback by his desire to touch her again. Would she react the same way—with embarrassment and avoidance? Such a reaction was exactly what he was afraid of so he left the draping to the dressmaker and her entourage, and he worked hard to keep his mind—and his eyes—on the fabrics and templates, not on the woman who in a few weeks would be his wife in every way but one.

Once a fabric and color were decided, Fenton perused the fashion plates and changed this neckline to that one and that sleeve to the other. Sometimes he would ask for the opinion of his mother or Maryanne, but most often he made the choices himself. Alice had well-formed shoulders, likely from her time in the garden, but she also had a small waist and a more substantial bosom than he had anticipated. The stays that had been applied made a difference. He kept even more distance after he discovered that detail and kept his eyes even more trained on the colors and styles. Each time Alice disappeared behind the screen he focused on the templates in an attempt not to think of her disrobing such a short distance away.

Through the entire fitting he could tell Alice was fuming, but she would not say anything with their mothers there, and so Fenton had his way with her new wardrobe which, if he did say so himself, was remarkable. He could hardly wait for the new gowns to arrive and see her realize his particular abilities. Would she admit he had done well? He doubted it, but he looked forward to trying to goad a compliment out of her.

Finally, with Alice nearly dead on her feet, they deemed the appointment complete. The dressmaker promised Fenton's top three gowns by the wedding day next week and said she would send a preliminary invoice to his secretary for approval before she began on the others. No matter how often he said he was not worried about the price, she seemed convinced he did not know the cost of women's fashions.

She *was* right—he did not know—but he also did not care. His father wanted him married and was footing the bill for the whole of the associated expenses; therefore, putting more and more invoices beneath his nose simply gave Fenton greater satisfaction, knowing this was painful for people beside himself.

Ironically, after admitting to Alice the whole of their arrangement, he had not regretted the marriage so very much. He found his bride-to-be quite amusing, actually, and somewhat of a challenge to keep up with in matters of their banter. How long it had been since anyone had appealed to his intellect? That the appointment today had showcased other of her attractions was something he tried very much not to think about. He could not afford such a distraction.

Alice looked exhausted and, despite his feelings of success regarding the day, looking at the three women's expressions as they walked to the foyer made him realize he may have pushed too far. Not a one of them looked overly impressed with the afternoon, and as he reviewed the day, he feared perhaps he hadn't been as successful as he'd expected. At least not in improving these women's opinions of him.

The Chariton carriage was waiting to take Alice and Mrs. Stanbridge home and Fenton helped them inside. Maryanne entered first—gracious enough that he did not believe she was too offended—leaving Alice and himself alone beside the carriage with a moment of relative privacy. She turned to step into the carriage without a word, but Fenton touched her arm.

"Alice?" He said it quietly enough that her stepmother would not hear him.

She faced him with an expression devoid of defensiveness—much how she'd looked before he'd told her the fullness—or narrowness, as it were—of his intentions for marrying. Only then she had not looked sad, and she looked very sad in this moment, enough for him to hate himself for being the cause of it.

"Are you all right?" he asked in a quiet voice.

She looked into his face, and he wondered if she were trying to gauge his sincerity. If so, what did she see? Was his expression as unmasked as her own in the moment?

"Does it matter?" she said in a tired voice, also quiet enough to keep it from the ears of others.

"Of course it matters," he said, but was uncomfortable crossing the line they had established by saying as much. "I didn't mean to upset you."

"Of course you did," she said, but she didn't sound angry. Just resigned. She raised a hand to her head, and he wondered if she had the very headache she had faked earlier in the week and then threatened to fake again at other events since.

Fenton didn't know what to say. He felt bad for making her feel . . . bad, and her not reacting with frustration and insults had him quite at a loss of how to communicate with her at all. "I'm sorry," he said lamely. "I suppose I got a bit carried away."

"I wouldn't expect less of a man who dresses like a court jester."

It was the first time she'd said anything that had truly hurt his feelings. Well, other than the fact that she didn't want such an idiot in her bed. That had stung. But since then their exchanges had been invigorating, not demeaning. At least they hadn't felt demeaning for him. This one did, however, and he was surprised, and irritated, to admit that he wanted her admiration and did not have it.

She held out her hand so he could lift her up, and he did so without meeting her eyes. He closed the door, nodded to the coachman, and stepped back so the carriage could pull away. He waited until it was some ways down the street before turning back to the house, hoping to simply retrieve his hat, gloves, and cane before making his escape. However, his mother was still standing in the foyer and her expression was severe enough that he stopped in his tracks.

Without a word, she turned to the drawing room, and, though Fenton considered making a run for it, he knew he had no choice but to follow her. Once inside, she waved him to a chair across from hers and pinned him with a piercing gaze.

"I believe you have something to tell me, Charles," Lady Chariton said.

Fenton squirmed and tried to think of what would satisfy his mother without revealing the whole of it, but she knew him too well and did not give him time to develop a believable falsehood.

"There is something strange between you and Alice," she said. "And it was not you simply turning the girl into a doll this afternoon." She let out a huff and shook her head. "I swear I have never seen anything like it. I nearly slapped you myself."

"I just now apologized to Alice for taking things too far," he said. "And I *am* sorry. I got carried away. You know how I adore fashion."

"This had nothing to with fashion, Charles. You were irritating her on purpose and very much putting on a show."

Fenton didn't know what to say to that and pretended to straighten the cuff at his wrist. He was twenty and seven years old and yet his mother could reduce him to a child in a matter of moments.

"And why did Alice not stop your ridiculous behavior? It was obvious she very much wanted to. Why, the girl was shooting daggers at you up until she was too worn out to do anything but stand up straight."

This time his mother did not rescue him and instead stared at him in silence until Fenton let out a breath. He knew that if he did not satisfy her questions, she would likely go to Alice directly, and who knew what Alice might say. And so he told her—well, he told her most of it. He left out the part about marital intimacies, for everyone's benefit.

"Oh, Charles," his mother said when he finished, leaning back against the cushion and closing her eyes. "A girl's heart is a tender thing."

"Not Alice's," Fenton said with a shake of his head and a quick exhale of breath. "I told her she could back out of the engagement and she assured me she was *quite* satisfied with the arrangement as it would do her and her family so much credit. I think she was relieved to know the entirety of it and glad she did not have to pretend feelings she did not have." It was his turn to level a gaze on his mother. "You and Father cannot expect me to be a gushing groom when you know I am here by force, not choice. And neither can Alice expect such a thing any longer. I am quite sure she is not heartbroken, and so everything is well." If his mother could hear the things Alice had said to him when they were alone she would not be seeing Alice as the victim. Part of Fenton wished he dared tell her, but then he might have to admit to the insults he'd thrown at her as well, and his mother would not be patient about that.

Lady Chariton opened her eyes, her mouth tight with disappointment. "Playing parts comes easy for you, Charles. I daresay it has become your nature to do so, but I had hoped you would not feel the need to hide from the woman you asked to become your wife." She paused and looked toward the fireplace. "I feel terrible for my part in this, the poor girl."

"The poor girl?" he repeated, lifting his eyebrows. "Do I not get any sympathy? This has not been easy for me either."

"It certainly was today," his mother shot back. She stood and moved to the window, keeping her back to him. "I do not want to speak of this anymore but I hope you will show Alice greater consideration as things move forward. Much as I regret how this has come to be, it is too late to be remedied." She turned back to him. "You and Alice shall have to make it work. You are to be *married*, and whatever *your* reasons for marriage might be, she does not deserve to be mistreated. You are to be good to her, Fenton. I had hoped—" She stopped and turned away again. "You may go."

Fenton stood, eager to leave this awkwardness, but hesitated near the door, feeling foolish for his behavior that afternoon. He wanted things to be better between him and his mother but was unsure how to convince her. "I'm sorry, Mama. I did not mean to disappoint you."

"It is not me I want you to worry about," Lady Chariton said, turning to face him again. "Alice deserves to be loved, Charles. Do you not see that in her eyes? Do you not see how she wants to . . . belong?"

"Love cannot be demanded, Mother. It cannot be forced." He had learned as much from his own father, who loved no one at all. Not his wife. Not his own flesh and blood. Part of Fenton worried he, too, could not love, especially someone forced upon him as Alice had been, and yet he *did* love his mother. He knew what it felt like to care for someone and to know that the love was returned. Only he did not know how to feel that way toward Alice or, in fact, toward anyone *except* his mother. Alice was part of the requirements that allowed him to retain his position and he could not foresee how that would change. Yet he needed to attempt it to satisfy his mother. He truly did feel bad for upsetting her with this disclosure, and he felt bad for upsetting Alice as well.

"But I believe love will come in time," he said almost flippantly, wondering if he really believed it. Could love grow out of something so complex and forced?

"Not if you treat this as a game to be played." Lady Chariton waved him to the door, shaking her head in disappointment. "Go," she said, fixing him with a stern look. "And do better."

CHAPTER 15

Alice's raw expression as she stepped into the carriage after the dressmaker's appointment and Lady Chariton's comments haunted Fenton for the rest of the day. Unsure how to make amends, he sent a note to Alice, inviting her for a ride in Hyde Park the next afternoon. It would be private enough for them to talk together, and though he was unsure of his exact goals for the outing, he hoped they could find more comfort with one another. His mother was disappointed in the way he had orchestrated things so far, and she clearly cared deeply for Alice and her feelings. Those were powerful motivators, and he very much wanted his mother's good opinion restored.

He also did not want Alice to think ill of him and realized that was what he'd created. While he enjoyed their banter and matching of wits in part because it protected him from feeling too close to her, thus preserving his control of both emotional and physical response, it did not lend itself to eventual camaraderie and friendship. There had to be a way for them to have accord without too much connection. Certainly there was a way to get the exact right balance of all of those things. Surely married couples did it all the time.

Fenton arrived at Alice's townhouse with high expectations of the afternoon, prepared to charm her into better graces. He helped her into his curricle—no easy feat as it required a four-step ladder—and she thanked him kindly, encouraging him. Perhaps she too was hopeful of a progression between them.

Once he was in his own seat and they were out of earshot of others, however, his hopes began to diminish as her expression soured and she let out a heavy sigh.

"So, for how long do I have to put up with your distinguished company, *my lord*," she said, fiddling with the string of her reticule and using the derisive address he knew full well she meant as an insult. "I looked over your list of my responsibilities and was disappointed not to see you outlining a time commitment for singular company, but I suppose your head is so full of colored stationery and fancy dresses you hadn't space to think of more important matters."

Fenton bit back a reply as rude as her own and instead pasted a smile on his face that he hoped looked genuine. "I have simply been thinking that—"

She let out a huff of air, and Fenton paused to steady his feelings before continuing. "As we are both aware of our situation, and about to join our futures, I thought we should work toward the level of comfort we hope to have one day. There is no reason for us to be miserable together. Don't you agree?"

"Certainly," Alice said, too conciliatory for Fenton to trust fully. "But I am not miserable. I am soon to be dressed in the height of fashion, the allowance I shall have in just another week's time will allow me all manner of frippery, and I am promised independence that most women only dream of."

"I meant there is no reason for us to be miserable in one another's company," Fenton amended.

"Well, I cannot agree with that," Alice said with a shake of her head. "I can think of *several* reasons for that type of misery."

Fenton's irritation rose. Here he was trying to improve their situation and be a gentleman and she was acting like a child. *For Mama*, he told himself, hoping the thought would stem his frustration. He was not used to being treated like this and wondered how he had managed to secure the one girl who would withhold the adulation and admiration every other young woman was eager to bestow. Never mind that Alice had seemed as smitten as any other girl until he'd confessed his reason for the marriage. From that point on she had walled herself off from him, which had served him too as it created a natural barrier between them. But he didn't want that barrier any more, at least not as much as was there now, and he felt sure he could break through now that he wanted their relationship to improve.

He must be more charming toward her, as he'd been in the beginning. That was it. He had given up charming her because he had felt pushed into this marriage. Now he would need to tempt and tease his way back into her good graces. Certainly he had not offended her to such a degree that renewed effort would not work. It had always worked.

"You look quite lovely, today," he said, adding the melody to his words that so many young women had enjoyed over the years. "Did you trim that bonnet yourself? It is an absolute vision."

She glared at him. "No, I did *not* trim this bonnet myself as well you know since you asked me that very same question the last time I wore it and I explained then that I do not trim bonnets. I work with real flowers, not silk ones." She faced forward again. "Or at least I used to before I came to this city of stone and cobbles and smog-ridden skies."

Fenton honestly could not remember having asked after the bonnet before, but it was not beyond belief that he would forget some flippant commentary they'd shared. He cleared his throat and tried again. "I do quite like that frock."

She turned to him again and tilted her head. "Oh, do you now," she said most condescendingly. "Even though it is yellow and therefore does not look well with my complexion? I choose it just for you, and am *oh so flattered* you remember it."

Fenton did remember teasing her about a yellow dress last week, but he hadn't looked at her so closely today to realize she'd chosen the same gown he had previously insulted. The woman was tying him up in knots, but he was not deterred. Surely after putting his foot in his mouth twice, he could rescue himself with one more attempt. "Is it not a fine day?"

To this she said nothing, leading him to believe he had confounded her with his good manners. He affected his feminine elocution and pushed his luck just as they arrived at the entrance to Hyde Park, already full of other members of the *ton* taking advantage of the fashionable hour.

"'Pon my word, I have not seen such a fine day in all the days I've spent in London this spring. It must be Divine Providence smiling down upon our outing, do you not agree?"

"Lord Fenton," she said crisply, squaring her shoulders and lowering her chin so she was fairly glaring at him. "Do not strike your dandy pose and flirt with me as though I am one of the silly females who blush at your look and simper for your attention. I am the woman you have chosen to take the position of your wife, and I am under no illusion of your interest in me or your desire for my company. I have every expectation to do what is required of me in the place I find myself, but it is *not* required—per your list of instruction—for me to play along with your ruse when we are alone, and therefore I will not do it."

"I am trying to become better acquainted with you," Fenton said between clenched teeth, his hands tight on the reins as his curricle—painted a deep red with bright yellow wheels—fell into line with other, more subdued, carriages taking the promenade. "I have invited you out so that—"

"We might be seen in the fashionable place expected of us, yes, I understand that." She smiled at an acquaintance in another carriage, but Fenton did not slow down to invite a conversation. Once they passed the carriage and could not be overheard, she continued. "I can only imagine that someone else has picked up on your indifference to me and so you are attempting to prove yourself. Is that right?"

He felt his neck heat up at the correct accusation but could not think of a proper response before she continued.

"Or, perhaps, you have set some silly wager with a friend regarding, oh, I don't know, how many times you can complete the serpentine, or maybe you expect to drive your curricle into the pond. Whatever your motivation is for this outing, I am certain it is *not* to become acquainted with me, otherwise you would have asked questions regarding my interests and expectations, not insulted me and then moved into your Macaroni persona which, I must tell you, I find very taxing."

Throughout her monologue, Fenton tried to keep his temper in check but by the time she finished, he was unable to keep his feelings to himself. "You are the most irritating woman I have ever met!" he said, too loudly, then looked around to see if anyone had overheard.

Mr. Corling and the young woman in his landau looked at him strangely, so Fenton smiled and nodded, grateful that Alice did the same, though her smile was just as polite and tight as his own. As soon as they were apart from anyone else, she spoke again.

"And here I thought I was the *least objectionable* woman of your acquaintance," she said sweetly, though her eyes remained narrowed. "Hmm. What an *aggravation* for you to have been so wrong about me, *my lord.*"

"Indeed," he snapped. He was about to continue his rant when familiar laughter caught his ear and his stomach sank. It took but a moment for the man on horseback to draw even with the seat on Fenton's side.

"'Pon my word, if it isn't Lord Fenton himself," Burbidge said, grinning widely. Newt suddenly appeared on the other side of the carriage next to Alice and gave an equally irritating smile. He lifted his hat and bowed as well as he could on horseback.

"And the soon-to-be Lady Fenton," Newt said when he replaced his hat. "You look right lovely today, Miss Stanbridge. I do so like you in that color. Why you look like the brightest daffodil of spring."

Fenton could have screamed, but Alice simply inclined her head and said hello. Fenton had tried to keep her away from his friends whenever possible. They were good for an evening at clubs and a round of drinks, but did not reflect well on him in company. Furthermore, though he had not told his friends of the arrangement concerning the marriage, they knew about the other requirements he was expected to fulfill—blasted rum—and suspected that his quick engagement was related. Fenton had tried to convince them otherwise, but after so many years of his making the most of bachelor-hood, neither of his friends believed him.

"What do you think, Burbidge," Newt said across the occupants. "Have you ever seen Miss Stanbridge looking quite so lovely?"

"I swear she grows in loveliness each time we see her, does she not?" Burbidge bantered back.

Fenton expected Alice to dress them down the way she had reprimanded him earlier, or at least give them a formal reply, but instead she lifted her chin and cocked her head coyly to the side, sending Fenton the slightest glance before smiling at Burbidge.

"Do you like it?" she asked, lifting the fabric of her skirt enough to swish it back and forth at her ankles. "I have so feared it does not do so very much for me." She pouted quite prettily as the two men flanking the curricle fumbled over themselves to assure her that she looked positively radiant, that the color brought out the flecks of gold in her eyes, and that anyone who said otherwise was a complete idiot.

"Oh, you do go on," she said, ducking her chin and waving away their ridiculous flattery. "But I must say my confidence is completely restored by your assurances. What gentlemen you are." She put a hand to her chest—amplified because of those new stays Fenton himself had purchased for her yesterday.

He could do nothing but breathe deeply for fear of making a spectacle of himself in dismissing his friends—though he vowed they would not be his friends much longer!

Alice leaned forward as though to look at Newt's horse and then summoned the most adoring expression Fenton had ever seen upon her face. "My, but that is a fine bit of horseflesh, Mr. Newtonhouser. Why, it's the very color of butterscotch, is it not?"

"Exactly as I describe her!" Newt said, his eyes alight. He began to prattle on about his horse, which was not nearly so fine a horse as either of Fenton's pulling their curricle—horses which Alice had said nothing about at all.

Alice listened to Newt's bragging and oohed and aahed as a silly girl would have done. When Newt was quite finished, she turned to Burbidge and asked him about the bottle-green coat he was wearing, claiming it made her think of the watercress that grew on the banks of a stream at her father's estate.

"And it fits you like a glove," she said. "You must tell me who your tailor is so that I can *insist* Lord Fenton attend him. The cut of your coat is far superior to his, I daresay."

Burbidge puffed out his chest and went on and on about a tailor who had nowhere near the skill of Fenton's man, and though Fenton attempted to ignore the three of them, Alice's simpering compliments were making him absolutely crazy. It wasn't jealousy, he convinced himself. What did he care if she found two men as idiotic as Newt and Burbidge entertaining? No, he was vexed that she would be so nice to them and not to himself, who *deserved* her attention. He was going to be her husband, after all, the least she could do was be as complimentary to him as she was to his stupid friends. Yet she ignored Fenton—who kept his teeth tight and his gaze forward—and held the other men's attention in the palm of her hand.

Just when Fenton was sure she had run out of things to say to Newt and Burbidge, she began telling them of the afternoon with the dressmaker the day before, exaggerating Fenton's already outlandish behavior so that even in his own ears he sounded like a complete dolt.

"Six hours?" Burbidge said, shaking his head at Fenton. His mouth stretched into a grin. "Why, the man is a tyrant."

"Oh, he is," Alice said with a pouty nod. "A *complete* tyrant. I was near tears when we left simply from the fatigue of it. But, I must say the man does know women's clothes. Why I wouldn't be surprised if he doesn't have a full closet of them made just for him, so in love he was with puffed sleeves and French stitching."

"I'm sure you're right," Newt said through his laughter. "I can see him now, spinning around in circle skirts and wishing he could wear a gown to the next—"

"I must see Alice home," Fenton finally said, snapping the reins so the horses would increase their pace. For a moment they pulled ahead of his friends, but they would catch up in a few more steps.

"Already?" Alice said with that same pout he'd never seen before today—and doubted she had ever made in her life. "It seems we only just arrived. Can't we do another round?"

"I promised your mother I'd have you home by half past three," Fenton lied as Newt and Burbidge drew even with them again. He glared at each man in turn, prompting them to throw back their heads with even more laughter before they split off looking like a couple of well-fed dogs. Fenton kept his eyes on the park exit while Alice settled herself in her seat with an arrogance he could feel like the heat from a fire.

"You see, Lord Fenton," she said with a lilt to her words. "Anyone can play the fool for another fool's entertainment, but it creates nothing of value and, from the outside, looks completely ridiculous."

"*You* looked completely ridiculous," Fenton retorted. "I could certainly see that."

"But did they not drink it up like milk?" she asked sweetly, lifting her eyebrows which widened her already large brown eyes. By George, they did have gold flecks in them. How had he not noticed that before? Why must he notice now? "Do they not feel fawned over and lifted up amid such insincere attention?"

He could not deny that, though he wondered at the point she was making.

Alice dropped her smile completely. "You have spent your life playing with people's affections, Lord Fenton. Though I do not understand why you have chosen such an insincere course to connect with the people around you, you *have* perfected your approach. However, such behavior will not work with me. We have agreed to a future together, and we shall have it regardless of how either one of us feels regarding the circumstance. If you should ever want to become acquainted with me—*truly* acquainted—you will not treat me as you do every other person in your life." She waved her hand to encompass his entire person—dressed in yellow breeches and a burgundy coat that matched the colors of his curricle. "*This*," she said with emphasis as she looked him over, "is a game you play, and while I have no choice but to play along in public, when and if we are ever alone, I expect the real Lord Fenton to be there, assuming you know where to find him. If all he can do is parry insults, so be it. I would prefer *that* man to the false one any day of the week." She lifted her chin and looked ahead.

Fenton did not respond. Could not. He felt vulnerable after her assessment, small in her accusation, and yet so angry he feared that should he open his mouth he would say things he would regret—not that she didn't deserve them. And so he said nothing and tried not to notice how deeply her words had penetrated his mind.

Did he know where to find the real Lord Fenton? Furthermore, was there truly more to him than he presented to the world? That he was unsure of the answer to either question left him irritated to the point that, after returning Alice to her home, he went to his rooms and poured himself a glass of brandy, swallowed it in one gulp, and sank onto the bed.

Here he had tried to do as his mother requested and "be better" and in the process he'd been humiliated. He would not make the same mistake again. These women—Alice and his mother—seemed to think there was more to his character, but what if they were wrong? What if he was the best man he would ever be?

CHAPTER 16

After their ride through Hyde Park, the time spent by Alice and Lord Fenton in one another's company became one long argument, picked up and dropped according to interruption by other people, for whom they were obligated to act as though all was well between them. That Alice could keep up with Lord Fenton told her two things: he was not an idiot—despite the role he played—and she could never let him win.

Every argument increased the stakes, and she continually fortified the wall that was to be her only protection against vulnerability. Despite how hard she tried, she could not help but feel the tingle of awareness when he was near her, nor could she ignore the warmth of his touch even though she knew his hand on her back when they entered a room, or her hand on his arm was only for show. Surely such physical reactions would diminish in time, and yet she worried she would miss that awareness when it was gone.

There was no end to the irony of her situation, and so she insulted him and baited him to keep her determination strong. The game was as ridiculous as it was necessary. She would not be made the fool again.

Sometimes their arguing was exhausting, and they would simply be silent, and yet other times they both seemed to relish it, seeking to win at something that was quite unwinnable. Nearly every event they attended together in the week before the wedding resulted in Lord Fenton stumbling to the carriage at the end of the evening, so saturated with drink he could not maintain his balance. Though Lady Chariton had said before she would speak to him, whatever she'd said was insufficient, and they all now simply ignored it.

As disgusted as Alice was by Lord Fenton's drinking, she envied it as well. For her part, she had no remedy for her discomfort. Other than a little wine with dinner now and again, liquor had never settled well with her, and it was inappropriate for women to overindulge. Her soberness only made her that much more aware of Lord Fenton's behavior, which she became more critical of every day, eager to berate him with whenever she had the chance. Now and then she would marvel at the change in her—from giddy fiancée to razor-tongued nag in a heartbeat—but that too she blamed on him. Her heart had been open until she realized he did not care for her. It was his disregard that had turned her so bitter.

Lord Fenton and his parents removed to the Chariton estate in Berkshire three days before the Saturday morning ceremony. Alice and her family would join them on Friday, and so on Thursday evening, she and her family enjoyed a final dinner together at the London house they had shared these last weeks.

It was a challenge not to give in to the growing melancholy she felt, and Alice found herself wanting to confide in someone. Surely there was something someone could say that would ease her troubled mind and heart. But each time the temptation beckoned, she would remind herself that to share her pain with her family would only hurt them too. She also feared that if she began, she would heap accusations upon them for their part in this. In some ways she could not blame them; she had been so genuinely happy for the match in the beginning that it made sense for them to believe all was well.

They finished dinner, and the ladies withdrew to the drawing room, leaving their father to his port and his pipe. After they entered the very room she had met in with Lord Fenton almost two weeks before, her sisters pulled the door closed. Alice did not think much of it as she sat in one of the lavender chairs facing the fireplace. She only realized their stepmother had not joined them when her sisters pulled two other chairs from different places in the room and set them in front of her.

"Where is Maryanne?" Alice began, looking in confusion from them to the chairs and then to the closed door.

Rebecca and Chloe exchanged a look, then, in tandem, sat down. Rebecca spoke first. "We thought it best—Maryanne included, of course—that we do without her company this evening."

"What would be best?" Alice asked. "I had wanted my entire family around me on my last night." She needed to feel that connection to the people who had loved her the longest and the best. With a loveless marriage on the horizon, she wanted to hold tight to what relationships she had—never mind that she had always felt a bit left out. She had often wished for a closer relationship with her family, and it was hurtful to think her family did not care to spend this time with her.

"You don't want Maryanne here for this, and I didn't want to do it alone," Chloe said. She looked at Rebecca, and they both smiled. Cold dread filled Alice's chest. They could not mean—

"Chloe is the one who spoke with me the night before my wedding," Rebecca said. "And so it is only fitting—though certainly not standard—for the two of us to speak to you on the eve of your great day."

"Two days from now your world will be so different," Chloe said. She reached for Alice's hand, and though Alice was tempted to pull away, she feared it would alert them to a problem. Already her face was on fire with embarrassment. She was grateful they did not know the true reason she was so red-faced.

Rebecca nodded from the other corner of the triangle created by their chairs. "You shall be a married woman, Alice, and certain . . . things that have remained a mystery to you until now will become a reality."

Alice forced a laugh even as her stomach pitched. "I don't want to spend our last night talking of such base things." She turned to Rebecca. "Tell me again of the dress you'll be wearing to the wedding. You said at dinner it had come just today from the dressmakers."

"There is no need to be embarrassed," Chloe said, ignoring Alice's attempt to change the topic of discussion. "It is better to know—"

"Oh, stop," Alice interrupted, finally pulling her hand away. "Let us play cards. Lady Chariton is a great lover of cards, you know, and I should like to be able to—"

"Stop trying to distract us," Rebecca said with a smile that did not seem to be fading at all. Rather she seemed to be enjoying Alice's attempts at deflection. They thought she was being coy. "As your sisters, we consider it our duty to reveal to you the mysteries of the marriage bed so that the experience might be a beautiful thing for you and Lord Fenton both."

Alice closed her eyes and felt her stomach burn. How would they respond if she told them the mysteries of the marriage bed were to remain a mystery for her indefinitely? How could she say that even when the time came that such relations would be necessary, that is all they would be? She had no joy or pleasure to look forward to, no love, intimacy, or warmth.

While one part of Alice wanted to divulge the truth and see the shock of it upon their faces, her pride would not allow it. Saturday would be a hard enough day to endure without seeing their pity when they watched her exchange vows with a man who did not want her except in name only. Alice took a breath and let it out slowly, dropping her head in surrender, which her sisters interpreted as consent.

"You'll thank us for this later, Alice," Chloe said, leaning forward and patting her knee. "Trust us. You will."

CHAPTER 17

Fenton paced back and forth in his bedchamber at Lakeshore—the family estate in Berkshire. He would be summoned to the drawing room for the wedding ceremony any time now, and he ran a finger beneath his collar in hopes it would relieve some of his discomfort.

It did not.

He'd allowed his mother to choose his wedding clothes and was dressed in conservative gray, which strangely made him feel more out of place than he had ever felt in shiny purple pantaloons or red-and-pink waistcoats. He did not feel like himself, but then he wasn't himself anymore so it was only fitting he look the part of a puppet—it was exactly how he felt today.

Since agreeing to his father's terms, Fenton had visited each of the family's holdings except for Foxcroft in Devon, which would have been his even without agreeing to his father's terms. His family had never spent much time at Foxcroft, and it was so far from London there had been no time to see it before the wedding.

Of the estates he *had* visited, however, he'd walked the grounds with bailiffs, sat across from solicitors, and come to realize the scope of responsibility that would be his someday. He had come to understand that a title was more than income; there were tenants' cottages to keep up, herds and fields to manage, and documents and contracts to read and understand and act upon. He was dizzy from all he had immersed himself in and anxious about rising to the challenge.

Anxiety aside, however, he was discovering abilities and interests about himself he had never explored before. It was invigorating to have purpose, and he even dared think his father might be impressed with how well he had done with his responsibilities so far, though he did not expect the earl to say as much. The old man was as sour as he had ever been, and so while nothing had been resolved between them, a level of mutual respect and tolerance might be forming. Perhaps.

You are getting married.

Fenton remembered as though he had forgotten, which on some days he had. Yet, somewhere in this house was Alice Stanbridge, the woman who would become his wife, the woman his mother said deserved to be loved. He pulled at his cravat again and swallowed nervously. His fingers tingled and he flexed them several times in hopes of improving the circulation.

His mother had arranged for the bridal couple to stay at a small cottage in Sussex for a short time. Only Alice and Fenton knew the door connecting their bedchambers would remain closed. After what would surely be an uncomfortable wedding trip, they would return to London until the end of the season so Fenton could continue familiarizing himself with the parliamentary procedures he had never been attentive to in the past.

Once they returned to London, he expected to live very much as he did now, spending enough time with Alice so as not to give rise to *on dit* about their companionship, but mainly focused on his responsibilities and spending time with his friends. He and Alice had only to make it through the next few days before they would settle in to their married lives with, and yet without, one another.

Married.

A husband.

Alice's husband.

It was all so unnerving.

The door to the chamber opened and his mother came in, forcing him to smile at her as though nothing were wrong. She had not spoken again of their discussion following the dressmaker's appointment, for which he was grateful, but neither had she lost the air of disappointment that had disheartened him. Today, however, her expression was soft, and he hoped she was happy enough about the union that she was not dwelling on the more uncomfortable portions. She embraced him, then pulled back and looked into his face as tears filled her eyes.

"Now don't turn into a watering pot on me, Mama," Fenton said. "You know I'll begin crying too and then the story of my emotional breakdown will be all over London by the time I return."

"I'm just so happy for you, Charles," Lady Chariton said, taking both of his hands with her own. "I hope with all my heart that you and Alice find happiness with one another."

Fenton forced his smile wider to cover his fears that a union that began as this one had could not experience great improvement.

Lord Chariton came forward, and his mother dropped Fenton's hands and moved aside. The way she curled up in his father's presence irritated Fenton to no end, and he wondered how things would have been for all of them if his mother had been more like Alice. Though Alice made him crazy, she was not a woman to be bullied. Until this moment he had not realized some part of him admired that.

"Shall we, Lady Chariton?" Lord Chariton said with no emotion at all, as though his only son's wedding were something to get through before he could return to his library and focus on more important things. Never mind that Fenton was feeling much the same, it irritated him that this day meant so little to his father.

"Yes, of course, my lord," she said with dainty submissiveness that set Fenton's teeth on edge. She gave Fenton a single kiss on the cheek and then ushered him out of the room at the head of the processional to the drawing room where they would wait for his bride.

His bride!

Fenton kept his expression mild as he stood before the front windows that looked over an immaculate English garden, robust with blossoms. *Alice would likely know every name of every flower,* he thought. The usual furniture of the room had been moved out to accommodate some forty chairs, which held the members of both families invited to witness the nuptials.

Fenton tried to appear relaxed even as tension built throughout his body. *This is all wrong,* he thought.

As the harpist began a processional hymn, every head turned toward the door. Alice appeared in the doorway on the arm of her father, dressed in a pale peach satin dress with pearl detail to the bodice and a train some four feet long behind her. The style suited her, but her expression was hidden behind a sheer veil. A bead of sweat rolled down Fenton's back, and he straightened his shoulders.

When Mr. Stanbridge handed Alice over to him, Fenton nodded his thanks while in his mind he groaned with the burden of this woman's future. His old schoolmate, Thomas Richards, had married this time last year and already had a child. He had written to Fenton to offer his hearty congratulations and stated quite boldly that matrimony was the single best decision he had ever made. But Richards had been in love with his bride, had wanted her in his life from almost the first moment he'd set eyes on her.

How could Fenton expect to have something similar when his marriage to Alice began this way? Would believing such contentment was possible set him up for even greater disappointment when accord did not come to be? Would he and Alice eventually make a life of comfort together, or was the entire situation already too sour to be redeemed? What if he somehow turned Alice into his mother, broken and small in his presence? What if Alice somehow made him into his father, cold and cruel and immoral?

It struck him that he had no idea how to be the right kind of husband. How could he preserve himself and lift Alice up when he had never seen such a thing before? He'd spent years in church and school and yet no one had ever taught him how he was to do this. Knowing he had already made a mess of it so far gave him no confidence whatsoever that he could find his way to a better course.

He and Alice turned to face the vicar, and Fenton fought against his rising anxiety. What if he'd taken the time to court Alice properly? What if he had not told her the truth in the drawing room that day but instead had tried to truly build an affection for her?

Alice's hand was in his and he could feel the tension coming from her despite the gloves they both wore. It was their wedding day, a date they would look back upon as a time of change, yet neither of them wished to be here. It was really quite sad. If Fenton had not asked for her hand, could Alice have found a man to love her the way his mother said she deserved to be loved? Had his selfishness prevented her happiness?

The clergyman talked of children in their future, and Fenton's stomach grew tight. The marriage would have to be consummated some time—in the eyes of the law and the church the marriage was not official until it was. That Fenton would ever feel comfortable with such intimacy seemed impossible. That he would ever feel capable of the possible result—fatherhood—seemed even more so. He had made a mess of his own life thus far. As of today, he was making an irreversible mess of Alice's. How could he expect he would not do the same for a child? How could he be capable of such responsibility?

They were instructed to face one another, and Fenton met Alice's eyes for the first time through the veil that covered her face. Her tight expression alerted him to his own, and he relaxed the muscles of his face. She focused on a point somewhere on his forehead, breathing quickly through her small pink lips and giving the impression she was trying hard to control her emotions.

The vicar began the final pronouncements, and Fenton wondered if perhaps he *could* love her, but his fears and anxiety stamped out such thoughts. What was love? How could it come of something like this?

Fenton could not look her in the eye, so twisted up were his thoughts, and instead stared at the slight widow's peak of her hairline while counting slowly in his head so as to keep from noticing the fine details of her face or the way she smelled of lilacs.

And then, in a moment, it was over. He lifted her veil and planted a very fast and very chaste kiss upon her lips. For an instant their eyes locked. He saw her sorrow and wondered what she saw in his eyes.

I am not ready, he thought with nothing less than despair. *This is not right. What have I done?*

CHAPTER 18

Alice spent the days of her wedding trip studying a book on herbal remedies. When the tedium of solitude overcame her, she visited one of the many gardens for which East Sussex was famous. She had studied up on the area so as to know where to direct the driver when the gardens were not within walking distance of the cottage. She would then spend hours sketching out different patterns and arrangements, noting how a certain shrubbery was pruned and wondering what the gardens of Fentonview would look like and if she would have enough summer left once they got there to start implementing her own designs.

It was strange not to be accountable to anyone when she left the cottage, but as a married woman, she could come and go as she pleased. She focused on the other benefits of her new station so as to not grow morose on the actual state of her marriage. She had independence, could wear a variety of colors and styles, travel, express her opinion more freely, and receive greater accommodation due women of title. She had an actual lady's maid of her own now, and Lady Chariton had asked Alice to call her Mama.

All in all, Alice had made out quite well in this arrangement, and yet when the hour was late and her thoughts moved to her husband just a closed door away, the loneliness would set in and her future would take on the gray tones of despair and regret. Though there were benefits to be sure, she did not truly have what she wanted.

For his part, she knew Lord Fenton had brought some ledgers and other documents to study, but Alice did not know what he did with all of his time. They saw one another only at meals and rarely spoke at all save for things like "Please pass the salt." The wedding trip may well have been the longest four days of Alice's life, and she was more than ready to return to London when the time came.

She and Lord Fenton did not speak during the carriage ride, which took the greater portion of the day, but they both greeted Lady Chariton with the expected humor of a newlywed couple. She had awaited them in the drawing room and called for tea as soon as they arrived.

Alice prattled on about how lovely Sussex was in spring. She had never been before, she explained, and hoped to return for a longer trip some day in the future. She spoke of the gardens and the weather and even the fine food of the cottage until she quite ran out of things to say.

Lady Chariton turned her attention to Lord Fenton who had let Alice do all the talking while he took a languid pose near the window. Only Alice noticed that he was nearly as far away from her as he could possibly be in the room.

"And did you like the gardens, Charles?" Lady Chariton asked.

"Of course," he said, waving flippantly, his lace cuffs looking as though he were waving handkerchiefs. "Why, I do not know when I have ever before admired gardens half so much."

"Which was your favorite?" Lady Chariton asked. "I quite admire the gardens at Pashley Manor myself. Did you see them?"

"Yes, Pashley was quite lovely," Alice supplied when Lord Fenton suddenly looked like a caught rabbit. "As it turns out, your son is a great lover of peonies, which were in full bloom."

"Yes," Lord Fenton said without acknowledging Alice's rescue. "In fact the peonies were so very fine that I have already asked Alice to find a way to add them to the gardens at Fentonview. I should also like a natural stone path to replace the gravel there. I found the pathways most pleasing in the priory garden."

Alice was surprised he knew anything of the priory, since he certainly hadn't seen it with her. As it was, she had also appreciated the flat stones of the walkways. However, she was careful to hide her surprise at his comment when Lady Chariton looked to her. She worried Lady Chariton suspected the charade between them, but the sharpened notice seemed to disappear as soon as it appeared, and Lady Chariton moved the topic of conversation to the social events she had accepted on their behalf while they were away—a ball the next night and a dinner party with an important statesman the night after that.

"From now forward I shall of course allow Alice to choose your engagements, but as these came while you were away, and were of the best society, I did not want them to go unanswered."

"But of course," Lord Fenton said with a nod. "Alice will be happy to take over that responsibility. She knows my preferences, and I trust her to respond accordingly."

Again, Alice was taken off guard. That he saw value in her opinions and ability to fulfill the role of Lady Fenton gave her increased confidence, and she dared think things were off to a better start than she could have anticipated. Once they excused themselves from his mother's presence, however, things did not remain so amiable.

"I've no interest in attending that ball tomorrow night," Fenton said as they walked arm and arm up the staircase to the family rooms.

"Your mother has already accepted on our behalf, and as it will be our first social appearance, we need to attend it."

"Balls are tedious, especially now."

"Because you shall *have* to stand up with me?" Alice said with a bite. "You *did* ask me to be your wife, my lord, and shall have to make the sacrifice of my company now and again."

"It is not that," Lord Fenton said without rising to her ire. "It is just that . . . how am I to get on as a married man? I cannot flatter and wink as I once did, it would be unseemly. But neither can I lose all my former manner." He let out a breath, which caused Alice to regard him a bit closer. She was unused to seeing insecurity in him or feel the sympathy such vulnerability on his part stirred within her.

"You shall not flatter and wink as you did before," Alice agreed. "But there is nothing amiss with giving compliments and making polite conversation. Married men are no longer on pursuit, but they are still agreeable. And there are usually cards to be played."

They reached the door to the room where Alice would stay and stopped, though they did not look at one another.

"You shall not insist on my continual company?" Lord Fenton asked.

Alice clenched her jaw, feeling as though they had circled back to the crux of his concern: that he would have to be at her side. "I shall insist against it to be sure," she said, releasing his arm as soon as she realized she was still holding it. "It is my deepest hope that with the legalities out of the way, we might do a better job of avoiding one another." His eyes narrowed and Alice was instantly determined to win this round of arguments, the first of their married life. "I think we both have an excellent example in your own parents as to how to lead independent lives and—"

Something snapped closed in Lord Fenton's expression so severely that it brought Alice up short and she lost her train of thought.

"That is your hope for us?" Lord Fenton said, as coldly as he had ever said anything.

"I only mean they do not socialize together frequently, perhaps once a week, if that." Even as she said the words, however, she knew they were wrong somehow. She could see in her new husband's face that he was not only irritated by the words, he was almost . . . angered by them. Somehow she had crossed a line without knowing exactly how. "Lord Fenton," she said apologetically. "I did not—"

"Enough." He stepped away from her, his expression cold as steel. "You have made your point. Once a week will be plenty of time together. I shall make it my *top* priority to stay out of your company otherwise." He turned on his heel and headed to the next doorway down the hall—his bedchamber, she presumed. It opened and shut with a snap, leaving Alice to stare after him and wonder what it was she'd said.

CHAPTER 19

Barker was tying Fenton's cravat in preparation for an evening at a friend's house when there was a knock at the door that connected Fenton's bedchamber with Alice's. In the past—all of his life until now, in fact—the wardrobes in both rooms had hid the connecting door. Fenton did not even know the door existed until they returned to London from their wedding trip nearly a month ago and found the furniture changed to reveal the connection. Of course, the door had not been used in the weeks since their return and to hear a knock upon it was so surprising that Fenton shooed his man from the room before hurrying to the door. He paused a moment to gather his composure before pulling it open. It would not do to appear too eager about this unexpected change.

Alice stood on her side of the doorway, dressed in an aubergine gown he had not seen on her before. It was one of the gowns he had chosen for her at the dressmaker's appointment before the wedding and was as fine as he had expected it to be. The square neck lined with black Italian lace and puffed sleeve with an wide cuff served her complexion and frame well, and when he waved her into his room—as though not shocked to see her there—he quite admired the movement of the fabric and the slight train to the skirt that elongated her waist. Yes, he did know a thing or two about fashion.

"I daresay I was right about this dress, Alice," he said with the whimsical tone she despised so much and which he therefore used often. "The purple plays upon the gold of your eyes to perfection and pairs well with your complexion. Yes, it is very well on you indeed."

She faced him with a surprised expression, which caused him to repeat what he'd said in his mind in order to determine what had caused such a reaction. It was only after the review that he realized he'd paid her a compliment that did not include any kind of jab. He hurried to remedy it. "Of course it does not compensate for your sour expression, but there is no gown capable of that, I'm sure."

She narrowed her eyes, souring that expression even more and looked away from him, which caused him a slight pang of regret that he could not pay his own wife a compliment. Of course, she held equal blame for the state of things because she chose to be contrary so he did not feel overburdened by his regret.

"I have come to talk with you about your mother," she said. "And I did not want to use any other room in the house for such a delicate conference."

Fenton's mind snapped to attention. "What of my mother demands delicacy?"

Alice clasped her hands together in a display of agitation, though it did not seem directed at him for once. Praise the heavens. "I have spent a great deal of time with her these past weeks, and you know I regard her quite highly. She truly is a woman of remarkable grace and respectability."

"Yes, she is," Fenton said, anxious to hear what sparked Alice's concern while attempting not to be distracted by the way the light from the window illuminated his wife's figure. It gave a sharp outline to her well-formed shoulders and graceful neck, to say nothing of her curves and softness when she moved in profile. The better stays he'd insisted upon were *very well* for her. He shook himself from such notice and kept his eyes on her face alone even as his pulse quickened despite his insistence that it not do such a thing. "I don't imagine her grace is what draws your concern."

"No." Alice began to pace back and forth in front of the window, keeping her figure in profile each time she changed direction. "I am concerned for her health." She went on to explain the thinness of Lady Chariton's frame, the sensitivity of her stomach, and the cough she had developed some days earlier that was getting worse. "I had her maid procure the herbs necessary for a tonic, and Lady Chariton says it has helped settle her stomach, but when I suggested a doctor for further assistance with the cough today, she refused. She said she had had quite enough of doctors." Alice stopped pacing and turned to face him. "But she would not expand and I did not feel it my place to press the issue. Has she been ill?"

It took a moment for Fenton to form an answer, though it was not that the response was difficult. Rather, it was the strangeness of this conversation—the normalcy of it. They had never experienced a conversation such as this. Only when Alice began to look unsure of his delay in responding did he hurry to answer her question. "She has been in rather good health of late but has struggled against a variety of illness these last few years."

"Why does she not want to find a remedy? Why not meet with

a doctor now that she is falling ill again? She seems quite set against it."

"Over the years, she has consulted with half a dozen doctors who have given her half a dozen treatments, none of which seemed to work and a few of which made things worse. One doctor in Berkshire nearly bled her to death, and it was months before she regained her strength. I had not noticed she was doing so poorly. You say it has been several days now?"

How could he not have noticed? What kind of son was he? But since he tried to stay out of the house as much as possible—lunching at his club, spending his days observing parliamentary business at the House of Lords, and enjoying the evenings as he always had—it was perhaps not so surprising. Avoiding Alice had led to his inadvertently becoming disconnected from his mother as well.

"I fear she is trying hard to hide the seriousness of her illness," Alice said with a sympathy he found himself envying. It surprised him to wish for regard equal to that which Alice held toward his mother. But wishing for what he did not have would only set him up for further regret. Though Alice was kind and concerned now, her razor tongue was certainly not forgotten.

Alice continued, "Prior to our engagement, and then moving into this house, I don't believe she was going out much, so perhaps she was feeling more the thing. Now she accompanies me on any number of visits several days of the week, and I fear it is taxing her far more than she will admit for fear we will not make the rounds. I know she enjoys the society of her friends and does not want to miss time with them."

"*Her* friends?" Fenton asked.

"I wanted to know her friends and associates, so we have spent most of our time becoming acquainted with them. She enjoy the visits very much, but it does seem to take her strength."

Fenton nodded to spare himself from complimenting his wife for being so solicitous. He was aware the relationship between the two women was deepening and, despite being continually at odds with his wife, he was glad for the companionship she offered his mother who, now that he thought more on it, had not been so socially motivated this season. "Does it seem her fatigue is increasing with these visits, then?"

"Yes," Alice said. Her hazel eyes confirmed her worry and solidified their truce on this one topic. "Today she began coughing at the home of Mrs. Hinson and could not stop for some time. Mrs. Hinson finally offered her carriage to return us home—we had walked over as it was only a few blocks, and the weather was fine—and your mother has been abed ever since. I took the herbal tonic to her a short time ago, and she was embarrassed for the situation and asserted I was not to be alarmed. But I am *quite* alarmed, Lord Fenton, and unsure what to do."

"I have worried over my mother's health—last season especially. It seemed her health declined as the season wore on." He paused, remembering more of that time; he had not thought of it much lately because it seemed the concern had passed. "It was not until she removed to Lakeshore after Parliament ended that she began to improve."

"So it is London, perhaps, that causes her decline," Alice said. "I know of others who feel lowered due to the smoke and smog. Today's cough, especially, makes me wonder if the city air is responsible for her difficulties. You once told me she often feels quite wrung out by the end of the season."

Fenton nodded. "To say nothing of the illness that spreads through the very society we all come to Town to enjoy."

"Which, if she has a weaker constitution, makes it even more of a concern. Perhaps she must leave London, then," Alice said, inclining her head as though it were all clear and decided.

"My father insists it is her responsibility to be in Town when he is."

"Would he not encourage her to go if it were for the sake of her health?"

"Perhaps," Fenton said simply, thinking of how much his father wanted things to look just right. Would he care more for his wife's health than how it might look for her to leave early?

"Could you speak with him about it?" Alice asked.

"I shall do what I can," Fenton said, hating the idea of conferring with his father. Any reason other than his mother would not be worth the aggravation. "Thank you for bringing it to my attention."

They held one another's eyes across the room, and though she stood several yards away, he found himself feeling closer to his wife than he had in all their weeks together. She looked away first, seemingly embarrassed for allowing the connection to last as long as it did. She moved toward the adjoining door, and in a reckless attempt to capture the moment, Fenton searched for something that would extend their conversation, which had been so surprisingly pleasant, regardless of the worrisome topic.

"I am to go to a dinner party tonight. Would you like to attend with me?"

She immediately shook her head as though she didn't even need to think of a curt reply she was so well practiced with them. "I shouldn't want to inconvenience you with more of my company than you have agreed to withstand, *my lord.*"

The way she snapped the last two words ended his feelings of camaraderie. "Thank goodness," he said, letting out a dramatic breath before turning back to his looking glass. "I thought you were dangling about in hopes of an invitation and am quite relieved to have misinterpreted. The entire evening is saved!" He looped a hand through the air, then pulled at his cravat. He would need to call Barker in to repair it but needed something to busy his hands with for the moment. He waved toward the connecting door. "Don't let me keep you, *my dear.*"

Alice sighed, and he felt sure she was rolling her eyes. "Just be sure to speak to your father." The door closed behind her, and he turned to face it, frowning over his own behavior while justifying the fact that she was the first to be rude.

"Barker," he called to his man, who was likely leaning against the door and listening to every word. The valet immediately entered the room.

"My lord?"

"My apologies for destroying the neck cloth. Could you please repair it as quickly as possible?" While Barker tended to the task, Fenton worried about his mother.

She would not leave London without Lord Chariton's consent, of that Fenton was certain, so it would do no good to try to convince her of it before speaking with his father. If Fenton could see for himself how she was faring, though, then he could present a clearer picture to Lord Chariton. For his own part, however, Fenton hated the idea of his mother leaving Town early. He would miss her, and yet he wanted what was best for her health.

"And hold my carriage another half an hour," Fenton added while his valet finished the knot. "I would like to visit with my mother before I go out tonight."

CHAPTER 20

Lady Chariton had deemed Sunday the best evening for the Theler family dinners, and so Alice took her place at the dining room table—reduced that one evening each week to fit just the four of them—and steeled herself for an uncomfortable meal. Lord and Lady Chariton sat opposite one another, while she sat at the lower end and Fenton at the upper end, as propriety dictated. Lord Fenton sat at his father's right and Alice sat at Lord Chariton's left.

Alice had had little opportunity to become acquainted with Lord Chariton, as he rarely entertained with the family and spent his days at the House of Lords or his club. That he had made no effort to get to know his son's new wife did not motivate Alice to make much attempt of her own. He was a bit severe, in her opinion, with little in common with Alice's father, who was far warmer in his demeanor than she had fully appreciated before.

Her family had left London the week after the wedding and she missed them. To distract herself from wondering what they were doing and wishing she were back at Warren House, she focused on learning how to be Lady Fenton. So far, it was mostly about meeting the right people, being exact in her manners, and trying to feel comfortable with a new level of attention.

Once she removed from London, she would need to run a household, but Lady Chariton saw to such tasks here in London. Alice tried not to think about how she and Lord Fenton would get on when it was just the two of them at a country estate. The thought of it made her stomach tight.

After the weather and the morning church service were discussed, Lord Chariton cleared his throat and looked directly at his wife. "Lady Chariton, it has come to my attention that you are unwell. I feel it best that you remove to Berkshire within the week to restore yourself."

Alice cringed at the directness of his order. It had been two days since her conversation with Fenton. She had expected Lord Chariton to approach the topic privately, and she glanced at Lord Fenton to see that he seemed equally surprised and equally irritated. In the silence that followed Lord Chariton's directive, Alice looked from one parent-in-law to the other. They were not a couple; they seemed as though strangers to each other. Alice wished she did not then picture Lord Fenton and herself decades in the future being just as disconnected.

"I do not wish to remove," Lady Chariton said after schooling her expression of surprise. "I shall stay until Parliament is ended as I always do." She raised her napkin to her mouth and attempted to hide a cough behind it, but with everyone's attention on her it was impossible. When she lowered the napkin a moment later, she looked across the table and spoke in a softer voice. "I simply need a bit more rest, my lord, and perhaps some adjustments to my diet."

"I will not have a repeat of last year," Lord Chariton said, his attention on his soup. "Nor the one before when the entire household became so distracted by your ailments that all order crumbled to the gutters."

"Father," Fenton said in a hissing kind of whisper, his eyes narrowed toward the head of the table. "This is not a punishment. She has done nothing wrong."

Lord Chariton shrugged. "She has not been attentive to her health or else she would be able to bear out the season."

"My place is in Town when you are here, my lord," Lady Chariton said. "I do not wish to leave until the session is finished and shall be attentive to my duties from now on."

"I have already decided," Lord Chariton said, picking up his wine glass and taking a hearty swallow. "I shall explain to our acquaintances that it was a matter of health. No one shall think poorly of such a reason as that. I have sent a note to the steward to have Lakeshore readied for your arrival. I expect you to leave in the morning with a single trunk and your maid. The remainder of your things shall be sent down within a few days' time."

"Surely she does not need to be sent in a rush," Lord Fenton countered, his tone sharp. "You have only just told her of this. Allow her some time to become acquainted with the idea."

Alice's heart ached at the way Lady Chariton's shoulders rounded in surrender. This had not come together at all like she'd expected it would when she'd decided to speak to Lord Fenton, and she felt responsible for the discomfort.

"What if I were to attend to Lakeshore with you, Lady Chariton?" she said, smiling. "I must say I am feeling quite worn-out myself, and as my family has left Town I have fewer associations I feel the need to pursue, though I have enjoyed meeting so many people through our visits. I was very much impressed with the portions of Lakeshore

I saw at the time of the wedding and regret that I did not have the chance to become more familiar with the estate."

Lady Chariton gave her such a grateful and hopeful smile that Alice felt more confidence in her impulsive suggestion. She looked from Lady Chariton's smile to Lord Chariton, who had a far less agreeable expression.

"You will stay in London and attend to housekeeping in Lady Chariton's absence," Lord Chariton said evenly.

"I thank you for your confidence, my lord," Alice replied, equally even in her tone. "However, as I have not yet had the proper training and—"

"And you are to attend to your husband," he said, cutting her off and returning his attention to his food. "That Lady Chariton is unwell is no excuse for you to set aside your responsibilities to your husband and this household."

Alice's face and chest burned from both anger and embarrassment. She had never been spoken to in such a way and did not know how to respond. The entire room was quiet while Alice looked at her soup and tried to think what to say. Only curt replies and sharp responses came to mind so she kept her mouth closed and her hands balled into fists in her lap. She could not speak to Lord Chariton with disrespect.

"Actually," Lord Fenton said, giving her the confidence to lift her head and look at him across the table. He focused only on his bowl as he scooped a bite of soup with a spoon held rather tightly. "Perhaps it would be better if Alice attended Mama to Lakeshore for the rest of the season. I would hate for Mama to travel alone, and we shall get on well enough. I believe Mama will be well cared for with Alice in attendance and therefore all her needs will be met."

"Your mother is not to be *your* concern, Charles," Lord Chariton said, not quite as loudly as he'd spoken to Alice but equally displeased. "And certainly not at the expense of—"

"My mother will *always* be my concern, Father," Lord Fenton cut in with the even, low tones more suited to a man not dressed head to toe in gold silk. Even when he and Alice were fighting over this or that he remained flippant. He was not flippant now, however, and despite the heaviness of the mood, Alice could not help but admire the strength of his defense even as she wondered at his motives for the argument. Was he truly eager to have Alice attend his mother, or was it the fact that he would not have to deal with his wife that encouraged this direction?

Lord Fenton continued, "I am greatly concerned over Mama's health and feel it imperative she remove from the city so as to recover. If Alice is willing to attend her, and Mama is comfortable with that arrangement, I shall support it."

"I shall not," Lord Chariton said. He glared at his son. "It is improper for a newly married man to be separated from his wife. And as I am the head of this—"

"I should like Alice to attend me," Lady Chariton cut in with quick words, as though rushing to say them before she thought better of it. Her voice was nowhere near the same volume or spirit as her husband's, but it sliced through his words nonetheless. Alice was surprised to see the intent expression upon Lady Chariton's face. Only moments before she had curled in on herself and offered no resistance at all. "But I should like to go to Foxcroft instead of Lakeshore."

Foxcroft? Alice repeated in her head. *What is Foxcroft?* She looked at Fenton for clarification, but his expression was equally confused. She looked at Lord Chariton, whose expression was nothing short of shocked. He put down his spoon and stared at his wife at the other end of the table. Lady Chariton straightened under his gaze and held his eyes. Though words were not spoken, something was exchanged between them. Lord Chariton's jaw tightened and his face reddened with anger.

"Absolutely not," Lord Chariton said in a low and rumbling tone that had Alice setting her spoon beside her plate for fear it would shake in her hand. Her family had been known to bicker and disagree, but not with such stormy countenances, cryptic looks, or thundering words. "I will not have it."

"And I will not be dissuaded," Lady Chariton said. "It had been my intent to go there after the session ended. If I am to leave London early, I should like more time at Foxcroft." She turned to her son as though her husband had not even spoken, and put a hand out to him, which he took. The display of gentle connection reflected their accord with one another, and for a moment Alice envied both of them. "Charles, I appreciate your support on this. Thank you." She rose from the table slowly and placed her napkin on her chair. "And thank you, Alice, for attending me." She had barely eaten any of her soup and there were three courses left. She did not meet the glowering eye of her husband but instead coughed behind her handkerchief while she walked out of the room.

Alice wanted to follow her, as she would have at the end of the meal, but she was unsure of what was expected of her in this situation and therefore remained rooted in her chair.

"I won't have it, Charles," Lord Chariton said. "When I agreed to her removal from Town I did not anticipate *this*." He cut his hand through the air.

Lord Fenton's expression was all confidence and certainty. "If removing to Foxcroft will ease her regret at leaving Town early, I mean to support her in a recovery of her health. As Alice will be there to help see to her comfort, I do not see why Mama should not be able to choose her own location of respite."

Lord Chariton glared at his son, then rose and threw his napkin on the table. It hit the handle of the spoon, which he'd left in his bowl, and splattered soup on the tablecloth. Lord Chariton stormed out of a different doorway than his wife had just departed and began yelling for his carriage.

"What is wrong with Foxcroft?" Alice asked Lord Fenton when they were alone.

"There is nothing *wrong* with Foxcroft," he said, sitting up a bit straighter. "Only it is rustic and located in Devon, near Whitestone. I have not visited it since I was a boy, and it is a two-day journey from Berkshire—a *long* two days by carriage."

Alice remembered the estate then, from the history she'd been given of her new family. "It is an estate that came through your mother's line, was it not?"

"Yes," Lord Fenton said, glancing at his mother's empty place. "Mother and I went every summer when I was a boy, but I haven't been back since I was . . . six or seven, I believe." He furrowed his eyebrows. "For years I would ask if we were going to visit Foxcroft again and she would say that perhaps we would the year following, but we never did. She seemed sad when she thought about it, so I assumed she did not want to return. I can't imagine why she would now want to go when she is feeling so poorly. The journey will be hard on her." He glanced at his father's empty place at the table, where a footman was attempting to restore order, and his expression shifted into one that Alice could only interpret as victorious. "Seeing as how my father is against it and my mother chose to insist makes me very much in her corner for this round, however. Regardless of her reasons."

He smiled slightly as he returned to his meal. Alice watched him, hoping the brittle camaraderie could sustain an additional question. "Why do you enjoy vexing your father so?" She had not seen much to admire about the earl, and Lord Fenton had not hidden his feelings for the man, but seeing him rise to his mother's defense made Alice want to know more about the motivation behind his actions. "Did something happen between the two of you that caused such a divide?"

Lord Fenton's eyes did not leave his bowl, but his movements slowed. After a few seconds, he looked at her and let out a tired breath that matched his expression of fatigue. "I do not care to speak of it, Alice. I cannot." His weary tone was enough that she did not press him—something that rarely was the case. As much as she wanted an explanation, she did not want to hurt him, and somehow she knew if she forced him to tell, it would be painful. "Please eat your soup," he said.

Confused but silent, Alice lowered her head and ate her soup.

CHAPTER 21

They finished their dinner in silence. Lord Fenton checked on his mother before he and Alice left for a card party at the house of a man Lord Fenton had met during his time spent observing Parliament. Lord Fenton had chosen this as the event they would attend together this week, which meant he expected it would be boring and Alice would need to help carry the conversation.

"The man is tolerable, I suppose," Lord Fenton mused as the carriage bounced along the cobbles. Alice watched him closely and tried not to be irritated by the increasing falseness in his movements and tone the closer they got to their destination. She wanted to see more of the man from dinner, the man who stood up for his mother. "But he only wears black breeches, and he snorts when he laughs." Lord Fenton shook his head and raised an eyebrow at Alice. "Can you imagine? Wearing black breeches day in and day out?"

"What does Mr. Beecher do in Parliament?" Alice asked, wanting to keep the conversation on topic.

"He is a clerk, but a well-connected one," Lord Fenton said, but he frowned. "You know, I do think I saw him in charcoal breeches once." He turned his head slightly. "Or was that Lord Pomproy's other clerk? Likely that. I'll have to check my notes."

"Notes?" Alice asked, confused.

"Yes, notes," Lord Fenton confirmed. "I spend hours in the House when I am there, you know, and much of it is dreadfully boring. I have begun taking notes on what the members wear, or don't wear. Lord Harrison did not wear a vest beneath his coat last Tuesday. How does a man not remember to put on a waistcoat? Where was his valet?"

Alice's irritation rose with every word. This was the Lord Fenton she could not stand, and by the glimmer in his eye, she suspected he knew her dislike and was goading her.

"You spend your time documenting what people are wearing? What of the laws and policy of the government? What of the issues brought to the body for decision?"

Lord Fenton shrugged and fiddled with the gold-colored fob hanging from his jacket cuff. "I do not hold a seat so it is of no matter. I am there merely for educational purposes. I studied such things to distraction while at Oxford—it is not such difficult material to understand that I need to be overly attentive."

"Therefore you spend the time focused on men's choices in fashion?" Alice said with disgust.

"Gads no," Lord Fenton said, pulling back in horror, his eyes wide and his eyebrows climbing his forehead. "There is no *fashion* in Parliament, well, except for me of course." He grinned, setting her teeth on edge. "I merely document their clothing, or, if you will, their *lack* of fashion. Honestly I do not know how they can expect to command respect from anyone when they all dress like a bunch of undertakers. For being the richest men in England, they do not invest very well in the things that truly matter. Speaking of which, how do you like the rest of the gowns from the dressmaker? You have not yet praised me for doing so well with them."

Praise was the last thing Alice was going to give Lord Fenton, though the dresses were quite exceptional and far finer than anything she had owned in the past. Fortunately, the carriage arrived at their destination and she was spared having to say anything. She could barely remember the soft feelings she had felt toward her husband at dinner.

Once they exited the carriage, Lord Fenton put out his arm as expected and Alice took it, also as expected. They made their way to the door of the house. "I do hope they are generous with their brandy and that there are enough couples that you and I can keep a distance for the evening, *my lord*."

"As do I," he said, patting her hand on his arm. "The brandy part especially. Sometimes it is the only way I can make it through."

The door opened, and they were both forced to put on their party faces, but inside herself, Alice admitted that she could not wait to leave London. She did not love society the way Lord Fenton did, and the energy it took to keep up the impression that all was well between them became more taxing by the day. Add to the falseness her discomfort at seeing parts and pieces of her husband that she longed for more of, and she was quite out of sorts and eager for the distance.

Lord Fenton amplified his dandy behavior for the benefit of the guests, and she felt her smile tighten. Yes, removing to Foxcroft was a good choice. And it could not come soon enough.

The next three days were filled with preparations for their departure and broken up only by an event here or there that Lady Chariton insisted they attend, though each one left her quite worn-out. Alice saw Lord Fenton very little, which was a relief, and when their paths did cross, they muttered their insults and rolled their eyes. It was by far their most comfortable form of interaction, and though Alice suspected more than ever that it was a protection on his part, she acknowledged that it protected her too. If he could remain the idiotic fool in her mind, she would not have to wonder or wish or hope for anything more between them. It was when other impressions trespassed into her thoughts that things became uncomfortable.

Lord Fenton oversaw the loading of the traveling coach Thursday morning, then shared a warm embrace with his mother. Alice turned away so as to avoid the feelings of envy their parting would inspire.

"Be well, Mama," he said. "And write to me as soon as you arrive. I shall miss you."

The boyishness caused Alice's heart to skip, and she quickly reminded herself of his drunken singing on the way home from the card party Sunday night. She'd ended up taking off her gloves and slapping him with them until he finally stopped. It had been ridiculous, and she was glad to remember the incident so as to not let her thoughts of felicity toward her husband get out of hand.

Lord Fenton handed his mother into the coach and then turned to Alice. The serious expression on his face made her brace herself, unsure what to expect. At least with the fop she could anticipate his behavior.

"I thank you for doing this, Alice," he said sincerely.

She wanted to reply with some insult, but how could she when he'd said something heartfelt? Instead, she centered her mind and responded with equal sincerity, though she felt tightly sprung and ready to jump forward with a retort if he turned the conversation. "I thank you for advocating for your mother's wishes. It will be good for her to remove from the city. I am very hopeful it will improve her health."

Lord Fenton put out his hand, and Alice was reminded of that day years ago when he had performed the same action, saying that to have a deal they had to shake on it—gentleman to lady. Taken off guard by the memory, and humbled by the graciousness of such a gesture, she lifted her hand, which Lord Fenton took in his own. Rather than shaking it in an official kind of way as she expected, he turned her hand and lifted it to his lips, causing her to startle at such an intimate touch.

Alice told herself he was performing for the benefit of those around them, but she'd been the subject of any number of those performed acts of affection and they had never felt like this. Warmth spread up her arm, through her shoulder and into her chest. She felt her cheeks heat up, betraying the intimacy she felt even though she knew it was not intimacy he'd intended. She vacillated between pulling her hand away and allowing herself to feel the fullness of the sensation.

He lowered her hand and then released it. "I shall join you both as soon as I am able," he said, further undoing her with his low voice. "Should anything change with my mother's health, please alert me immediately."

"Of course."

He held her eyes in a way that made her feel incredibly vulnerable, and when he smiled she felt it all the way to her toes. He handed her into the carriage, and she tried to make sense of the competing feelings in her chest. She had looked forward to leaving for Foxcroft because it would take her away from him. She would not be irritated by his nasally tones, or put off by his peacocking about town. And yet, as the carriage pulled forward, heading to Lakeshore where she and Lady Chariton would stay the night before continuing on to Foxcroft, Alice realized that she would miss Lord Fenton.

She would *miss* her husband.

Oh, dear.

CHAPTER 22

After leaving Lakeshore the next day, the journey to Foxcroft was uneventful other than the stops to change horses, eat a meal, and stay a night. Lady Chariton rested a great deal, even in the carriage, but when she was alert she reminisced about Alice's mother, growing up in Essex, and, especially, Lord Fenton as a boy. Through her memories, Alice could see why Lady Chariton and Lord Fenton were so close—his mother only saw the best side of him and did not factor anything else into her opinion.

Alice, of course, did not try to mention his less favorable attributes, but the question of why he behaved as he did became bigger and bigger until she was of half a mind to write him a letter that demanded an explanation. But one did not send letters such as that, and she could not expect he would reply to it if she did. That there was more to him than he chose to share with her, with everyone other than his mother, was interesting and aggravating and, at its core, irrelevant. Alice could not make him trust her, and certainly her willingness to engage with him in their endless arguments did not earn her that right.

But the more she heard of his mother's affectionate memories, the more she wished she had not demanded the truth of their arrangement from him that day in the drawing room. He had said he expected they would grow in accord for one another, and perhaps they would have. But she had demanded the truth and reacted with vigor to the hurt she'd felt. How did one undo such a thing? Could it be undone?

On the morning of the third day of travel, Alice and Lady Chariton climbed into the coach and made the last of the journey. It was midafternoon when they turned into a somewhat pitted drive flanked by yew trees in need of pruning—two were completely dead and needed to be cut down.

Lord Fenton had described Foxcroft as rustic, and the unkempt drive attested to that very thing, so as they rounded the final bend of the drive, Alice was surprised by the two-story, butter-colored house, complete with a slate roof, dormered windows, and a covered porch that hung over an elaborate fan-shaped stone staircase with wrought iron railings on both sides. It was not the largest estate house Alice had seen, and perhaps not quite as big as Warren House, but it was far more expansive than she had expected, though it did show signs of neglect in the overgrown hedges and peeling paint about the door and windows.

"What a beautiful house," she said.

Lady Chariton nodded, a look of expectation and . . . sadness about her eyes. Alice remembered Lord Fenton saying that his mother seemed sad whenever she spoke of Foxcroft. Alice wondered why, if it made her sad, had she insisted on coming?

The carriage stopped before the fan-shaped steps, and the coachman who had accompanied them from London handed both ladies from the carriage while a line of servants gathered at the base of the stairs. Alice looked upward along the front of the house with stones so perfectly set one upon another that she could not make out the mortar between them.

A man stepped forward, and Alice moved behind Lady Chariton out of deference.

"Lady Chariton," the man said, bowing toward her. "I hope your journey was well. I am Mr. Mumford, the steward for Foxcroft estate these fourteen years. I am very pleased to meet you after all these years of written correspondence between us."

"I am pleased to meet you as well, Mr. Mumford," she said. She introduced Alice as her daughter, Lady Fenton, and said she would be assisting with the household. Alice hadn't expected that, but it made her feel important so she nodded and tried to stand with bearing fitting her title—a title that still felt surreal to her.

Lady Chariton moved first to the woman servant furthest to the right. Because of the navy dress and pressed white collar the woman wore, Alice assumed she was the housekeeper. She appeared surprisingly young—perhaps no more than thirty years of age.

"Mrs. Gale," Lady Chariton said with a nod.

"Your ladyship," the woman said nervously as she curtsied.

Lady Chariton kept her eyes on the woman until she straightened and looked at her mistress again. Something passed between them, though Alice could not guess what, and Lady Chariton moved to the next servant in line.

Alice kept her eyes on Mrs. Gale, who watched Lady Chariton warily. *How did they know one another?* Alice wondered. Mrs. Gale was not old enough to have been even a chambermaid twenty years ago, which is how long Lord Fenton had said it had been since Lady Chariton had visited Foxcroft.

Alice's attention was drawn away from Mrs. Gale as Lady Chariton took both hands of an older woman with silvery hair not caught up entirely beneath her ruffled cap. She was nearer to the age Alice would expect for a housekeeper, but she wore the apron of a cook.

"I am so very glad to see you, Mrs. Banner," Lady Chariton said with a smile of such warmth that Alice was quite astounded. She had never seen such connection between a servant and a mistress. Yet it had been twenty years since Lady Chariton had been here? "You are well?"

"I am well. We are both very well." Mrs. Banner inclined her head and smiled back. "I am glad you have returned."

Both? Alice repeated in her mind, her eyes sliding back to Mrs. Gale. Did she mean herself and the housekeeper? Alice was so confused.

"As am I," Lady Chariton said. "Very glad indeed. We shall speak later."

"Yes, my lady," Mrs. Banner said with a nod.

Lady Chariton moved down the line of staff members organized by rank—each of whom Mr. Mumford presented to her. Alice remained distracted by Mrs. Banner's softness and Mrs. Gale's wariness each time they glanced at their mistress.

When Lady Chariton had finished with the introductions, Mr. Mumford dismissed the servants, advising that he would certainly expand the staff now that Lady Chariton was in residence. Lady Chariton agreed that was a good course and then asked to be shown upstairs.

Mrs. Gale hurried to lead the way up the outside steps to a large foyer that seemed chilly compared to the fine day. Lady Chariton barely glanced around before heading for the stairs to the left that led to the second floor.

"I would like to stay in the rose room, if you please," Lady Chariton said.

Mrs. Gale's nervousness increased, though she stayed a step ahead of her mistress. "In the absence of specific instruction in your letter, we have prepared the countess's bedchamber for your ladyship."

"My apologies for not including such information," Lady Chariton said, taking hold of the handrail with one hand and her skirts with the other when they reached the first step. She was so thin that her dress hung about her shoulders. "But I should like the rose room. Lady Fenton may take the countess's chamber if she likes."

Mrs. Gale glanced over her shoulder at Alice, who tried not to show her surprise at Lady Chariton's invitation. Surely she should not have better accommodations than the countess.

The staircase to the upper floors was on the left side of the foyer, and Alice and Lady Chariton followed Mrs. Gale up, taking the stairs slowly as Lady Chariton was quite worn out from their travel. The cough still plagued her, but already it seemed better than it had been when they were in London.

"I'm afraid that the blue room and the countess's chamber are the only two rooms we prepared for your arrival," Mrs. Gale said when they reached the landing. The group paused to allow Lady Chariton a rest before they climbed the second set of stairs. "The other rooms are still in Holland covers."

"I am sure the rose room can be put to rights before I retire for the evening, though I would like to look in on it now."

Mrs. Gale looked doubtful, but all she said was, "Yes, my lady."

They passed a set of double doors left open to show a very large and well-appointed bedroom done up with heavy brocade fabrics dulled with age—the countess's chamber, to be sure. Lady Chariton did not look inside.

They turned a corner and entered another hallway. The first door on the left was also open, revealing blue silk on the walls and more blue within the pattern of the coverlet and drapery around the large bed. This could only be the blue room Mrs. Gale had spoken of. It looked very well, but Alice did not spend a great deal of time looking in on it, as Lady Chariton and Mrs. Gale continued down the hall.

At the final door to the right, Mrs. Gale stopped. She looked as though she might ask one more time if Lady Chariton were certain of this room, but then thought better of it and opened the door, pulling it wide to allow them entry.

The curtains were drawn, leaving the room in darkness. Mrs. Gale hurried to the window and pulled back the sash. Daylight burst forth along with a puff of dust released from the fabric of the drapes. Alice, standing just a bit over the threshold, looked around the bedchamber that was much smaller than the other two they had passed.

In addition to its small size, it was also long and narrow. The bed and wardrobe, both in covers, were set on one side, and a small sitting area, also covered, was set on the other side near a stove rather than a fireplace. It was barely fit for the lowest-ranking guest invited to a house party, never mind the countess. The walls were whitewashed, but an upper corner showed a water stain spreading between the wall and ceiling. Two rings on the drapery were broken, leaving a section in the middle bowed like an old horse. The room—the entire house really—had an air of abandonment and disregard.

Alice felt she could keep her peace no longer. "Mama, will this room be the best for your comfort? It is the farthest from the stairway and rather confining."

"I shall be quite comfortable here," Lady Chariton said as she crossed to the window. She gazed through the glass for several seconds. Alice shared a concerned look with the housekeeper. "Yes," Lady Chariton said softly, still looking out the window. "This will do very nicely. I shall reserve my instruction to the staff until tomorrow so that all efforts to put this room in readiness can be attended to." She turned to Mrs. Gale and smiled, though her fatigue drew heavily on her expression. "I believe luncheon has been prepared in advance of our arrival?"

"Yes, my lady. It is set in the morning room."

"Very good. Following luncheon, Lady Fenton can tour the other rooms and choose whichever she prefers for the duration of her stay."

"I shall stay in whatever chamber is closest to her ladyship's," Alice said.

"The blue room is in readiness," Mrs. Gale said, though hesitantly. Alice could appreciate the housekeeper's concern at needing to ready two rooms for the night. "And it is part of the only other adjoining apartments besides the countess's chamber."

"That is right," Lady Chariton said with a nod of remembrance. "I had forgotten that, so it must be the room you take, Alice. Unless you prefer the countess's chamber. Charles can take the adjoining room to either one when he arrives."

"I could not take the countess's chamber," Alice said, her cheeks heating up at the implication that she and Lord Fenton should have adjoining rooms.

"Lord Chariton will not be joining us here if that is what concerns you," Lady Chariton said casually. "The blue room is very comfortable I am sure, but you truly may have your pick. There is no cause for standing on ceremony."

Alice considered arguing for a room closer to Lady Chariton's, but the blue room was only a bit further down the hall. "The blue room will be very well," Alice said with a polite smile to the housekeeper, who looked relieved.

"Very good, my lady," Mrs. Gale said. She turned her attention to Lady Chariton, who was still looking out the window. "I took the liberty of planning tonight's dinner: braised pork and a vegetable stew. I hope it will be acceptable."

"Of course," Lady Chariton said. She finally turned and followed Mrs. Gale out of the room.

As the other two women left the room, Alice moved to the window, thinking perhaps an extraordinary view had prompted this choice of Lady Chariton's. She frowned over the fields and outbuildings that made up the scene below the windows. Close by stood the stable and carriage house as well as what looked like servants' quarters, likely reserved for the grooms and gardeners. In the distance she could just see the rooftops of what must be the village, with at least a dozen tenants' cottages. It was certainly not the view one would choose if one could avoid it. And yet Lady Chariton had chosen it.

After another perplexing moment of observation, Alice turned from the window and hurried after Lady Chariton. She had come to Foxcroft to attend to her new mother. She must maintain her focus, but she hoped that in the process of seeing to Lady Chariton's comfort, she might reach a better understanding of why they had come *here* at all.

CHAPTER 23

It was four days before Alice had time to explore the gardens on the west side of the house, and she was near to bursting by the time she finally set out for them. She had seen the gardens from the drawing room on the main level each time she and Lady Chariton retired there. Alice felt the pull of them, but there were too many other tasks she had to take care of before she could reward herself with the comforting solitude of the plants and shrubs.

Lady Chariton had made clear that Alice was to be intimately involved in running the household, and Alice was overwhelmed by the details she was to oversee: linens, staff concerns, approval of meals, shopping lists, and which members of staff went to the nearby village and which did not.

New servants arrived each day, menus were drawn up, instructions were given, and Alice was at the center of all of it. She met with Lady Chariton several times a day to discuss how to do a thing, and then left the rose room with her head high and her heart pounding as she undertook yet another task of household management. It was as exhausting as it was rewarding, and Alice wondered how she would ever have learned to run a household without such an opportunity as this.

Her questions concerning Mrs. Gale and the odd reception between her and Lady Chariton were soon nothing more than a vague memory as the housekeeper patiently and respectfully worked side by side with Alice as she learned the way of things. It must have been very tedious for a woman who had run the household carte blanche for so many years, but Mrs. Gale never gave the impression she was put out by such training.

Today—finally—Alice had accomplished everything on her list that needed to be done before supper and asked permission to explore the gardens. Lady Chariton told her she did not need to check as though she were her governess. Alice kissed her on the cheek and then let herself out through the west entrance, intent on exploring the paths she could see from the drawing room window. Her fingers itched to dig in the soil, and she thought of her working frock packed carefully away in the blue room wardrobe.

At Warren House she had full use of the gardens, and the servants were used to having her work beside them or take charge of a corner here and there on her own. In London that was not an option, of course, though when she first arrived she had helped the gardener expand the herb garden behind the small house. The man had not been as open to her help as she would have liked, which is why she had not continued her work there.

Now, she was back on a country estate, with earth and gloves and sunlight at her disposal—only she worried working in the garden would undermine her position with the staff. She was no longer the middle child of a noble but modest family who was allowed to please herself in whatever way she chose, now she was a woman of title and respect.

The gardens had more walking paths than greenery, with some well-weathered statues and a bench set beneath a sun-bleached trellis. She wandered through the footpaths flanked with rose bushes and frowned. The shrubs were placed too close together for the roots to have proper room to grow, and the tufts of lavender further in were sorely in need of being divided come fall; the centers were quite woody. The hollyhocks and a great patch of irises also needed to be divided.

Alice broke a bud off an anise bush and put in her mouth, savoring the licorice flavor on her tongue. It was not surprising that without a resident to walk the gardens it had fallen into neglect, but it would not be so difficult to restore, and already she could see the potential. The soil was good, as was the placement of the garden itself. She could even see how to incorporate a few details of design she had been particularly fond of in the Sussex gardens she had sketched while on her wedding trip.

Alice's excitement for the project grew, though she remained mindful that they would not be at Foxcroft long, perhaps six weeks at the most. There was no telling how long it would be after that before she—or any other family member—would enjoy the gardens again. Yet the desire to take the gardens in hand wrapped itself around her like a warm blanket. Surely she could help Lady Chariton see how important the time out of doors would be for her. She already felt nourished by the venture after so many weeks in London.

The hedges had been recently trimmed but were in need of proper pruning that would encourage the thinner portions to grow in. Because of the sparse patches, Alice could see that the shrubbery divided the gardens and the working portions of the estate. There was a gap in either corner, to allow the gardeners in and out she supposed, and she went through the southern gap so as to get an additional tour of the remaining grounds.

She approached the carriage house as soon as she recognized the barnlike building with large doors that allowed for the coming and going of coaches. She and Lady Chariton had arrived in the family's traveling coach, which she saw straightaway, but Alice was curious as to whether there were other carriages kept at the estate and, since the large doors were open and no one stopped her, she entered the cavernous building.

There was a wagon and a gig meant for just one horse—surely used by the staff. There was also an old barouche, which did not look as though it had been used in well over a decade, and a sleigh, equally neglected. She ran her fingers over the curved wooden rim, smiling to herself over the memories of being pulled in her father's sleigh as a girl. Wondering whether or not Lord Fenton had similar memories gave her pause, but she smiled, knowing he would never know her thoughts had so unexpectedly turned to him.

Lady Chariton had written Lord Fenton of their safe arrival, but Alice considered writing to him herself. She could tell him that all was well with their journey and that his mother, though still fatigued, seemed very content to be here. *What could I say besides that?* she wondered. He would not want to hear of her plans for the gardens, and to mention the disrepair about the estate would make her sound as though she were complaining. What else did she have to talk about?

"Good mornin'."

Alice came up short, startled to have her thoughts interrupted by an unfamiliar voice, though it should not have surprised her so much, as she was in such an unfamiliar place. She looked up into the eyes of a man who grinned at her in a way that was most disarming.

"Good morning," she said carefully, backing up a step; he stood very close to her. She could tell from his working clothes that he was a servant, but he was not addressing her as a servant would. She had not seen this man before, as she had met only the house servants. She could think of nothing else to say other than to introduce herself so that he might know of her rank. "I am Lady Fenton."

"Please tah meecha Lay-dee Fen-ton."

He spoke with a slow cadence that gave equal weight to each syllable of each word. He stood with his hands at his side and that same smile on his face, oblivious to her discomfort. She looked at him a bit closer and realized that his eyes looked strange, as though they were spaced too far apart on his exceptionally round face. A moment later she realized the man was simpleminded and a new kind of fear settled about her. The simpleminded were unpredictable and unseemly in their behavior. And she was alone in the carriage house.

"I should return to the house," she said quickly, walking backward so as not to turn her back on him. "Good day to you."

"Gooday!" he called after her.

She turned finally, but after a few paces, she looked over her shoulder in time to see him languidly exiting the carriage house behind her. He raised his hand to wave, but she only lifted her skirts and walked that much faster.

She entered the back door of the house and closed it soundly, waited a moment, and then pulled it open just enough to see if he'd followed her. He had not; the path was clear.

She closed the door again, reviewed the encounter, and went in search of Mrs. Gale. Why would they employ a man such as he was?

Surely there was no shortage of workers in this part of the country. The entire thing had unsettled her. Lord and Lady Chariton were so proper about every other aspect of their lives, yet so many things about this place were just not right.

"Oh, that's Adam," Mrs. Gale said. Alice had found her at her desk below stairs, where she was making a list of new linens Lady Chariton wanted ordered. The ease of Mrs. Gale's expression showed she did not feel the same discomfort around the man that Alice had felt. "He is Mrs. Banner's son."

"The cook?" Alice said, remembering Mrs. Banner as the woman with whom Lady Chariton had exchanged such a warm welcome. "Is Adam not a worker, then?"

"He does odd jobs about the place," Mrs. Gale said, seeming finally to realize Alice's displeasure. "He is especially fond of the animals and oversees their feed and water."

"He is a simpleton."

"Yes," Mrs. Gale said with a slow nod. "He has the mind of a child but a heart of gold."

"Do Lord and Lady Chariton know a simpleminded man is in their employ? Perhaps it was not a concern when there was not family in residence, but surely now it should be considered. It is ill-advised to try to keep them from this knowledge. I surely cannot condone it." A spark of shame rose in her chest at the disappointment she saw on the other woman's face. No, she would not be shamed for feeling as she did, and her opinions were no different than that of anyone else in society.

"Lord and Lady Chariton are well aware of Adam's position here," Mrs. Gale said, sounding both confident and uneasy at the same time. "His father left, you know, after he saw what his son was, but Mrs. Banner was allowed to stay. They have the use of Gray Cottage, and Adam has lived here all his life. He and Mrs. Banner are the longest-employed servants at Foxcroft—going on forty years for Mrs. Banner."

Alice was shocked to hear that Lord and Lady Chariton could have made such an arrangement. It was not their responsibility to make Mrs. Banner's situation so comfortable, and she would have been a much lower servant when Adam was born and her husband deserted them.

"I found him rather frightening," Alice said, but she felt silly saying as much due to Mrs. Gale's obvious affection for him and the confirmation that he was welcomed by the family. "He stood very close to me and did not address me as he should."

"Adam does not understand all matters of decorum, but he would never hurt anyone," Mrs. Gale said, her voice taking on a touch of concern. "It's only that he's not used to strangers. He would not ever be cruel, mind you—but he is curious, you know. Like a child."

"He is not the size of a child," Alice said, thinking of stories from her childhood. There was a man in the village near Warren House who could communicate only with grunts and gestures. It had been uncomfortable to be near him and so Alice, and every other child, made a point to run when he came close. How could a man who could not speak as he should be trustworthy? How could a man with the mind of a child be any more so?

"My lady, I can assure you that he is a good boy."

"He is a man!" Alice said, unable to hide her frustration.

"And he is a *good* man," Mrs. Gale said hurriedly. "Please don't set your head against him. Mrs. Banner has been at Foxcroft since she was a scullery maid. There is nowhere they could go and still find a living."

Alice paused, not having realized her assertions were very much pointed in the direction of finding a way to rid the estate of this man. Alice thought of the greeting she had seen between Mrs. Banner and Lady Chariton when they had first arrived at Foxcroft. The regard the women shared was genuine. Mrs. Banner had *great* cause for such gratitude, but why should Lady Chariton be so warm? And why had Lady Chariton not warned Alice of Adam's presence?

Alice was tired of keeping so many questions to herself. She was acting the part of a mistress here, why should she not better understand the dealings of this household? "How long have you been at Foxcroft, Mrs. Gale?" she asked with boldness. "Forgive my notice, but you seem very young for your position."

Mrs. Gale was instantly uncomfortable. She looked at the top of her desk while preparing an answer that Alice did not think should need so much thought. "It shall be nine years come October, my lady."

"And when did you rise to the level of housekeeper?"

Mrs. Gale shifted in her seat. "Three years ago, my lady."

"What is your age, then?" She kept her eyes fixed on the woman and waited for an answer.

"I am thirty and six years old," she said quietly, nervously.

Housekeepers rose to their station after years of service in the household, after they knew every room of the house and every nuance of the family they served to the degree that they could manage it without disruption. Surely things would be different at a country estate without family in residence, but to hire a woman *so* young? After only six years of employ in the house? Alice had never heard of such a thing. "What recommended you?" Her own boldness made her uncomfortable, but it *was* her right and her place to address a servant this way.

Mrs. Gale swallowed and looked at the floor. Alice let her take her time to answer. "I was employed in another Chariton house prior to coming to Foxcroft as an upstairs maid nine years ago. In total I have worked for the family nearing twenty years. When Mrs. Mumford passed away three years ago, I was the most senior maid on staff, and Lady Chariton offered the position to me. I accepted."

Alice furrowed her brow. It *was* an adequate explanation, and yet she was as confused as she had ever been. "Why were you moved to this location, so far from the other estates belonging to the family? Which house did you serve in before coming here?"

Mrs. Gale's nervousness suddenly changed to fear, and she held Alice's eyes with a pleading look. "Please let me be at peace with my past; it was overcome with great difficulty and I do not want to upset Lady Chariton with giving rise to it. I have worked hard to be pleasing here. Might that be enough to settle your mind?"

Alice blinked. *Her past? Upset Lady Chariton?* Obviously, Alice had been kept unapprised of Mrs. Gale's circumstance on purpose, and though she felt justified in continuing to press the issue until she was satisfied, she was also reminded that, though she was managing the household, she was not the mistress here. The woman who *was* the mistress seemed to be aware of these odd circumstances, in fact she had apparently played a part in the arrangement of them. To question those decisions would be disrespectful of Lady Chariton, and Alice would not do that. She made a conscious effort to soften her expression and nodded at Mrs. Gale. "I shall ask no more of you."

The woman was instantly relieved. "You won't recommend against Adam? I know it's not my place to ask such a thing, and in the end it is the decision of the family, but do think of what it would mean to him and his mother."

"You overstep your bounds, Mrs. Gale."

Mrs. Gale dropped her head. "Forgive me, I did not mean to be impertinent."

Alice felt as out of place in her own head as she did in this house and let out a breath, regretting the whole of how she'd handled the conversation. Mrs. Gale had Lady Chariton's blessing and had been nothing short of kind and accommodating to Alice. It was unfair for Alice to take out her frustrations on the woman, regardless of their respective stations.

"Forgive my tone, Mrs. Gale. I am simply finding this place very mysterious and letting my frustrations take too great a hold of me."

Mrs. Gale seemed as though she wanted to speak, but then returned her gaze to the floor. "I'll see that Adam does not bother you further, my lady. He's been told not to cross the hedge so, perhaps if you would do the same you will not have to suffer distress in the future."

Alice nodded, feeling sufficiently reprimanded for having crossed into the working portion of the estate. That was the staff's domain, not hers, and therefore Adam would be easy enough for her to avoid. That no one else—not even Lady Chariton—had issue with him being a resident of the estate made Alice feel silly for having brought it up. "You may return to your duties, Mrs. Gale."

"Thank you, my lady," she said before returning to her list.

Alice took the stairs to the second level. Despite the rose room being so small and oddly set, Lady Chariton was quite content there and had spent the better part of the last four days within it. She had come down for dinner last night, but had taken the rest of her meals in her room, claiming that she wanted to recover sufficiently from the travel before moving about too much.

Alice found an upstairs maid and was assured that as of fifteen minutes earlier Lady Chariton had been reading in her room. Confident she would not wake her ladyship, Alice dared knock on the door.

"Come in," Lady Chariton called, and Alice let herself in, glad to be greeted with a smile.

"How did you like the gardens?" Lady Chariton held out her hand, inviting Alice to join her. She set the book she had been reading in her lap and turned her full attention to Alice.

"They are well, my lady," she said, casually moving toward the window. A fire had been lit in the stove despite the day being quite fine, making the room uncomfortably warm.

"Please have a seat," Lady Chariton said before coughing discreetly behind her handkerchief.

Alice could not sit and instead looked down on the outbuildings. By knowing what to look for, she could see the cottage that Mrs. Gale had said Mrs. Banner and her son lived in. It was the only building of gray stone, set directly behind the other servants' quarters and very commodious for a cook and her simple son.

"Are you well, Alice?" Lady Chariton asked. "You seem anxious."

Alice turned away from the window and moved to sit in one of the chairs, trying to decide how best to go about this conversation. "I am well," she said, then paused before deciding to continue. "Only I met one of the servants—Adam—when I was inspecting the carriage house. I'm afraid it has shaken me."

Lady Chariton's face froze for a moment and she leaned forward slightly. "You saw him?"

The expectation—dare Alice call it excitement?—in Lady Chariton's face caused even more confusion for Alice. It was very similar to the reaction of Mrs. Gale, who had shown an acceptance, no, a fondness for the man Alice found so unnerving.

"How was he?" Lady Chariton asked. "Was he well? Did he seem happy?"

"He seemed happy," Alice said after she recovered from her surprise. Had anyone in all her life asked her about a servant's happiness? "But I found him a bit frightening."

Lady Chariton leaned back in her seat, a serene smile on her face. "Oh, there is no need to be frightened of Adam. He is gentle as a lamb."

She knows him well enough to know his disposition? "I understand from Mrs. Gale that he remains here under Lord Chariton's generosity."

Lady Chariton's expression tightened. "*My* generosity," she clarified with a hint of sharpness. "I manage this estate, not Lord Chariton. I make the decisions here."

Alice was even more surprised and pulled back in her chair. "*You* manage Foxcroft?" She had never heard of a woman managing an estate and though she knew Foxcroft had come through Lady Chariton's line, that did not necessarily separate it from her husband's holdings. Did Lord Fenton know his mother managed the estate?

Lady Chariton nodded once but did not expound.

"So, Adam and his mother are here under *your* benefaction?" Was that the proper word to describe the arrangement? Alice didn't know how else to define the situation.

"Yes."

Another answer that Alice found lacking.

"And you agree that it is safe to have him about the place? Do you not worry he will lose control of his limited mind?"

"I do not worry about that at all," Lady Chariton said with confidence. She raised her handkerchief and coughed again.

Alice could think of nothing else to say and realized in how many ways her world had turned upside down since she'd married Lord Fenton. Her marriage was nothing as she'd expected it to be, and Foxcroft was far more complex than she had imagined when she'd agreed to come. Lady Chariton was not as Alice expected either. She was more than a woman of society—she managed an estate, she gave unwarranted charity to a simpleminded man and his mother, and she had convictions Alice had not seen in London and did not understand now. Lady Chariton had secrets.

"What did Adam say to you?" Lady Chariton asked, as engaged as Alice had ever seen her before. Over a simpleminded servant she had not seen in twenty years? He would have been a boy when Lady Chariton last saw him. Was that why she was so certain he was harmless? Did she not realize he was no longer a child but a grown man?

"He said he was pleased to meet me. Oh, and he said good morning."

Lady Chariton smiled and leaned back in her chair. "He is a sweet boy."

Alice felt a distinct discomfort in her chest. How she wished Lord Fenton were here; she would insist upon answers from him that she could not demand from Lady Chariton. "I do not understand this,

Mama," Alice finally admitted, surrendering against the chair back. "There are so many things about this place that do not make sense to me, that go against everything I understood about the way of things. I do not understand why a woman as young as Mrs. Gale has been entrusted to manage this household, or why you would go to such pains to keep on a woman with a simple son. Neither seems to be a wise choice, and yet everyone is so comfortable with the arrangements. I seem to be the only one who questions any of it. Why have you not been here for twenty years? Why did you want to come now?"

Lady Chariton's expression became both serious and sympathetic. "Do not let these things upset you, Alice. I assure you that all is well here at Foxcroft. The longer I am here, the better I know the wisdom of having come. I could not have come at all without you, and so I would ask that you ease your mind and take peace in my comfort here."

Alice appreciated the compliment, but her frustration was not eased entirely. If Lady Chariton was so grateful for Alice's help, why did she not try harder to ease Alice's mind? "Will you not confide in me?" she asked quietly, hurt that she had to ask so boldly rather than Lady Chariton offering the explanations without such direct supplication. "I know there must be some reason for Mrs. Gale being here and Adam and his mother being kept on. Will you not tell me the whole of it?"

Lady Chariton fixed Alice with such a thoughtful look that Alice felt her breathing become short as she anticipated the answers to her questions. Finally, Lady Chariton's thin hand touched her arm and she shook her head. "Not yet. I am sorry, Alice. It is not that you do not deserve to know, it is only that I have promised myself I should tell no one the whole of things until I've told Charles."

"He does not know?" Alice had not considered whether he did or not, but obviously the reasons for such oddities were enough that Lady Chariton had decided, perhaps long ago, how she would explain them.

"I cannot adequately explain myself to you right now, Alice. But I would ask that you trust me all the same. I hope you grow to love this place as I do so that when the whole of it is revealed, you do not judge any of us too harshly."

Us? Who? But Alice did not say it out loud. She'd been told not to ask, she'd been told she would not be answered, and therefore she could not press. Alice could also not ignore the fact that Lady Chariton *did* trust her enough to tell her this much. She also trusted Alice to be patient, to accept that she would know the answers she wished for in time. "Very well," Alice said, somewhat gratified by the softening of Lady Chariton's face.

"You are a good woman, Alice," Lady Chariton said, leaning back in her chair. "And such a blessing for this family. Have you any idea how much we all need you?"

Alice did not know what to say. She could see nothing about herself worthy of such a statement, and yet it spoke to her core so strongly that she clung to the hope of its truth. "I truly want to help," she said.

"And you *are* helping," Lady Chariton assured her. "In more ways than you can imagine. You are the daughter I never had, and Charles will have such need of your strength and kindness."

Alice had to look in her lap to hide her expression. Lord Fenton did not need her. He did not even want her. Lady Chariton's words only awakened how very much Alice wished he did.

She could hear the change of topic in Lady Chariton's tone of voice when she spoke next. "I'm afraid I have not yet recovered from our travels, Alice. Would you call for my maid so I might take a nap before supper? I'm afraid they haven't yet adjusted the bellpull correctly and my summons goes to the kitchen."

"Of course," Alice said, glad to have something to do. She stood and turned toward the door. "I'll see she is sent up straightaway, and I'll make sure the bellpull is properly routed."

"And Alice?" Lady Chariton reached out and took Alice's hand. Alice looked at the woman's soft eyes, the same color as Lord Fenton's but reflective of wisdom he did not have. "I cannot thank you enough for attending me here. I do not think Lord Chariton would have allowed it had it not been for you and Charles appealing on my behalf."

The honest praise humbled Alice, and she smiled down at the woman who had become so dear to her. "I am glad to be of help."

Lady Chariton smiled. "Once Charles joins us, I shall be as happy as I have ever been, surrounded by my children in a place I dearly love."

Being counted as one of Lady Chariton's children caused Alice's heart to soften to the point where she could not in good conscious remind Lady Chariton that she and Lord Fenton would not be with her for long.

Though Fenton would come to Foxcroft after his time in London was finished, and stay for perhaps a week or more, the plan was to return his mother to Lakeshore before the two of them removed to Fentonview. That Lady Chariton spoke as though they would be staying at Foxcroft made Alice uneasy. She did not want to be the one to remind Lady Chariton of their limited stay when Lady Chariton was obviously so glad to be here.

Lady Chariton gave Alice's hand a squeeze, then released it and lay back in her chair with her eyes closed.

"I shall retrieve your maid," Alice said. She hurried down the stairs and wondered if she shouldn't write to Lord Fenton about extending their stay at Foxcroft, or perhaps ask that he join them sooner than planned. He was expected to remain until Parliament was finished, which was still a fortnight away, but quite unexpectedly, Alice felt in need of his help.

She also determined that she would find time to attend to the gardens. Though she still worried how it might influence the servants' opinion of her, she needed the comfort that growing things had always given her. She would unpack her working frock and secure a wide-brimmed hat to protect her from the southern sun, but she would find time each day to attend to the gardens so that for some portion of each day she might quiet the questions that worked up a frenzy in her mind.

CHAPTER 24

Alice waited a few days more before she wrote to Lord Fenton. At first the delay was because she was unsure of the best course, but when they had been at Foxcroft for nine days and Lady Chariton's health had not improved, Alice felt she should not wait any longer to write.

Lady Chariton had left the house to attend church on Sunday, but she was quite spent the rest of the day and did not eat much supper. The coughing was more frequent, and though Alice had made a coltsfoot tea that seemed to help, it was not giving the relief Alice had hoped for. She had also prepared a tincture, but it would not be at full strength for a few more days. Alice had studied all manner of herbal remedies in hopes of finding something that would be restorative to Lady Chariton.

Four days passed before Alice received Lord Fenton's response to her letter, and when she first saw her name written across the front of the robin's-egg blue envelope in his flowing script, she felt a rush of girlish affection. The burst of fancy was quickly followed by the qualm of reality—this was not a love letter. It was simply business between a husband and wife.

Alice was glad for her conscious reminder when she opened the letter to find it short and to the point: Lord Fenton would come as soon as he could, and he and Alice would stay on at Foxcroft until Lady Chariton was fit for travel again but would not be in any hurry. He thanked her for the update as well as her continued care and signed the letter "With regard, Lord F."

The letter did not contain much by way of compliment and affection, yet Alice read the closing three times. Time apart had left her regretting that the time they'd spent together had been filled with so much bitterness. She hoped they would not return to such ways when he came to Foxcroft. They would have only each other—no society, no friends, no distractions. It would be the two of them and Lady Chariton—if their exchanges were filled with resentment and irritation, they would be hard-pressed to find any solace here. Even working in the garden would not be enough to remedy the discord.

It wasn't until after Alice and Lady Chariton had enjoyed breakfast in the rose room, which had become their routine, that Alice found an opportunity to speak of Lord Fenton's impending arrival. Alice did not mention that she'd asked him to come sooner, only that he would come sooner than originally planned.

"That will be wonderful," Lady Chariton said, taking hold of the handle of her teacup with thin fingers that trembled slightly. Before she lifted the cup, though, she looked at Alice. "Might I ask why you continue to refer to Charles by his title? I don't believe you have ever referred to him by his Christian name."

Alice looked at her own cup of tea, unsure what to say. The truth of it was that Lord Fenton had never invited her to use such informality and she would not do so without his invitation. "I suppose

I simply want to show him due respect. Do you not refer to Lord Chariton with his title?"

"Yes, but that is different." She waved off Alice's comment without explanation. "I should think comfort with one another would be of more value than formal respect between you and Charles, don't you?"

Comfort? What would it feel like to find comfort in Lord Fenton's company? Pondering the possibility left Alice feeling out of sorts and conspicuous. Not wanting to prolong the awkward conversation, Alice stood. "I think I should check on supper. You said the beef bothered your stomach last night, did it not? I want to make sure it's not on—"

"Oh, sit down, Alice," Lady Chariton said, though her tone was humorous. "I shan't tease you, then. You may call Charles whatever you like. And dinner will be fine—the new herbal tonic you've brewed for me seems to be helping my digestion."

Alice was eager for the change of topic and gratified to hear such a positive report regarding Lady Chariton's health. "Fennel tea is a relatively easy aid for digestion, and the coltsfoot and peppermint should help to mellow the cough."

"And that is precisely what it has done," Lady Chariton said with a smile that Alice did not believe. She turned to the side table and picked up a book, which she held out to Alice. "Would you mind reading to me for a bit? I do so like Henry Fielding, but my eyes are weary."

Lord Fenton sent word a few days after his first letter arrived that they could expect him on June twenty-sixth. He would leave as soon as Parliament closed session and stop only for overnights and fresh horses. Though Alice was minding the household—and feeling more confident about her abilities every day—Lady Chariton insisted on organizing the necessary preparations for her son's arrival personally.

Alice, still worried about Lady Chariton's health, was torn between wanting to relieve her of any additional burdens and wanting to respect her wishes. In the end, the light she saw in Lady Chariton's eyes when she spoke about her son convinced Alice to acquiesce to her wishes. Though she promised both herself and her mother-in-law that she would be ready to assist at a moment's notice.

As each day drew closer to Lord Fenton's arrival, Alice could feel her nerves becoming more and more tightly wound. She tried to blame her anxiety on the continued mysteries of Foxcroft, none of which had begun to feel more resolved in Alice's mind, but she knew her nerves were because Lord Fenton would be coming soon. Their last exchange in London had been so . . . civil that she could not adequately anticipate how they would react to one another when he arrived. Would that civility continue, or would they both be on the defensive for having let down their guards enough for the farewell to have taken place at all?

It had been their allied concern for Lady Chariton that created the commonality; therefore, the fact that he was returning in consideration of his mother's health gave Alice hope that such civility would continue. And yet, if Alice expected such a thing and he reacted with his defensive teasing, she would feel foolish for not having been prepared and likely respond with greater venom, which would undo any tenuous accord between them.

It was all so vexing that she was worked into a great state of distraction and worry by the time June the twenty-sixth arrived.

After breakfast, Alice joined Lady Chariton in the drawing room where they would await Lord Fenton's arrival. It was the first time in almost a week that Lady Chariton had come to the main level of the house. She was enjoying the sun coming through the window while Alice sketched a plan for a gazebo in the west corner of the walking garden.

She had first begun improvements by clearing out several areas overgrown with morning glory. Rather than attempt to save the shrubbery in the west corner, she had the gardener pull out the whole of it, revealing a level area large enough for a gazebo that would allow an outdoor tea from time to time.

Mr. Mumford knew of a carpenter in the village for the construction if she could provide him with a drawing, and, once Lady Chariton had agreed to the expense, Alice began sketching. She was excited about the prospect—the gazebo would serve as a focal point that she could then arrange the paths and plants to support—but the excitement could not ease the tightness in her chest regarding Lord Fenton's arrival.

The drawing room afforded a view of the drive, and at the sound of wheels on the gravel, Alice stood and crossed to the window to confirm that it was Lord Fenton's silly curricle. What a ridiculous carriage to use for such a long journey. She turned back to announce his arrival only to see that Lady Chariton had fallen asleep in her chair. She had been awake a few minutes ago, but her eyes were closed softly and her chest rose and fell in a calm and steady rhythm.

Lady Chariton had not been sleeping well at night—her cough was at its very worst then—and so rather than wake her now, Alice made the decision to greet Lord Fenton herself. Lady Chariton had done so much to prepare for this moment, surely Alice could step in and help in some small way.

And perhaps it would be best to confer with him before he saw his mother, so that Alice might better prepare him for Lady Chariton's lack of improvement.

Alice stood alone in the foyer, attempting to hide her nervousness at seeing her husband for the first time in weeks, when the footman opened the door and Lord Fenton came inside. She had been prepared to see him in a shiny blue coat or perhaps the canary yellow one he liked to sport when driving his curricle—it matched the wheels—but instead he was dressed in boots, buff-colored breeches, a navy coat, and a waistcoat striped with both colors. He looked positively . . . attractive, and Alice felt her cheeks heat up at the intensity of the realization.

Lord Fenton handed his hat to Mr. Mumford and ran his hand through his hair, which was not waxed and shaped as was usually the case in London. For lack of a better way to summarize his appearance, he looked masculine—like a man *should* look. He held her eyes with the barest half smile on his lips, and Alice felt the fire of her continued response. Goodness but he was handsome when he wasn't dressed like an idiot.

"Do not be alarmed," Lord Fenton said in his foppish drawl, pointing his finger at the ceiling for emphasis. "For it is I, your prodigal husband only *dressed* like a country gentleman since my fashion is truly lost in the wilds of the country outside London."

Alice was surprised he had so correctly assessed her reaction. "You do not wear your colors and lace when you are not about in London?"

"Good grief, no," Lord Fenton said, putting one hand to his chest and waving the other hand through the air. "Who would appreciate it here?" He gave an exaggerated sniff, and Alice could not hide her smile.

"I, for one, appreciate this"—she waved toward him, encompassing him from head to toe—"far more than your costumes."

He clucked his tongue behind his teeth. "Careful," he said. "If you compliment this drab stuff too much I might well go back to London to fetch my silks and lace after all."

She shook her head, and he winked, bringing a rush of blood to her cheeks. What did he mean by that wink? As her last interaction with him had been that soft kiss on the back of her hand, this made two unexpected gestures that quite sent her thoughts to bouncing.

The sound of footsteps spared her from answering, and she let out a breath she did not realize she'd been holding. Alice turned toward the approaching servant, likely Mr. Mumford or Mrs. Gale coming to greet the man who would act as master of the house during his stay. She was surprised they had not been waiting on his arrival already; surely Lady Chariton had put them on alert.

"Your mother has been awaiting you in the drawing room," Alice said. "But I'm afraid she has—"

His sharp intake of breath caused Alice to look over her shoulder. Lord Fenton's eyes had grown wide and his cheeks flushed. Unsure what had caused his reaction, she looked around in alarm, only to see a very similar expression on the face of Mrs. Gale, who had stopped short some distance away. The housekeeper recovered herself first and looked at the floor while fidgeting with the fabric of her collar.

Attempting to create an explanation for their reaction to one another, Alice remembered that Mrs. Gale had worked in another estate before coming here. So, Lord Fenton and Mrs. Gale must know one another, but that alone did not explain their unusual reaction. A wave of jealousy swept through Alice at the idea they might have a past connection that exceeded what it ought to have been, but she hurried to act her part; it would not do for anyone to see her so discomfited.

"Lord Fenton," Alice said, her mouth dry as she pretended not to have noticed anything amiss. "I should like to introduce you to the housekeeper of Foxcroft Manor, Mrs.—" Her words were cut off by the sound of the front door opening. She turned in time to see Lord Fenton's back disappear the way he'd come in only minutes earlier. Alice faced Mrs. Gale, who looked absolutely terrified as she too stared at the open door.

"Lady Chariton is in the drawing room?" Mrs. Gale managed after a few moments.

Alice nodded, but Mrs. Gale was already moving in that direction, leaving Alice alone in the foyer again. She had not told Mrs. Gale that Lady Chariton was asleep. Her thoughts jagged and spinning, Alice looked in the direction where Mrs. Gale had disappeared and then to the open front door through which her husband had fled. What should she do? What aspect of this situation should she address first? There had been no training whatsoever for how she was to handle such a thing as this. It did not escape her notice that her hopes of Lord Fenton bringing with him clarity and answers to the many questions she had about this place had not been realized. Instead, his arrival had served to create even more.

CHAPTER 25

When Fenton first left the house, unable to stand there and look at *her*, he thought to jump on a horse and ride away as fast as he possibly could. But the groomsman had already taken his carriage to the back of the estate, and he could not simply leave after working so hard to get here. But he still had to get away. He needed distance enough to pull himself together. What was *she* doing here? His mind spun, tripping over itself as he tried to make sense of this. Mama had wanted to come to Foxcroft knowing *she* was here? *Knowing it?*

He reached for his flask in the inside pocket of his coat, but there was barely a swallow of brandy left. He drank it dry and then cursed and threw the flask at the hedge, gratified to see the bottle dislodge a shower of twigs and leaves on impact. He wished he had twenty more to throw after it but instead he began pacing back and forth in the garden, which was where his feet had taken him.

By the time Fenton heard his name being called he feared it had been said many times. His chest was heaving, only in part because of the exertion of his escape, and he bent over with his hands on his knees in an attempt to catch his breath and recover some measure of control. He had not expected Alice to follow him and tried to still his mind enough to think of what he could possibly say to her. Did she know? Had his mother told her?

His stomach burned and his jaw ached from holding it so tight as he stood and faced her. She had picked up her skirts, revealing stocking-covered ankles, and was moving toward him almost in a run, coming to a stop when she was but a few feet away. He had to force himself to look away from her bosom, which was lifting and falling too quickly not to be noticed. That the woman responsible for his determination *not* to be attentive to such things was only a short distance away ignited his rage all over again.

"What?" he snapped at her, causing her to pull back slightly.

"I-I don't . . . What is wrong?"

"What is *wrong*?" Fenton replied, throwing his hands up. "I am trying to gain a bit of peace and you have chased me down like a hound. Can I not have a moment?"

"You can have all the moments you want once you explain to me what that was," she snapped back, just as he'd known she would. It somehow calmed him to see that she was the same Alice she had been before. Everything else was changed however, and her consistency could not repair it completely. Why had his mother wanted to come here of all places? And Mrs. Gale—where had such a name as *that* come from?

Alice continued. "It was completely improper for you to—"

"Do not lecture me on propriety," Fenton said. He pointed to the house. "Do you know who she is? Are you a part of this?"

Alice's eyebrows pulled together. "Do I know who . . . ? You mean Mrs. Gale? She is the housekeeper."

Fenton snorted and had to turn around and close his eyes. His thoughts were racing and he could not slow them. "Do you know who she *was*?"

Alice was quiet long enough that his thoughts finally did slow as he awaited her answer. "Was she your lover, Lord Fenton?"

He spun back around and felt his mouth go slack. Alice regarded him with a blank expression, as though she were holding every thought she had inside herself. For an instant, he was disappointed she would think it—had he not convinced her that he did not pursue dalliances? That he was a man of moral character above that? But he'd no sooner thought that then he remembered how little they knew of one another. She did not know his heart, nor did she know his pain, and though he had sworn he would never speak of it, he knew he could not keep it from her. If for no other reason than to convince her that it was not *his* sins he would be hiding should he refuse to discuss it.

"She was not *my* lover," he said, the word burning his tongue. How he hated reliving this! A circumstance that had defined his course in so many ways. Why was *she* at Foxcroft?

The brief look of relief on Alice's face heartened him. She wanted him to have good character; it mattered to her. But she was still confused, and he owed her an explanation he was unsure how to give. With no time to plan out what he would say, he tried to distill it in his mind so as to present it clearly at least, if he could not say it kindly.

"Mrs. *Gale*," he said, unable to keep the derision out of his voice, "used to be a chambermaid at the London house." He tried to find additional words but did not know *how* to say it, did not *want* to say it, had *never* said it before. The words were not prepared to be spoken.

After a few seconds, Alice's expression became irritated. "I see. Chambermaids are most certainly vexing." She crossed her arms over her chest. Had he ordered the neckline to be cut so low when he ordered this particular gown? What had he been thinking? "I can see why you are so upset and withdraw any objection that was certainly not warranted for such a crime on her part."

He narrowed his eyes at her sarcasm but did not really mind it so much. Most women would be covering their ears and having a fit of the vapors over such a discussion as this, and he was grateful that whatever her failings—and surely he would be able to focus on them once again—Alice was built of stronger stuff than most. The recognition of her ability to withstand the sordid details gave him the confidence he needed to continue. "I discovered this particular chambermaid in a very compromising discussion with . . . my father when I returned home from school a day earlier than expected."

"A compromising *discussion*?" Alice repeated, though he could see she was beginning to understand where the conversation was heading.

Fenton took a breath and looked at the ground, kicking at a pebble. "She was being sent away, but promised an income for her and . . . her child due to the exemplary service and companionship she had provided the *oh so honorable* earl during his time in London." Fenton met Alice's eyes, holding her gaze for the few moments it took her to realize the whole of it.

Alice's lips parted, and she looked as though she would speak, but then she did not, and closed her mouth. The pity that moved into her expression both embarrassed and softened him to the point where he had to look back at his pebble.

"I did not fully understand the implications of what I heard that day, but as the reality of it descended upon me, I came to hate my father for it. All my life I was taught to be respectable, to conduct myself with the finest of manners and decorum. I had interpreted that to mean that I was to behave that way, not simply appear as though I did. To find that my father was so contrary to the instruction he had drilled into me all my life is impossible for me to describe. The betrayal of my mother . . ." He swallowed. "And the desecration of our home was abominable."

"When did this happen?" Alice asked. "How long ago?"

"Nearly ten years. I was sixteen years old." He paused for a breath. "I had hurried upstairs to surprise my parents with my early arrival, which is how I happened upon the study where my father and Jane were closeted. I began to open the door until I heard crying, then paused and overheard the portion of discussion. Perhaps a wiser young man would have tiptoed away, but I did not. Instead I listened for a time and then threw the door open, surprising them both. Jane ran past me—I never saw her again. My father chastised me for intruding and then assured me he'd done nothing wrong. He was only being a man as any other man would be."

Alice flinched. Fenton could not believe he was having this conversation with a woman, let alone his wife. The ways of men were to take place away from the tender ears of the fairer sex. Yet he was telling her the whole of the affair, which he later learned was only *one* of his father's dalliances.

No longer blinded by belief in his father's character, the young Fenton had pieced together other memories that had once seemed odd, but then made a horrible kind of sense. The time he had discovered his father with another man's wife in the library a few years before. He'd thought she was sitting on his father's lap, but had convinced himself she had not been. There were occasions when Fenton had found his father speaking softly to a woman at a party—once he'd even seen a woman slip his father a note during dinner—though later neither the woman nor Fenton's father were in the drawing room with everyone else. Any number of things he had easily looked over before had then fit into his growing understanding, and it had left him confused and embarrassed.

"Oh, Lord Fenton, I am sorry."

He had nearly forgotten about Alice and looked up at the sincere compassion of her expression. "Do you think your father has . . . kept her all these years? That perhaps Mrs. Gale's function as the housekeeper is a ruse?"

Fenton shook his head. He was in possession of one additional piece of information that made that possibility an unlikely one. "I have only ever told one other person of what I saw and heard that day."

Alice pulled her eyebrows together. "Who?"

The guilt of having heaped his burden on his mother, without realizing how much heavier it was for her to bear, cut through him all over again. His heart truly ached for it, and yet he could not change what he'd done.

Still holding Alice's gaze, Fenton let out a breath and admitted the further shame. "I told the very person to whom Foxcroft belongs—my mother. Jane—Mrs. Gale—can only be here because my mother made it so."

CHAPTER 26

Alice did not know what to say. Everything Fenton had told her was confirmed in the anxiety of his movements, the expression of his face, and the pain in his eyes. Alice was of course aware of such indiscretions taking place beneath the notice of proper society. Her family had dined with a family in Sheffield whose daughter had run away to Gretna Green with a footman some years before. And a landholder not far from Warren House had married a woman who had once been his late wife's lady's maid but who had stayed on even after there was no lady to look after.

Alice had never encountered such a thing herself, but she could not get out of her mind the image of that straw-haired boy with lanky arms and charming eyes. Lord Fenton had said he had discovered this ten years ago—near the time he had given Alice her first garden. She was sad to think of that boy having to make sense of such sordidness.

"I am so sorry," she said again, causing him to stop his pacing and look at her. He held her eyes, and she saw more of that boy she'd first fallen in love with than she had seen ever since. She wanted to touch him so he might feel the level of her sympathy and regret in his behalf and yet it felt like too much. As though even the smallest touch might shatter the paper-thin bond she felt between them. He had trusted her with something he had not trusted to anyone else . . . well, anyone but his mother.

Alice could not even begin to make sense of how that factored into the current situation, but she had seen the guilt on Lord Fenton's face when he'd admitted to having told his mother, surely hurting her with the information. Alice also felt his confusion at the present circumstance. Afraid he had not heard her, she repeated herself a bit louder. "I am so sorry for the burden you have carried and for the turn it has taken."

"Thank you," he said in response, but he sounded nervous— vulnerable—and Alice feared he regretted having told her now that the initial fervor had passed.

She had not given him much reason to trust her since their conference in the London drawing room where she had learned the truth of his proposal, and for the first time, she felt bad for shutting herself away from him so completely. If it had been someone else who had followed him to the garden, would that person have become his confidant? The thought made her sad and tempted her to lock herself behind the barrier she'd constructed against him once again, but his expression was still soft, and she could not deny the longing she felt that things might always be this way between them.

He took a step toward her, and she held her ground, wondering if he would come closer and yet knowing that what they had discussed still lay heavy between them. "I need to talk to my mother," he said.

Alice nodded slowly. "I think that is a wise choice. She can better make sense of what has happened." She thought of Mrs. Gale seeking

Lady Chariton and wondered what *that* conversation had consisted of.

He looked past Alice to the house, took a breath, and then looked back at her. "Will you come with me?"

Alice was surprised. Part of her did not want to attend such a personal discussion, but for him to ask made it a request she could not deny. She nodded, and the relief that entered his expression lowered her defenses even more.

They removed to the house, where Lord Fenton asked Mr. Mumford for a glass of whiskey. Alice chose to say nothing of the drink; it was difficult to fault him wanting the strength of it now. Once the glass was in hand, Alice followed Lord Fenton to the drawing room, fearful that Mrs. Gale would still be there. Alice was unsure Lord Fenton was prepared to see the housekeeper so soon after the shock of encountering her in the first place but did not want to add to the difficulty by suggesting the possibility.

Lord Fenton opened the door, and Alice was relieved to find Lady Chariton alone in the room, sitting in the same seat she had occupied all morning. She smiled wanly and held her hand out to her son. "Please come and sit down, Charles."

He hesitated, but recovered in time to cross to her and take her hand. He made to sit but then seemed to remember Alice still standing in the doorway and instead invited her to join him. Alice glanced at Lady Chariton, wondering if she would ask her to leave, but the woman simply nodded toward her in acknowledgment.

Alice crossed the room and sat on the end of the settee furthest from the matron. Lord Fenton sat on the end closest to his mother, and though he looked as though he wanted to say something, he did not seem to be able to find the words. He took a quick swallow of his drink and looked at his mother expectantly.

"I am sorry for the surprise of this," Lady Chariton said, sounding sincerely regretful. "I had hoped to speak with you before you encountered Mrs. Gale. I fear I made a difficult situation even more so by not better preparing either of you."

"Why is she here, Mama?" Lord Fenton asked, sounding like that little boy Alice had once known.

Before she answered, Lady Chariton's gaze slid to Alice, who felt quite conspicuous.

"I told her," Lord Fenton said. "Just now."

Lady Chariton looked back at her son, her expression pained. "The whole of it?"

Lord Fenton tightened his jaw, but then forced it to relax. "Obviously I do not know the whole of it, but I told her of the . . . disgrace."

Lady Chariton's eyes went to the floor, and Alice wondered if she was gathering her own strength. She felt sick for Lady Chariton. How would it feel to know your husband had done something so disgraceful? That your son had discovered it in your own home?

"Shall I go, Lady Chariton?" Alice asked when seconds ticked by on the clock resting on the mantel. "I won't stay if it will make this more difficult."

Lady Chariton looked at her with sad eyes, eyes that looked old and tired. She opened her mouth to speak, but coughed instead, though she quickly recovered. "Your presence will not make this more difficult, my dear, and as you are part of this family, I am afraid this becomes your burden too."

Alice did not know what to say. She wanted to refuse it—she did not feel capable of carrying more burden than she had been these last weeks—but she felt instantly contrite to be so selfish. She *was* a part of this family and the trust extended to her was humbling.

Lord Fenton finished his drink and set it on the end table before he spoke to Alice. "I did not tell you what happened after I told my mother of what I'd seen and heard." Guilt flitted through his expression again, but Alice could see he was resisting the pull of it. "Jane—Mrs. Gale—was removed." He looked back at his mother. "At least, that is what I believed."

"She *was* removed," Lady Chariton said with a nod. "Lord Chariton had arranged for a tenant and his wife on another estate to look after her during her confinement and help her find her way after the child was born."

The child, Alice repeated heavily in her mind. *Lord Chariton's child. Lord Fenton's half-sibling.*

"Father told you of the arrangements?" Lord Fenton questioned, leaning forward. "You spoke to him about it?"

"I did not speak to him," she said with a shake of her head. "But through those staff members loyal to me I learned of the arrangements. I tried to cast it from my mind, to not think on it at all, but I could not stop thinking of this poor girl and her child."

Lord Fenton grunted and stood up quickly. Lady Chariton watched him pace for a few turns before she spoke again. "Whatever you might think of her, Charles, she was a girl seduced by a man she could not have refused."

Lord Fenton stopped pacing and faced his mother. "You did not see them, Mama. She was not . . . regretful. She begged him to come for her after the child was born. I heard it. I told you."

"She was young," Lady Chariton replied. "And unprepared for

the situation she found herself in." She paused for a breath, and Alice wondered what it was costing her to speak of this. "I understand your prejudice against her, but I do not share it. She was an innocent and did not deserve the ruin that would have been her fate, a ruin *he* gave no consideration for." The last words had a bite to them. It was her *husband* she was talking about.

"I have never encouraged you to be disrespectful of your father, Charles, but he is the only one who deserves your censure. He is the one who desecrated our family home and took advantage of a servant. He is the one who sent her and her child away to spare his own difficulty."

"I have no trouble heaping judgment on my father, but why is *she* here?" Lord Fenton asked, his eyes intent on his mother.

"Because Foxcroft was the one place I could send her that your father would never know. He has not been welcome here for many years." Lady Chariton's eyes drifted to the window, and Alice and Lord Fenton shared a look of confusion. She could ban her own husband from the estate? Lord Chariton did not seem to be a man who would heed such orders, and yet he had not argued much to keep Lady Chariton from removing here.

Lady Chariton continued. "It was months after Jane's removal when I decided to find her and be sure she was well. I felt I had a duty to her, being mistress of the house and wife of the man who had ruined her. Her mother had worked for us in London too, you know, and died just a few years before all this took place. I knew Jane was alone, and I did not trust that your father had cared for her in a way that would truly remedy what he'd done." She looked at her hands in her lap. "As it turned out, Lord Chariton had only paid for one year of her care. After that year ran out, she was to be turned out to find her own way in the world." She met Fenton's eyes. "He had no concern for her future, or for her child . . . his child.

"So I found her and offered her a place at Foxcroft. She agreed and I sent a note to Mr. Mumford explaining that she was to be hired on as a maid, with lighter duty until her child came. No one knew the paternity of her child, only that she was under my recommendation. I expected she would leave in time, once she had adequate recommendation to afford her another position elsewhere. That she stayed has been both a blessing and a hardship, I admit, but when Mrs. Mumford passed away, it felt right to offer Jane the position. She has done a very good job of it and, until I decided to return to Foxcroft, she was quite content.

"I fear she has found my presence disconcerting, however. And then, when you arrived, it nearly unraveled her completely. She knew you were coming eventually, but I had not prepared her for it so soon, and she was taken off guard. I have given her the afternoon to collect herself. We will speak again in the morning. She is prepared to leave, but I am hoping she will reconsider."

Lord Fenton did not comment, but Alice felt sure he did not share that hope. Though Alice could appreciate what Mrs. Gale's presence meant for him, Lady Chariton's mercy felt the better course. It seemed as though Mrs. Gale had paid a very dear price for what had taken place.

When no one spoke for several seconds, Alice dared ask another question. "What of her child?" Alice had been there three weeks and had not seen a child of nine years old about the estate.

"The child came too soon and was not strong," Lady Chariton said, looking toward the window. "She lived only a few weeks' time."

The sincere sorrow in her voice and her expression aged her more than Alice had seen before.

Another silence descended upon them as all three seemed to be waiting for another to be the first to speak. Finally Lord Fenton returned to his place on the settee, though he did not relax into it. "Why did you not tell her of my coming today?"

"For fear she would leave before you came," Lady Chariton said. "In fact, I told no one of your arrival for fear Mrs. Gale would hear of it. I had planned to speak with you first and explain." She fixed her eyes on her son. "I am sorry for the shock of this for you, Charles, but it would help if you would show her acceptance. If her intent is to leave, I shall not try to stop her, but I believe she would stay if she felt your agreement with that course. She has lived here for nearly a decade, it is her home, and her child is buried here. She has lived a difficult life but has been able to rise above her disgrace. She is well respected in this household and in the village. I would be sad for that past disgrace to become the reason she leaves this haven."

Lord Fenton said nothing, resting his elbows on his knees and letting his hands and head hang down. He too seemed to have aged this past hour, and Alice hated that she knew not how to comfort him, how to help him.

"I am sorry," Lady Chariton finally said, placing a hand on her son's shoulder. Lord Fenton lifted his head to look at her. "I hate to have been responsible for so much discomfort. As I said, I had expected to speak with you before you encountered her. Perhaps that was the wrong course all together."

Alice realized this was exactly why Lady Chariton had insisted on handling her son's arrival, and upon reflection, was unsure how else it could have been done. It did not seem fair for Mrs. Gale to have left for fear of confronting Lord Fenton, nor did she think Lord Fenton would have reacted well if he'd been warned of Mrs. Gale's identity. Perhaps Lady Chariton's decision was truly for the best, seeing as how the shock would have been felt regardless of how it came about.

"She is not a villain, Charles," Lady Chariton said, still looking deeply into his face. "She does not deserve your censure."

"Perhaps not," Lord Fenton said, though his words were tight. "But I do not know how you can face such a reminder of the heartache, Mother. I do not know how you can look at her and not think of what he did."

"It is not his character I think of when I see Mrs. Gale, it is my own. I was in a position to attempt to remedy a horrible wrong, and I believe I acted as a Christian woman should. That is all I think of; it is all I allow myself to think of. Any other thought only perpetuates the pain, and I have no room in my heart for that."

Lord Fenton held his mother's eyes a few moments more, then nodded his understanding, though Alice was unsure he truly did understand. He stood and let out a heavy breath. "I believe I shall remove to my bedchamber and try to rest before dinner. My mind does not yet seem to have caught up with all that has happened, and I shall need some time to make peace with it. To which room will my trunks be delivered?"

"You will be in the blue room with Alice tonight. I shall have the staff ready the gold room adjoining it for you tomorrow."

Alice's breath caught in her throat as her eyes darted to meet Lord Fenton's, which stared back at her only a moment before he looked to his mother again.

"I mean no disrespect, but I prefer my own bedchamber, Mama. Surely something can be readied for me in the space of the next few hours. I would be pleased with a guest chamber if it would be an easier task than the gold room."

"Certainly not," Lady Chariton said in a voice of authority. She began to smooth her skirts, which Alice saw as a way to excuse why she would not look her son in the eye. "The household is in disarray as it is, and Mrs. Gale has the afternoon off. As the gold room is the one connected to Alice's, it would be foolish to put the staff to so much trouble only to move you the next night. It is bad enough that I am the reason newlyweds have been apart for such a length of time."

"Mama," Lord Fenton said, his tone betraying both his exhaustion and an embarrassment only he and Alice understood. He opened his mouth to continue, but then met Alice's eyes. The awkwardness of sharing her bedchamber with him pushed her nerves over the crest they had been climbing toward this last hour, but as Lady Chariton was quite determined, and Lord Fenton was silently appealing to her, she felt she had no choice but to acquiesce.

"It shall be perfectly agreeable to share my chamber, of course," Alice said with a nod, avoiding meeting the eyes of either one of them. "We can discuss future accommodations tomorrow, when things have settled better than they are right now." She rose and shook out her skirts. "I shall speak with Mr. Mumford about the removal of Lor—*Charles's* trunks and make space for them." She looked at her mother-in-law. "Perhaps Lord Fe—*Charles* could help you to your bedchamber. I worry about what this has taken from you, Mama. If you are not quite recovered by supper, I shall have a tray sent up."

Lady Chariton reached her hand out and Alice took it in both of her own. "You are a dear girl, Alice. Thank you."

Alice wanted to say something of how sorry she was for the pain Lord Chariton had inflicted through his actions, for the toll it must have taken on Lady Chariton all of these years, but it seemed in-delicate to try. Instead, Alice leaned in, gave Lady Chariton a quick kiss on the cheek, and then quit the room, her head full of many thoughts. Yet one alone caused her heart to race and her palms to sweat. Lord Fenton would share her bedchamber tonight. *Her bed.* How on earth should she feel about such a turn as this?

CHAPTER 27

Lady Chariton did not come down to supper, but Fenton didn't think her presence would have changed the heaviness of the evening. The entire household seemed smothered by it, with the servants casting glances at each other, and Fenton and Alice not knowing what to do or say while still attempting to keep to the expectations of a typical country evening.

They ate in the dining room with peeling paper on the walls and a cracked windowpane and said very little. Alice removed to the drawing room upon completion of the meal, then looked surprised when Fenton joined her after only one glass of port. He'd wanted the whole bottle. Two. But his awareness of Alice and the shock of all they'd learned in so short a time had him worried about her. He wanted to somehow ease her discomfort and yet didn't have the slightest idea how he could do so.

The awkwardness stretched between them for a few minutes before he gave himself a stern talking to and turned to face her. "When I spoke with Mr. Mumford, he said you are designing a gazebo for the garden."

Alice looked up from the book she'd been reading and nodded in a shy way Fenton found rather endearing. "Mr. Mumford knows a carpenter who could build it. I hope it can be a place outdoors where we can take tea now and again."

"That sounds lovely," Fenton said, though he wondered at the construction. They did not plan to stay at Foxcroft long. "I did notice there were several places in the garden that had been dug up. Was that your doing?"

"Mine and Mr. Ambrose. He's the head gardener and accommodating of my ideas."

"So you have been able to dig, then?"

He watched the smile form on her lips and felt sure she was remembering that conversation from all those years ago when she had said she loved to dig. A glimmer of pride pricked his heart to realize that the garden he'd arranged for her then had been a part of something much bigger through the course of her life since. He knew of the herbal remedies she had made for his mother and had heard her speak of her love of plants and trees on more than one occasion. Though it was not a passion he shared, he admired it in her. Admired that she was not embarrassed to pursue a hobby that most people in their station would not admit to, much less brag about.

"Yes, I have been able to dig some," Alice finally said, breaking eye contact to look at her skirt.

"And does Mr. Ambrose limit your use of his implements to Tuesdays and Fridays?"

She laughed then—a true and honest laugh that caused Fenton to draw a quick breath for the effect her reaction had on him. "In fact I am allowed to use them any day but Sunday. He explained that as a

God-fearing man he could not justify my working in the garden on Sundays."

Fenton raised an eyebrow. "And you let him get away with such tyranny?"

She laughed again, and Fenton felt the same reaction as he had the first time. He realized he had not heard her laugh since those exchanges in their childhood. Once they'd met again in London, she'd been too reserved and—dare he say it?—adoring, before the fateful conversation in the drawing room. After that discussion, she'd been too cold and defensive. Yet she'd laughed now—twice, in fact. What did it mean? Had they moved past their earlier defenses against one another?

"I daresay I had no argument," Alice admitted. "I'm too much a God-fearing woman to do such work on Sundays, only I found his insistence rather diverting. And how was London?"

Fenton went on to relay the closing of the parliamentary session. "My father was irritated that I left so soon after the close." He felt his lips tighten at the reminder of his father. He wondered how they would get on when they saw each other next. It was not as though Fenton had learned anything new, but knowing the repercussions of his father's actions made those things heavier than they had been before. He could feel Alice watching him, awaiting further explanation, and so he smiled to hide the tightness he still felt.

"He had some work left to do in Town that he wanted me to witness, but I shall have other opportunities for that. After seeing Mama again I am quite concerned over her health. I am glad to have come earlier than expected."

"As am I," Alice said, smiling softly—sincerely—at him from across the room. "I believe she will improve with you being here. It is remarkable the effect the two of you have on each other, as though you bring out one another's best qualities."

"I hope you are right," he said, touched by her compliment. "Between the two of us, I believe we shall give her the right medicine of companionship and comfort."

Alice smiled, he smiled back, and when the silence became uncomfortable, she turned her attention to the book in her hands, tucking her feet beneath her in such a way that she showed her youth—she was only twenty—and looked like a painting. *Lady in Repose,* Fenton thought it might be called. Or perhaps *Lady Reading.* It was almost surprising to realize that she was a *Lady*—Lady Fenton—not just Alice. Not just the woman he had joined in banter and insults. She had conducted herself with such decorum today, not going into hysterics or casting judgments about. She simply listened, and asked questions without making the hardship harder.

"What is it, Lord Fenton?"

Fenton blinked, realizing he'd been staring, and looked about for something to explain his interest. There was nothing else in the room other than faded furniture and limp drapes. The house was very much in need of some attention. He certainly could not tell her that he was imagining her as a painting. "Nothing," he finally said. "Just woolgathering, I suppose."

The smile she gave him was sympathetic, and he sensed she wanted to talk of the day while at the same time not wanting to talk of it ever again. He could relate but did not know how to address the complexities of this new type of interaction.

She watched him a moment longer and then closed the book and set it aside while untucking her feet. "I believe I shall retire," she said, unable to hide her nervousness.

It was early yet, but Fenton could not deny his own fatigue. Only he wondered if he would get any rest tonight. The anxiety of sharing a room—*a bed*—with Alice made it difficult to imagine he would be comfortable enough to sleep. Yet, between the travel and taxing nature of the day perhaps he would fall asleep as soon as his head hit the pillow. Especially if he could settle his stomach with a bit more brandy or rum.

He'd done better these last weeks controlling his desire for drink as he'd focused more resolutely on Parliament and his future duties there, but he could already feel that Foxcroft would test his fortitude. While drinking was often social and frivolous in Town, here he could sense it was the inner turmoil that would drive him to the bottle. Tomorrow, he would need to look at that a bit more closely. For tonight, he simply *needed* a drink, and since he knew Alice did not approve, he would need to pursue it without her company.

"Will you send your maid for my man when you are . . . prepared for bed?" he asked, his gaze sliding away from her face and that far-too-low neckline. He wondered if she could not tuck a scarf about the edges, but was too embarrassed to request such a thing as it would betray his thoughts.

"Yes, my lord."

The words caught his attention and he looked at her, wondering if she realized this was the first time she'd addressed him that way without turning the words into an insult. If she didn't realize it, he didn't want to make her mindful of it, but he could not help but wonder if Foxcroft, and the rawness of this day, might be a starting point for the two of them. A starting point for what, he did not know; but for the first time since offering marriage to Alice Stanbridge, Fenton did not feel as though he were here only by force. Perhaps rather than allowing the brandy to numb his growing feelings, he ought to consider those feelings with greater attention. The idea frightened him, in a curious sort of way.

CHAPTER 28

Alice tried very hard to hide her nerves as her maid assisted her in getting ready for bed. She chose the peach nightdress with the matching dressing gown. Her sisters had given her a nightdress of gauzy white for her wedding night, but it was tucked deep into a drawer since Alice had no use for it. The peach set was far more modest and appropriate for what was a very strange and awkward situation.

Alice chose to wear her hair in a braid over one shoulder rather than rolled into curl papers. Lord Fenton had never seen her in such a state as this, and she did not want him taken aback by papers sticking out here and there, to say nothing of the stray papers that would litter the bed in the morning. As silly as it was—and it was most certainly silly for her to want to impress him somehow—she wanted to appear attractive in her state of . . . undress? That did not sound right and made her cheeks heat up. Attractive in her state of bed-wear? That did not sound right either. It was not as though she expected him to . . .

She shook her head and stood up so quickly she knocked the vanity with her knee, sending a hairbrush to the floor. Her maid picked it up and replaced it. Alice clasped her hands together to keep from appearing so jittery, and pasted a smile on her face.

"Please send up Lord Fenton's man when you return below stairs," Alice said, assuming the valet would alert his master on his way up. "I shall look in on Lady Chariton."

Lady Chariton answered Alice's knock with an invitation to enter. She was reclined against the headboard, her face wan. Alice arranged pillows not in need of arrangement, moved Lady Chariton's slippers a bit closer to the bed in case she should need them, and straightened the edge of the coverlet so it was perfectly parallel with the footboard. Lady Chariton coughed, and Alice assisted her with a drink of warm milk her lady's maid had left for the countess.

Once reclined again, Lady Chariton took hold of Alice's hand. Alice looked at her mother-in-law's hand—thin, bony, and corded with veins and tendons—then looked up into the woman's weary face.

"Alice," Lady Chariton said in a soft tone that calmed Alice like a blanket. "Charles is not his father."

A lump came to Alice's throat. "I know that," she replied while realizing that she *did* know that. In that embarrassing interview they shared in the drawing room prior to the wedding he had told her he was not a rake. She had been so overwhelmed by everything else that day that she had not given that particular detail much attention, but she did now. He was *not* his father. In fact, she felt sure that because of his father he was very different indeed.

And yet he played a role too. While Lord Chariton wanted all the world to think him respectable and proper with his family exactly as it ought to be, Lord Fenton wanted to appear irresponsible, silly, and all things that opposed his father's wishes. Or at least he had until accepting the terms of the agreement that had brought Alice into the situation.

Now, he was being forced to change. She felt she had seen the real Lord Fenton today, but wondered what it was like for him—not playing a part. Did he notice the changes in himself? Did he like them? Did he fear that giving up his façade would bring him closer to the type of man he did not want to be—a man like his father?

Lady Chariton squeezed Alice's hand, bringing her focus back to present. "I fear he might need you to remind him of that from time to time," she said, releasing Alice's hand and lying back on the pillows as though the action had taken what was left of her energy. She closed her eyes, and Alice noted how visible the delicate veins of her paper-thin eyelids were beneath the skin.

"Can I get you anything else?" Alice said.

Lady Chariton shook her head and coughed twice. "You have already done so much." She opened her eyes and looked at Alice with watery blue eyes. "Do you know why I wanted to return to Foxcroft?"

Alice did not know, especially after today's revelations.

She smiled. "I wanted to come to Foxcroft because it is the place where I have had my greatest happiness."

Alice felt her eyebrows come together. How could that be? She had not been here since Lord Fenton was a boy, and she had sent her husband's lover here to get her as far away from him as possible while still doing what she felt best in that charitable heart of hers. The estate itself was unkempt and in no way seemed to proclaim happiness. And yet Alice had no reason to doubt the comment. There must be happiness within this place for Lady Chariton—perhaps childhood memories, or the fact that it was her own and therefore untouched by her husband—if one did not count Mrs. Gale. It was still so very confusing.

"Having you here," Lady Chariton continued, "is but one more bit of joy to add to the whole of it. Life will always serve us best to look for the joy, Alice. And when we find it, we should hold on to it with both hands." Her smile slipped away. "Do not let anyone take it from you, no matter how good their reason."

Lady Chariton's strange advice followed Alice out of the room and down the hallway. Of course Alice would hold on to joyful things. But what had she meant about people taking it from her? Could someone take away joy from another? Was she alluding to Lord Chariton's indiscretion? Was she speaking of Foxcroft itself?

Alice puzzled over Lady Chariton's words but had not drawn a conclusion by the time she pushed open the door to her bedchamber and drew up short when she found it occupied.

Both Lord Fenton and his man turned to her in surprise before she looked at the floor and mumbled an apology. Lord Fenton was only in his shirtsleeves, the tail of his shirt hanging loose almost to his knees. She had forgotten he would be there and was embarrassed to have burst into the room. She began to back out of the doorway when Lord Fenton stopped her.

"You may stay, Alice," he said. If there had been a teasing lilt to his voice or a hint of anger she'd have continued her retreat, but rather his tone communicated his own vulnerability, perhaps wrapped around a wish to overcome it.

Alice did not want to disobey him in front of his valet or give the impression that she did not want to overcome their difficulties, so she nodded and slipped into the room, shutting the door behind her. She turned toward the fireplace, before which two satin-covered chairs were placed, and sat in the chair that kept her back to Lord Fenton's disrobing.

She was glad he could not see her blush and wished she'd brought her book from the drawing room. As it was she had nothing but the fire to claim her interest. It was only her eyes that were drawn to it, however. Her other senses were trained on the men behind her.

They did not speak much, a sign of how well the valet knew the tastes of his master, but she could hear the rustle of fabric as Lord Fenton removed his shirt and breeches. She felt her body tensing and then heard the sounds of his putting on a nightshirt. This was followed by a brief discussion of what Lord Fenton would wear the next day—gray breeches with a green coat and waistcoat.

No pink, Alice said to herself with a smile. *Or embroidered honeysuckles.* She very much approved of his country dress.

Finally, the valet left.

"Are you quite ready for . . . bed, Lady Fenton?"

Alice stood and turned toward him. He stood on the left side of the bed, dressed in an ivory-colored nightshirt devoid of ruffles or flounces but with an open V-neck, the tie strings hanging down his chest. Seeing even that small section of his chest invited feelings of intimacy she did not know what to do with, and she could barely look at him.

Instead, she looked at the bed, which was big enough for the two of them to be quite comfortable without touching one another even by accident. The realization brought a stab of disappointment—much to her continued embarrassment. Searching for a way to belay the growing awareness, she moved toward her side of the bed.

"You call me Lady Fenton now?" She offered a smile so he would know she was not trying to start an argument. Her weary mind could not expend energy for their banter tonight, and she would be sad for the more pleasant interactions to be cast aside. "Is that part of your country manners too?"

"Well, seeing as how you continue to call me Lord Fenton, I suppose I thought it only fair that I should return the formality."

Alice looked away from his gaze and fidgeted with the cuff of her nightdress. "I do not mean to be critical, Lord Fenton, but you have never given me leave to call you anything else."

He lifted his eyebrows in surprise while looking thoughtful. "Have I truly never done so?"

She shook her head.

"Well, then I must remedy such an oversight." He put a hand to his chest and bowed quickly. "Would you please call me Charles?"

It was so silly—his asking her to call him by his first name after nearly seven weeks of marriage—that she could not hide a smile. "Yes, my—Yes, Charles."

He smiled and it dazzled her. Not that he had not smiled at her before, but this was perhaps the first one she believed he meant. She turned her attention to the bed already turned down. There was an oil lamp on the nightstands on either side of the bed, and Alice turned the one on her side down until the flame was extinguished, then looked across the bed at Lord Fenton—at *Charles*—in the muted light. He held her eyes a moment then turned down his lamp as well, leaving only the glow of the dying fire to light the room with moving shadows. They were both still a moment, then sat on the bed in tandem.

Alice removed her dressing gown and laid it over the chair beside the nightstand before sliding beneath the cool sheets, which made her shiver. She felt sure Charles was staying as close to his side as she was to hers. Once she was settled, she glanced his way long enough to confirm that they both lay there, on their backs, looking at the ceiling like a pair of corpses. She did not know how she would ever fall asleep for the tension and was relieved when she heard Charles clear his throat as though preparing to speak.

"I am sorry for today, Alice," he said. "I had never expected you would be burdened with our family's dark history. I have told myself for years that it was in the past, that I should overcome it. To learn it was not so much in my past, but very much part of the present was shocking for me. I'm not sure I handled it well."

"I am not sorry," Alice said. Fenton was quiet and so she clarified. "I am sorry that it *happened* all those years ago, and I am sorry for the pain so many people have suffered, but I am not sorry to know of something that shaped your family in so many ways."

"Shaped us?"

The darkness of the room, the vulnerability of the day, and perhaps even her level of exhaustion gave her little reason to withhold her thoughts. Her brief discussion with Lady Chariton came to mind and empowered her further. "You are not your father, Charles, and I have come to realize today that the fact that you are so different from him was a very determined decision on your part."

He said nothing, but the silence between them was not heavy, and though she could think of several other things to say, she remained quiet. She wanted her words to wash over him, cleanse him of the fears that his father's sins were somehow his own. Finally, when the silence had dragged on far too long, his soft voice cut through it.

"I have tried so very hard not to be the kind of man he is." He paused. "But sometimes I fear that despite my efforts, I will become him. I fear that the same appetite that drives him and disgusts me is simply hiding in a corner of my soul somewhere, waiting to awake, at which point it will demand to be fed to the peril of my character. The day I discovered him and Jane—Mrs. Gale—in the library he told me that all men do as he had done, that one day I would do the same. It is our right, he said, it is our nature."

Alice was grateful he could not see the surprise on her face as the realizations she had been making rather slowly suddenly fit together so perfectly, so seamlessly, she wondered how she had not connected the pieces before this moment. The fear that he would become his father, insatiable and immoral, was what had come between him and her from the start. It was not that Charles did not want a wife, it was that having one put his fear into play—the fear that the intimacies of marriage could wake a beast within himself and put him on a course to be the very thing he hated most in the world.

In an instant Alice felt even more of the barrier she'd built between them crumble. She wondered just how much of this man was a result of his father's choices. But was the result necessarily a bad one? Was it a weakness for a man to be virtuous?

"You are not your father," she said again when she feared he was regretting having spoken. The words weren't enough. She knew they weren't enough, but she could not think of the words that would be sufficient. Perhaps because there were no words that could convince him. This fear was something he had harbored for a very long time. She could not undo it with a pretty phrase or a reassuring thought, but she could try.

"I believe men can control their appetites, Charles," she said. "I have seen it in my father and in my sister's husbands, and I believe that for any man to say he cannot control his passions is a lie. A dangerous lie as it speaks to none of us being able to overcome our human frailties. I admire your determination to rise above the carnal instincts that prevail among your sex, Charles. I admire and appreciate that very much. I also believe that nothing can *make* you become what you so very much do not want to be." It still felt insufficient, but she did not know what else she could say.

"I hope you're right, Alice," he said softly. His tone remained unconvinced, but she did not expect that one reassurance after a decade of fear would be sufficient. "I hope that very much."

CHAPTER 29

Fenton blinked awake, taken aback by the unfamiliar room until he remembered where he was. He turned his head to the side where Alice—his *wife*—lay only a few hand widths away. They had both moved closer to the center of the bed in the night, and she now lay on her side, facing him and still very much asleep.

If he wanted to, he could reach out and touch the lacy collar of her nightgown—the same color her wedding dress had been—that had fallen to reveal one smooth white shoulder. Or he could trace his fingers across her lips, soft with sleep. This painting would be *The Lady Sleeps* or perhaps *Sleeping Beauty*, though that title had been used before.

She *was* beautiful, however, though he had been slow to acknowledge it in the time they had spent together. He hadn't wanted to acknowledge it, if truth be told, so that he would not lose himself in the stirrings she created within him. But he realized now that if he had wanted the security of not desiring his wife, he should not have married Alice Stanbridge.

"Nothing can make you become what you so very much do not want to be."

He was not sure he believed it, was not certain he dared risk such a belief. But he had never felt so very pulled toward a woman before, toward any woman. And she *was* his wife. In the eyes of God such feelings were right and good. In the eyes of the country, such feelings were necessary to solidify their marriage. And yet, how did one let go of boundaries and protections so many years in the making? How did one convince oneself that a monster was nothing more than a figment?

Alice shifted in her sleep, snorting in a most unladylike fashion in the process, and Fenton smiled. He lifted himself on his elbow and with his other hand reached toward the end of her braid resting on the sheets between them. He ran two fingers down the length of it, smooth as silk. He had never touched her hair before, had never even seen it worn down until last night.

Feeling brave and unable to resist the draw of her, Fenton brushed a finger lightly against the lace collar of her nightgown. He looked at her face to confirm she had not awakened, then touched the lace again, outlining the way it rimmed her neck and feeling a shivering tingle rush through him.

The kiss from their wedding day came to mind, the quick perfunctory kiss that had sealed their agreement and made them husband and wife. What if he had gone about this marriage differently? What if he had allowed himself to see these facets of Alice he had seen only recently—her compassion, her steadiness, her patience and grace? What if he could have fallen in love with her? What would a kiss made up of *those* feelings have been like?

He felt his heartbeat increase due to the direction of his thoughts and the temperature of his body followed suit. What if he were to kiss her now? Could he press his lips upon her sleeping ones and then know the difference between an obligatory kiss and a willing one? Would she welcome it? How would it change them?

The moment caution came to his mind he pushed it aside, uncaring for the future consequence of this morning kiss. All he knew was what he wanted, and the more he looked at her face and played out the fantasy of it in his mind, the more he felt pushed and pulled and coiled upon the course. His lips on hers. Her breath as his. His hands on her skin. Her sigh in his ear. So strong was the compulsion that he began to lean into her, began to feel the tingle of the kiss on his lips before it had even happened. He was near enough to hear the movement of her breath between those soft lips, could feel the heat of her body reaching out for his, and then, in a moment, the very monster he feared was before him and he wanted far more than one kiss.

The beast flashed its eyes in his mind and smiled a wicked grin that looked very much like Fenton's father. "Men are creatures of desire," Lord Chariton had said all those years ago. "One day it will take you too."

For one instant Fenton wanted Alice in every way a man should want his wife. In the next instant he was frozen by the fear of what that wanting would begin in him. An instant after that, Fenton scrambled backwards off the bed. He needed distance; he needed physical space between them so as to think clearly.

His foot caught in the bedclothes and sent him falling into the bedside table, dislodging the oil lamp that fell despite his fumbling attempts to catch it in midair. The lamp shattered on the floor, spraying oil and glass everywhere while he untangled his foot from the sheet. Once free, he danced in a circle, avoiding the debris until his legs met the back of the bed, and then he jumped forward as though the bed might burn him. He hop-stepped, hop-stepped out of the way of the mess and the bed and the monster and—

"Charles?"

Her voice was like honey and fire and London smog and he spun around to see Alice sitting up in bed, her eyes wide as she surveyed the spectacle he was making.

He lowered his arms to his sides as though he had not been hopping around like a frog and tried to force a smile. "Oh, did I wake you?" The hem of his nightdress was doused in oil, and he tried to pull it from where it was sticking to his bare legs.

Alice's eyebrows pulled together. "You're bounding around like a rabbit and asking if you woke me?" She looked him over and then leaned forward to see the state of the floor. "What on earth's happened?"

"Nothing," he said, pulling his shoulders toward his ears. "Well, I mean, I did knock the lamp off the bedside table and, well, there's glass and oil everywhere, but other than that nothing's happened, I wasn't doing anything at all."

She stared at him in confusion, and he wondered if she were repeating the words in her head and trying to make sense of them just as he was.

"I think I shall call for some help with this," he said, looking at the mess on the floor and aware that Alice had gotten out of bed on her side. She came up behind him, and his whole body tensed with her proximity.

"Are you all right?" she asked, placing a hand on his arm that seemed to burn as the oil might have had the lamp been lit and the oil hot.

He turned his head to look at her, but only briefly for the rush he felt when he met her eyes and saw those golden flecks within them. *You could kiss her now*, a voice said in his mind, and he snapped his head to look forward again. *See what happens when you let go enough to admire her!*

"I'm all right," he said too quickly. "Of course I'm all right, why wouldn't I be all right?"

"Well, you shattered a lamp on the floor," she said far more calmly than he had been able to speak. "Oh dear," she continued, sudden alarm in her voice. "You're bleeding!"

"I'm what?" He looked down and saw the small pool of red spreading out from beneath his right big toe. Even as stars began to snap in his vision he looked over the portion of floor he'd covered in his idiotic dance and could see smears of red there also, testifying that he'd stepped on some glass. The room began to spin and he felt Alice's hands, so warm and small, at his waist as his knees went weak and he explained that he'd never been one to do well with the . . . sight . . . of . . . blood.

CHAPTER 30

Alice tried not to laugh as Lord Fenton suddenly came to, some two or three minutes after he'd crumpled to the floor. The footman she'd called after extracting herself from Fenton's unconscious form had pulled him to the rug in front of the fireplace, keeping his injured foot over the wooden floor so that another rug was not ruined.

Now Lord Fenton was blinking and turning his head with eyes as wide as Christmas morning while his brain seemed to attempt to catch up with what had happened. Alice was kneeling beside him and placed a hand on his shoulder, causing his wide eyes to focus on her.

"Be still," she said. "Breathe."

His disorientation remained, but he took a deep breath and then let it out slowly.

"Good," she said after breathing along with him for several seconds. "Are you all right?"

He looked around wildly, and she once again had to press her lips together to keep from laughing at his behavior. He looked toward the footman and maid cleaning up the mess, at Alice, at the bed, and back to Alice again. "What happened?"

"You don't remember?"

"I remember *you*," he said, and though she knew he was simply not yet coherent enough to be choosing his words, she was taken back to the moment when he'd hovered over her in the bed—was it only minutes ago?

She'd been awakened by a snort she feared was of her own making, only to realize before she opened her eyes that Lord Fenton . . . *Charles* was watching her. He had been very close—close enough to touch her hair, close enough to run his finger across the lace of her nightdress. It was all she could do to feign sleep for fear that if she indicated she were awake, he would pull away.

And then he came closer, and she felt sure he was going to kiss her. She could smell the scent of yesterday's cologne mingled with the smell of his breath that in another circumstance would not be so very welcome. She could feel his desire and would have tolerated any number of imperfections to have that kiss she felt sure was only moments away.

She had wondered what it would feel like and how it would change them . . . and then he was out of the bed as though he'd been shot . . . and the lamp . . . and the jumping about. There was no need to pretend to be asleep after that. Then came the blood and the fainting. Yet when she'd asked him what he remembered of it all, he remembered *her*. The man was undoing her one button at a time and yet the suspense might just be the death of her.

"You remember *me*?" Alice repeated quietly, hoping the servants wouldn't hear them. "What do you remember of me?"

The flush that crept up his cheeks along with a full return of his faculties was as validating as it was vexing. Why had he not kissed her? Why had he pulled away at the very last moment?

Then his face paled. "I remember the b . . . bl . . ."

"Blood?" Alice supplied for him.

He closed his eyes. "I'm not very good with blood."

She did laugh then and removed her hand from his shoulder, though she allowed her fingers to trail down his arm in the process and was rewarded with a slight tremor on his part. "Yes, you said as much as you were falling to the floor." She nodded toward his foot. "There's a piece of glass in your toe."

He groaned and clenched his eyes shut as though to spare himself the sight.

"Mrs. Banner is coming to tend it for you, but I think it is safe to say that you shall survive this near-fatal injury and go on to wear your high-heeled London boots yet again."

"I shall need whiskey."

"For your foot, perhaps, but not for your belly. It's eight o'clock in the morning."

His eyes opened and he scowled at her. "I do not awaken at eight o'clock in the morning."

She kept her tone strong and authoritative. It would not do to communicate in vague terms her determination that he control his drinking. "Apparently, you do. But you do not drink whiskey at such a time of day."

"I drink whiskey whenever I choose to."

They stared at one another, and Alice felt the argument building in her head if he were to press this. She enjoyed the sober and clear-headed Lord Fenton so very much that the idea of losing that man to the drink was impossible to endure. They were saved a potential argument when Mrs. Banner came into the room carrying a basin, cloths, and, in fact, whiskey for cleaning the wound.

Alice rose to her feet to make space for the woman. As Lord Fenton's injury was not significant, the cook's ministrations would be well enough.

"Thank you," Alice said, meeting Mrs. Banner halfway across the room, relieved that she had not had to call for a doctor. "I hope he will be a good patient."

"Can't be any worse than the others I've had," Mrs. Banner said. "Only, could we get him into a chair? Oh, and Lady Chariton's maid was asking after Lord Fenton. I assured her his injury was not serious, but Lady Chariton would like you to come speak with her when you've a moment, Lady Fenton."

With the help of the footman, Lord Fenton limped and moaned his way into one of the chairs by the fireplace while Alice turned her attention to supervising the remaining cleanup. The glass had been picked up and the maid had gone to fetch sawdust to absorb the last of the oil that made the floorboards shine in the morning light. Alice directed the footman to remove the soiled rug and to send up a maid with fresh bed linens while Fenton gasped and grunted from the chair by the fire.

Alice was in good humor when she went to Lady Chariton's bedchamber, and she told the story with amusement. When she finished, Lady Chariton was smiling, only adding to Alice's contentment with the morning so far—other than the kiss that did not take place and Fenton wanting a drink so early in the day. She hoped Mrs. Banner would not give him one and wished she'd left that instruction. Alice had no doubt Fenton could charm a drink from the cook if he had a mind to.

"You are a good partner for him," Lady Chariton said. "How glad I am that he chose you."

Not many days before, Alice could not be sure she would have agreed. It still stung to know Fenton had not chosen her for her own merits. And yet, perhaps he had just not known that he had. And perhaps the choosing was but one part of matrimony. They had shared hardship yesterday, and he had nearly kissed her today. Certainly, things were improving enough for her to dare be optimistic.

"As am I," she said, then stood from where she had been sitting on the edge of Lady Chariton's bed. "Now, if you'll excuse me, I think I should look in on my husband and make sure he has not sweet-talked Mrs. Banner out of her whiskey."

On Alice's way to the door, however, Lady Chariton coughed, deep and hard enough that Alice turned back to her. Lady Chariton waved her toward the door as though wanting her to leave, but Alice came back to the bed when the cough did not end right away.

"That was different," she said with certainty once the fit was past.

Lady Chariton nodded slightly, trying to hold back another cough, which she was unable to do. Her whole body shook. Alice picked up the water glass from the bedside table and helped Lady Chariton sit up enough to take a sip. With her hand on Lady Chariton's back, Alice could feel every bone of the woman's spine and ribs; she had lost so much weight.

"I will be fine," Lady Chariton said somewhat hoarsely when Alice helped her lay back on the pillows. "Only call my maid and—" She began coughing before she could finish her sentence.

Alice hurried to the bellpull to call the maid but quickly returned to the bed and assisted with another sip of water.

"When did the cough change to this, Mama?" Alice asked.

Lady Chariton tried to wave Alice from the room again.

"When did it change?" she insisted. "I shan't leave until you tell me."

Lady Chariton took a breath, though it was ragged and strained. "During the night," she finally admitted. "I'm afraid that my chest is quite aching from it. Perhaps if I sat up a while the position would do me good."

Alice assisted her in sitting up, supported by pillows to keep her inclined, but noted through the process how weak Lady Chariton was. Had she struggled all night and been unable to reposition herself?

"We need to call a doctor," Alice said when Lady Chariton was finally settled against the pillows.

Lady Chariton shook her head. "They can do nothing for me."

"You do not know that. We should at least get an opinion regarding what has changed."

There was a tap at the door and Larkson, Lady Chariton's maid, opened the door.

"Oh good, Larkson is here. You may go, Alice."

Alice moved away to allow the woman with far more practiced hands to see about her mistress's comfort, but was hesitant to leave.

"Go see to Charles," Lady Chariton said, waving toward the door. "I am in good hands now."

"Yes, Mama." Alice did not quit the room for fear that Fenton's toe was in great distress, however. Rather she realized that if anyone could convince Lady Chariton to see a doctor, it would be her son.

It was not until late afternoon that Dr. Jeffs, a young, jovial man, could attend them. For good measure he inspected Lord Fenton's foot and assured them that Mrs. Banner had tended it well and the injury would give his lordship no undue trouble. Charles did not seem altogether convinced of it, but was far more concerned about Lady Chariton and the cough that had changed overnight and left his mother weak as a newborn calf.

Dr. Jeffs examined Lady Chariton in her bedchamber, and then joined Fenton and Alice in the drawing room. "There is something impeding her breathing. Fluid to some degree, but an additional blockage in the lower quadrant of her left lung, I think. I gave her some laudanum for the pain and to help relax the lungs. I shall return in a few more days to see how she is faring. My hope is that the medication will help relieve the blockage, at which point the fluid can be better absorbed by the body and she should be restored to health."

"And if the blockage is not cleared?" Charles asked in too loud a voice. He'd been nursing one drink or another all day and now he swirled rum in his glass while he awaited the doctor's answer.

Alice had not commented on the drinking, justifying it with his injury and concern for his mother, but she was not at peace with her silence any more than she was with his indulgence.

Dr. Jeffs's expression remained optimistic. "We shall approach that if we need to, but let us be hopeful of the benefits of the laudanum. Often rest is the great healer, and I understand she has been well attended by Lady Fenton here and her tonics and such." He smiled at Alice, and she ducked her head, embarrassed as well as complimented. "I suggest you carry on with such ministrations along with the laudanum and see if a bit more rest does not lead toward improvement."

Though not completely appeased, both Alice and Charles agreed to the doctor's course and then saw him out. They moved up the stairs side-by-side and deep in thought.

"Did you know she was in pain?" he asked as they turned at the landing. He put the now-empty glass on a small table and Alice hoped that meant he was not going to fill it again.

"No," Alice said, deeply troubled to know that Lady Chariton had kept it from her. "She never said as much."

"And that she was not sleeping?"

"I know she's had a night now and again where she did not sleep as well as she'd like, but I did not suspect it was ongoing. Perhaps the laudanum *will* help, then. Perhaps all she needs *is* rest."

Charles nodded, but his brow was still furrowed when they entered the rose room. Lady Chariton was asleep, looking no bigger than a child in the large bed, propped up by half a dozen pillows so as not to lie flat upon her back. Larkson showed them the medication and relayed the measurements. Alice would take responsibility for that part—too often such medications were used improperly and led to greater damage than that which they were to appease.

While Alice conferred with the maid, Charles sat in the chair beside his mother's bed, watching her with a look of concern. "I should like to stay with her for a little while," he said once Larkson had left the room. He looked up at Alice, and the expression on his face made her heart catch in her chest. "I just want to make sure she is resting well. I don't want her to be alone."

"Of course," Alice said. "Perhaps we could make a schedule so she is always attended until she is recovered."

"Very good," Charles said with a nod. "I thank you for seeing to it."

"Of course," Alice said, touched by his sincerity. She quit the room, looking back just before closing the door to see Charles take his mother's limp hand in his and raise it to his lips. Alice swallowed against the lump in her throat but did not allow her mind to wander down the dark pathways of what might be in store for the lot of them if Lady Chariton did not recover. Sometimes, it was better to keep one's mind on the present.

She and Charles had supper in the dining room, with Larkson sitting with Lady Chariton, and then Charles stayed with his mother for the remainder of the evening while Alice wrote a letter to Rebecca and made a list of the things she would need to do the next day. She was no longer consulting with Lady Chariton on the daily tasks of the household but was anxious about performing her duties as efficiently as she had when she could ask the countess's opinion.

When Alice next looked in on Lady Chariton, Charles was gone and Larkson was in his place. Lady Chariton was awake. Alice asked Larkson to bring up some broth and then took the chair closest to the bed.

"I do feel much better," Lady Chariton said, attempting to look bright. If she knew how poorly she appeared, she would not have even tried. Then she coughed, deep and hard enough that Alice helped her lean forward. The spell passed, but Alice's concern did not. Larkson returned with the broth, but after only a few sips Lady Chariton waved away the spoon and sank into the pillows.

"Should you like another dose of the medicine?" Alice asked. "I believe it will help you sleep."

Lady Chariton nodded, then coughed again before Alice gave her a spoonful of the tonic. Alice read aloud by the light of the lamp beside Lady Chariton's bed until the woman was fully asleep. By the time Alice returned to the blue room—Larkson having resumed the vigil—Charles was already asleep.

With all that had taken place that day, the gold room had not been readied for him to occupy, but Alice was disappointed he had not waited up for her. She had hoped he might be eager for her company, perhaps even renewing his attentions from that morning. Despite the concerns for his mother, they had worked as a team today, and Alice had enjoyed the accord of it. And yet, he had fallen asleep.

Rather than wallow in her disappointment, Alice pinned her hopes on the morning. Perhaps he would again attempt to work up the nerve to kiss her. Perhaps this time he would succeed against his fears.

Alice called her maid to help ready her for bed as quietly as possible but soon realized that Lord Fenton was not just asleep, he was passed out. The realization turned her hopes into sharp irritation. What if Alice had needed his help? What if his mother had asked for him? How were they to work toward a greater connection if he drank himself into a stupor? It was so very much like London, and all the irritation from that time wrapped around her disappointment of this night until she was fuming.

After the maid left, Alice found two empty wine bottles hidden behind the wardrobe and scowled at them while adding one more item to the list of things she needed to do the next day. She'd had no control over his drinking in London, but she could certainly make a statement about it here.

Once in bed, she looked across the darkness to the form of her husband, his mouth open and the light from the dying fire reflecting off a line of drool connecting his mouth to the pillow. She huffed in disgust and turned her back to him, feeling the resurgence of irritation while also entertaining the fantasy of snuggling up to his unconscious form and draping his arm around her waist. Even if he would not know it, she longed to feel the comfort of his embrace, his warmth. But her pride—and his drooling—would not allow it.

She closed her eyes and tried to think of other things, but she could not silence the longing she felt for the real Lord Fenton—the man she had seen since he'd come to Foxcroft. If he would avoid the drink, surely she would get to see more of *that* man.

CHAPTER 31

Lady Chariton seemed improved the next day, much to the entire household's relief. She ate a simple breakfast of porridge and coltsfoot tea in her room and was sleeping and breathing easily when Alice looked in on her afterward.

Alice then coordinated the menus with Mrs. Gale and set about the other items on the list she'd made the night before. The task she had added to her list when she faced her drunken husband was to ask Mr. Mumford that all the liquor in the house be locked up in the wine cellar. Her father had done the same once when his brother—who could not resist the drink, almost to his complete ruin—had come for an extended stay. Without liquor on hand he had been uncomfortable at first, but after a few days' time his eyes were brighter and his laughter more genuine.

"Everything?" Mr. Mumford asked in surprise.

"Yes," Alice said as though it were not such a strange request. "I want the brandy taken from the library, the whiskey removed from the cabinet in the study, and all wines and champagnes inventoried and locked up. I shall approve the supper wine with you each day, and apart from some sherry for Lady Chariton when she requests it, and whatever Mrs. Banner needs for cooking, any other requests are to be cleared with me." She held his eye to make sure he knew this was a serious request.

"Very good, my lady," he finally said, but he was not happy with it. She did not let the steward's feelings influence her own, however. Since London she had been irritated by the degree of Lord Fenton's drinking. Now it seemed clear that by keeping himself intoxicated he could avoid troubling feelings, such as his mother's health and, perhaps, his growing attraction for his wife. Alice would not deny him drink completely, of course, but she would not allow him to indulge to such degrees as he was used to either.

Lord Fenton, for his part, woke with puffy eyes and a pounding head he took a powder to alleviate. Though he did not feel well, he still toured the estate with Mr. Mumford and Mr. Ambrose, the head gardener. The years of nonresidence had taken a toll on the estate, and there were a great many things that, thanks to recent education on details of management, Lord Fenton was well versed to remedy. Work orders were given, permissions to hire granted, and a timeline developed so that in a month's time most of the neglected elements would be repaired. He told Alice the details of his day and the whole of his plan over supper, for which she had approved a red wine to go with the lamb and then worked hard to keep her husband distracted enough by conversation that he did not have more than two glasses.

When it was time for Alice to remove from the dining room, and he to enjoy his port, she suggested they look in on his mother before she fell asleep for the night. Alice hoped that if Fenton stayed with his mother through the evening, he would not seek out a drink. Then, tomorrow he would awake with a light head and open countenance and they would get on as they had the first two days after his arrival.

Lady Chariton was in good spirits, and Alice enjoyed hearing stories of Lord Fenton's youth. He was the perfect blend of the good humor of his London self and the truth of the man she'd seen in recent days. She liked it very much and encouraged him by asking more and more questions about his childhood and schoolboy antics. Alice even felt brave enough to tell Lady Chariton the story of how the two of them had met thanks to a grass fire. Fenton tried to stop the telling but Lady Chariton had listened with rapt attention. When it concluded, she shook her finger at her son. "You were a rascal."

"I'm sure there is no argument against that," he said with a shrug, obviously relieved his mother did not reprimand him more strongly for the fire. They laughed and talked a bit longer until Lady Chariton was ready for her evening dose of medicine. Her cough did not seem to be so evident today, thank goodness, but they all agreed she should do what she could to sleep well. Larkson would stay with her tonight, allowing Alice and Fenton to retire.

"I would like to speak to you privately tomorrow, Charles," Lady Chariton said once he gave her a good-night kiss. It was a rather formal request, which Alice could see surprised Fenton.

"I hope that you would not *not* speak to me tomorrow," Fenton said once he recovered from his reaction.

"Might we say ten o'clock? In the drawing room if I am up for it, here in the rose room if I am not."

Fenton looked concerned, but he nodded, gave his mother one more kiss, and then wished her a good night.

It was not until they were walking down the hall side by side that Alice realized the one task neither of them had seen to—readying

Lord Fenton's bedchamber. She knew the moment Lord Fenton made the same discovery due to the way his step slowed. He rolled his shoulders.

"It is all right," Alice said, moving ahead of him to open the door. "The bed is big enough for the two of us, and we can endure it for one more night." She smiled to show that the arrangement was unobjectionable to her. Very unobjectionable. His expression did not seem much relieved, however.

"I had meant to see to the gold room myself as I know you have been so busy with other matters," Fenton said, following her into what had become an intimate space when they were in it together. She wondered if he noticed the feel of it too or if it were just her feminine fancy. He stayed just inside the doorway and shifted awkwardly from one foot to the other. "I'm afraid it slipped my mind what with the estate duties."

And the foggy head left over from two bottles of wine, no doubt, Alice thought to herself. "I will see that it is readied tomorrow," she said aloud, and when she saw the relief on his face, she had to turn away to hide her disappointment. Yesterday morning he had nearly kissed her, today he would not even step into the room with her. Apparently soberness alone would not release his feelings. Or perhaps his feelings were not as she hoped them to be.

He didn't speak, and she didn't look at him as she moved to the bellpull to summon her maid. She began removing pins from her hair, knowing it was wicked to want him to admire her hair loose about her shoulders and feeling greedy to want more than amiability to continue to grow between them. But she wanted all of it—his friendship, his admiration, his touch.

A few more pins and her hair began to tumble down her back in soft curls. She sat at her mirror and watched his reflection while he stared at her, as mesmerized as she hoped he'd be. She had just begun to smile to herself, feeling victorious, when he took a step backward toward the hallway.

"I shall busy myself in the library while you prepare," he said, then turned on his heel and left the room, closing the door behind him. Though disappointed, she felt her little game had been successful too. He'd noticed her—he'd been affected—and that could only lead toward good things. Better understanding his fears helped her to feel more patient too. He would need to learn to trust himself, and her as well, before they would be ready for such things as her sisters had explained to her on the night before her wedding. When he was ready, however, she would make sure he knew she was willing.

Her maid came to assist her, and minutes later, Alice was undressed but for her thin linen chemise when the door to the bedroom was thrown open. Both she and the maid squeaked in alarm as the door hit the wall behind it. Alice grabbed for the first piece of clothing big enough to cover herself—the petticoat she'd worn beneath her day dress. That it was her husband glowering at her from the doorway did not make her feel any better.

He took two long strides into the room and put his hands on his hips while his eyes shot daggers. "You locked up my whiskey?"

"Will you give us a moment?" Alice said to her maid, who was only too happy to leave. She scurried out of the room, pulling the door closed behind her.

Alice faced her husband, not wanting to have this conversation with her petticoat clasped to her chest but not wanting to reveal herself so indecently either. Not when his mood was dark. "Will you turn so that I might put on my dressing gown?" she asked.

He narrowed his eyes a bit tighter, but then turned his back to her, allowing Alice to run a few steps to grab her dressing gown from where it lay across the end of the bed. Once the sash was tied about her waist, she cleared her throat. "I think you drink too much," she said simply. Calling him Charles felt too familiar to be used during an argument. But since she'd adequately turned "my lord" into a derogatory term that did not sound right either.

"I've hardly a drink at all since coming to Foxcroft."

"Other than the three glasses of wine at dinner, the port to follow each meal, and the glasses of whiskey you carried about with you all day long yesterday, you mean?"

"That is how men drink, Alice," he said. "Especially in the country where one cannot trust the quality of the water."

"And the two bottles of wine you drank between your mother's sickbed and my bed last night? That is not excessive? Did you not feel their effects all day? Because I can assure you the servants took note. I am attempting to spare your reputation."

"You do not dictate my habits," he said in a cold and calm voice. "And I will not be locked away from the liquor in my own home."

"It's not your home, it is your mother's," Alice said, but her resolve faltered. She could not claim greater authority over the estate than Fenton. It was too late to back down, now, however, and arguing with this man was familiar enough that she quite easily fell into it. "I have taken over the household management and feel it would serve all of us well if you would control your appetites."

It was the wrong word. She knew it as soon as she said it. It was the same word he'd used when speaking of his fears that he would become the kind of man his father was.

She felt her cheeks grow pink with the implication and attempted to remedy it. "I only mean that you should—"

"I know what you mean," Fenton said, his arms crossed over his chest. "And I do not appreciate such high-handedness. Do you not know how this makes me look to the servants? Could you not discuss it with me so that I would not make a fool of myself to ask for whiskey only to be told by Mr. Mumford—who was as embarrassed as I was—that I am not *allowed*? As though I am a child?"

Alice had not even thought to speak with him about it. She'd made the decision last night in a fit of disappointment and irritation. She had embarrassed him, and yet her pride was such that she could not back down.

"Are we not discussing it now, *my lord*?" She cringed to hear the familiar condescension in her own voice. And yet she could not stop—the only other result of this conversation was for her to berate *herself* for her actions, and that would return her to her feelings of inadequacy. "I cannot imagine why I did not think we could have a reasonable discussion about this. Now, if you are listening, I am aware of some remedies for the desire for drink—herbal tonics and things that . . ." She could not finish under the weight of his stare, which had grown even stonier than before.

He regarded her for several seconds, then shook his head in a gesture so soft and almost tender that she felt it to her very core. "I had believed we had made progress these last days, Alice. That we were working alongside each other in a way that was both comfortable and congenial. I had gone so far as to think that the insults and goading were a thing of the past, a role we played when we were too unsure of our place with one another to be otherwise. Perhaps conciliation is the role you were playing all along. I wonder why I dared trust it at all."

He spun on his heel and stalked out of the room, leaving Alice to stare after him and feel every inch of the descent her heart made as it fell to her toes. Tears rose in her eyes. Why had she *not* simply talked with him? Was she still so unsure of herself that she needed to assure her control? And now what should she do? Open the cellar and let him drink himself sick? Or keep it locked and rebuild the barriers she seemed so very good at creating between them?

CHAPTER 32

Alice did not know where Lord Fenton slept, but when she asked after him the next morning, her maid said he was out riding already. The maid kept her eyes on the floor when she spoke, which told Alice that the argument with her husband had been discussed below stairs.

Alice asked nothing further but continued to reprimand herself for not talking to Fenton about her concerns before taking such extreme, and disrespectful, measures. And yet her concern with his drinking *was* justified. If she'd handled it better, however, she might not have destroyed all the progress they had made. The only course was to apologize and attempt to make things right. How Fenton would react to her attempts to repair this would be up to him. The entire thing made her stomach burn, and she regretted her independent ways, which in this circumstance had not served her well.

Alice went down to breakfast, alone, and then looked in on Lady Chariton, who was dressing for the first time in several days. She was determined to have her mysterious discussion with Fenton, so once she was readied, Alice assisted her down the stairs slowly and carefully, feeling with each step that a twist to one side or another would snap the woman's bones in two.

Alice sat with Lady Chariton in the drawing room and tried not to show her anxiousness as she worked on her gazebo sketch, which had been all but forgotten, and waited for Lord Fenton. He arrived at two minutes before ten o'clock dressed in navy breeches, scuffed boots, and a shirt with only a simple knotted cravat. The edges of his hair were damp with sweat and he did not look at Alice when he entered the room.

"Oh, Mother, you look as radiant as the sun this morning," he said with his effeminate tones as he bowed elegantly over Lady Chariton's hand. Alice knew his behavior was for her benefit—a reminder he was not bending to her will—and she placed her sketch pad on her chair.

"I shall leave you to your discussion," she said, smiling respectfully at her mother-in-law but avoiding Lord Fenton's gaze as she quit the room. She waited outside the room until she heard the murmur of their voices, then set off to find Mr. Mumford.

Allowing Fenton to drink with abandon was not a solution, and she feared it would be worse than ever after he'd been denied, but they would find no accord if she did not treat him as a grown man. When Lord Fenton was finished talking with his mother, Alice would offer her apology and hope her humility would repair the damage she had done.

She found Mr. Mumford below stairs and tried not to show her embarrassment as she asked that the whiskey and brandy be returned to their usual places and the wine cellar unlocked.

"Yes, my lady," he said and then eagerly moved off to open the stores.

That task complete, Alice found Mrs. Gale. There had been no further discussion of Mrs. Gale's past, but Alice bore the woman no ill will. She was good at managing the household, and Alice felt admiration for the woman's ability to rise past her difficulties.

"Could you see that the gold room is readied for Lord Fenton by this evening?" Alice had once promised herself that she would do well in her role of Lady Fenton; she only hoped her husband would recognize her attempts at correcting what she'd thus far done wrong.

She and Mrs. Gale then discussed the day's menu, the matter of the new scullery maid who had not returned after her half day off, and whether or not they should add some chickens to their flock now that there were three people in residence and the cook was having to buy eggs from a tenant.

When that was finished, Alice headed for the stairs that would take her to the public level, mentally making plans to spend some time in the garden for the first time in several days, when she heard heavy footfalls across the upstairs foyer. She paused, then hurried up the remaining steps and into the foyer in time to see the front door slam shut. The floor reverberated in response, and though Alice had not seen who had exited, she could ready a guess due to a very similar circumstance that had taken place just a few days before. She hurried to the drawing room and gasped to see Lady Chariton bent over in her chair, her head in her hands as she sobbed.

"Mama," Alice said, hurrying to kneel beside her chair. She placed a hand on the woman's thin back and rubbed it in slow circles as she looked toward the door, wondering what could have happened.

Lady Chariton began to cough, that deep racking cough that shook her entire body, and Alice was soon calling for water. She helped Lady Chariton to the settee where she could lay down. Lady Chariton's chest was heaving as she attempted to take a breath.

"You must calm down," Alice said, rubbing the woman's hands in hers.

Every few seconds Lady Chariton would cough again, her whole body shaking when she did so. Mrs. Gale brought water, which did not help very much.

"Fetch the laudanum," Alice said to the housekeeper, then shook her head and came to her feet. "Ask Mr. Mumford to help me get Lady Chariton to her room. I'll give her the medicine there so she can rest in her own bed."

It was several minutes until Lady Chariton—carried by the steward when it became apparent that she was unable to navigate the stairs herself—was lying in bed, her breathing normal and her cough diminished, though tears still leaked from her eyes as they all waited for the medicine to take its effect. Mr. Mumford and Mrs. Gale hovered by the doorway, awaiting further instruction, while Alice sat on the edge of the bed and brushed hair off Lady Chariton's damp forehead. Dr. Jeffs was not due until tomorrow, but Alice would send for him today. In the space of an hour, Lady Chariton's condition had become extreme.

"Charles?" Lady Chariton finally said, meeting Alice's eyes with anguished ones of her own.

"He . . . went out," Alice said. She hesitated before deciding to push forward. "What happened?"

Lady Chariton closed her eyes. "I had to tell him," she said, her voice breaking and her chin trembling with such emotion that Alice's fears doubled. "After all these years . . ."

Alice waited for Lady Chariton to continue but she did not. "Tell him what?"

Lady Chariton began to cough again, and Alice nursed her through it until finally she calmed again. The medicine's effect was increasing, and Alice worried Lady Chariton would not be lucid long enough to speak of what had happened. Alice felt sure she very much needed to know.

"What did you tell Charles? If I'm to help him, I have to know."

Lady Chariton nodded, slow because of the medicine. "I told him of Adam."

"Adam?" Alice had all but forgotten about the simpleminded man she had encountered in the carriage house. She had not ventured past the garden since and he had not ventured past the hedge. "What about Adam?"

"He insisted," Lady Chariton said, looking up at Alice with unfocused eyes. "I had no choice."

"I don't understand," Alice said, shaking her head and trying not to sound as frustrated as she felt. "Who insisted? Adam? You had no choice in what?"

"No choice," Lady Chariton said, her eyes fluttering closed and her expression going slack. "I had to give him up. I had to leave him here."

A sprinkling of understanding began to rain upon Alice's thoughts, but she felt herself resisting, unwilling to go the direction they beckoned her. "Who?" she asked sharply, shaking Lady Chariton's shoulder enough to rouse her, though her head began to loll to the side. "Who did you leave here?"

Lady Chariton blinked her eyes and for a moment became present. "Adam must stay at Foxcroft," she said, her voice soft and sad and unsteady. "He can be happy here. He can be safe. We shall have another son in his place."

Alice was unsure if the gasp came from her own mouth or that of Mrs. Gale, who stood behind her. Alice stared at Lady Chariton as the woman's eyes closed again and she slept. Alice's chest begin to tremble as a fullness of understanding filled her up.

"Oh, heavens," she breathed. Alice gently released Lady Chariton's hand she'd been holding and laid it on the quilt. Then she turned to face Mr. Mumford and Mrs. Gale. That they were as shocked as she was told her that Adam's parentage had been kept secret from them as well, but it was not *their* reaction that had her concerned.

"Do either of you know where Lord Fenton went?" She was already moving toward the doorway. How must it be for him to have learned this?

"No, my lady," Mr. Mumford said, shaking his head. "Shall I ask the other staff?"

Alice considered that, but Fenton had been gone for nearly half an hour. He'd left through the front door, which meant it was reasonable to assume he'd taken the same trajectory as when he'd realized Mrs. Gale was here at Foxcroft.

"I'll find him," she said. "Please summon Dr. Jeffs immediately, and tell Mrs. Banner what's happened in case she does not know that Lady Chariton had been planning to divulge this information." She looked at them and managed as much of a smile as she could. "Thank you," she said with sincerity, her eyes lingering on Mrs. Gale's a moment longer. "We are indebted to you both for your service to this family, and I know that we can count on you in this. Please see that Lady Chariton is not left alone while I am gone."

"Yes, my lady," they said in unison.

Alice hurried down the stairs and through the front door. She hoped Fenton would not dismiss her when she reached him due to the tension of last night's argument. She prayed that by the time she arrived she would have thought of how she could help him make sense of this latest discovery.

CHAPTER 33

Fenton knew Alice was there before he heard the swish of her skirts over the grass. Some other sense alerted him to her presence. He closed his eyes and dropped his head, not feeling fit for company and yet touched that she'd followed him through the garden and the wood, over the brambles and finally to the edge of the stream where he thought he had been hidden. He should have known she would come after him, as she had when he'd encountered Mrs. Gale, as she had in another way when he'd admitted the fear of having inherited his father's weaknesses. Even with last night between them, she had come.

He lifted a shaky hand to wipe the sweat from his forehead and ached for a drink. The hard ride this morning had been in hopes of somehow outrunning the discomfort of not having a drink on hand to even out his feelings. It had not worked and instead made him wonder if Alice were right. He could not remember the last day he'd spent without a drink every few hours to calm his nerves; and his want of a drink was extreme when he did not have one in hand. The thoughts had been uncomfortable, but little had he known how much more discomfort awaited him this day. Little had he known the way his desire for oblivion would claw at his insides once his mother had told him the secret she had kept from him all his life.

Fenton stood from his place on a fallen tree, turning toward Alice in time to see her—skirts lifted—step onto what looked like solid ground until it sucked her shoe and foot into it. She immediately pulled her foot out, but thick mud dripped off what had been a very nice slipper completely unfit for the wilds where she had followed.

She scowled. "Could you not have simply gone to the garden again?" she asked, moving to the side and testing that bit of ground even as Fenton came to her aid.

He took her hand and supported her elbow, leading her around the front of the log. Once seated, she leaned forward, gathered her skirts to her knee and sighed at the ruined slipper before reaching down and peeling it off her foot. The stocking was quite saturated too, and she lifted a single eyebrow at him. "You may want to turn away, my lord, or risk being quite scandalized when I remove this stocking."

He wished he could tease her in response, but he could not. This newest wound was far too fresh. However, he *could* help her with her stocking, and so he knelt in front of her, ignoring the wetness that immediately seeped through the knees of his breeches.

She pulled her foot away when he reached for it. "I can attend to it."

"I have no doubt that you can," he said, reaching for her foot, which this time she allowed him to take. "But if I can help, you can keep your skirts from getting any more soiled than they already are." The intimacy of the touch surprised him, and he looked up to see her staring back at him with flushed cheeks. "Though I'm afraid I do not know precisely how one removes a woman's stocking."

Alice leaned forward, reached under her skirt, and fiddled with the garter he could not see but felt as though he could. His chest became hot for a different reason than it had been feverish so far this day, then his neck, and his ears as she unrolled the stocking from somewhere high on her leg.

When it reached her knee, Fenton took over, gently folding the sheer silk around itself as he peeled it from the delicate skin of her foot. He stared at her knee, calf, and ankle—naked before him—then cleared his throat and moved to the stream where he wet his hand-kerchief and returned to wipe the streaks of mud from her foot. As soon as he finished, she pulled her leg away and brushed her skirts back down to cover herself.

"Thank you, my lord," she whispered so breathlessly that it quite took his own breath away too.

He knelt, holding the soiled stocking until remembering himself. He took the stocking and slipper to the stream and rinsed them both as best he could before laying them over a sun-dappled rock to dry. He splashed some of the cool water over his face in hopes it would relieve the variety of ailments besetting him, and then came to sit beside her on the log. He stared forward, feeling her eyes move from him to the stream and back again while she waited for him to speak.

She knew about Adam. If she did not he felt sure she'd have asked what prompted his run, and he was relieved he did not have to explain to her something he could not fully form in his mind. *His brother? Not dead. Abandoned.*

"I feel as though I am repeating myself," she said after a few minutes had passed without a word from either one of them. "But I am so sorry."

He grunted at the understatement. "How many more surprises await me, I wonder?" He moved his elbows to his knees, hung his head, and wished for brandy, which only irritated him further. He did not want a drink because it calmed him. He wanted a drink because it could *numb* him. He could forget about his father's debauchery, could ignore his attraction to his wife, could block out the discomfort of his own silliness and now block out this new awareness. Numbness had become an escape for him, the way he coped with every difficulty, but it made him weak. He was tired of weakness. Tired of playing the fool so very well.

Alice broke into his thoughts. "I would like to assure you that there are no more surprises such as this, but I felt sure that was the case after the discovery about Mrs. Gale. I do not know what to make of this newest turn." She paused. "A few days after we arrived here, I met Adam. He frightened me, and when I spoke to your mother about him, I added all my questions about Mrs. Gale's youth and why we had come here at all—Foxcroft was a strange place and I found it very disconcerting. Lady Chariton told me that she needed to talk to you before she could explain the confusing elements to me. After the situation with Mrs. Gale, I assumed *that* was the whole of the oddity about the place. I had forgotten about Adam completely in the uproar of it all. Have you met him?"

Fenton let out a breath and nodded. He had seen Adam in the stables the day of his arrival when he'd gone to check on the horses, and he'd caught sight of him again this very morning. Fenton had not spoken to him on either occasion, only seen him from a distance and wondered at his disability as it was obvious he was not whole.

Fenton closed his eyes. Adam was his brother—older by four years, which was the length of time it took for his parents to accept he was not fit to be heir and see to making a replacement. Lord Chariton had insisted on Adam's removal and the subsequent story of Adam's death. Lady Chariton had insisted he go to Foxcroft, where she established Mrs. Banner's care for their son.

Fenton had not yet begun to come to terms with the half-sister buried somewhere on the estate, the unwanted child of his father as the result of his infidelity, yet now he had to face the prospect of a full-blooded brother, living out his life here as the son of a cook. It was all so twisted. It was all so wrong. He could not make sense of it.

Fenton reached for Alice's hand and for a moment he felt as though he should explain his need to feel her touch, but instead decided to let it be. "Adam should be me," he said. "He was the first-born son. He should be Lord Fenton."

"Oh, Charles," Alice said, her voice drawn and sympathetic. "Whatever it is you are feeling, I know you must see that Adam is too . . . limited to fulfill the requirements of an heir."

"I see that he could not bear the responsibility," Fenton acknowledged, raising his head to look at the sky through the trees. "But that the only course my parents saw was that he could not be their *son*—could not be *my* brother—makes me hate this world to which I belong." He shook his head and closed his eyes, repulsed by everything that had combined to make this circumstance a reality. Despite his disgust of it—that *both* his parents would go along with such a thing—he understood why it had been done, and that was perhaps the most unsettling part of it. "The only reason I am the heir is because of his . . . limitations. Had he been whole, I would not be me."

"You would not be *Lord Fenton*, but you are not your title,

Charles. You have a soul and a mind and a will of your own, apart from your place in society and the order of your birth."

He looked at her, closing one eye against the sun that hit him just wrong. "Do I?" he asked. "And if I had been born simple, what then? Would they have had another son and discarded me as well?"

Alice's hazel eyes were full of tenderness and her forehead pinched. It was hard to believe when she looked at him this way that just last night she had announced him unfit to manage his own health. In this moment she seemed to be the best friend he had ever had, and he wondered if that were the true gift of matrimony—another person connected to your troubles as directly as you were. Someone who would feel your same pain, and mourn your same grief even when at odds with you.

And yet, marriage had not been thus for his parents and that raised his fears once again. Was what he felt for Alice now because of how broken he felt for all that had happened? Would a week pass, a month perhaps, and they would be at one another's throats again? Would he go back to the drink and the disconnect it afforded him in her company? Would sharing such closeness now only serve to make the inevitable divide more cutting? More tortuous?

"We cannot explain such things," Alice said, saving him from his thoughts. "Why one son would be born as Adam was, or why society puts such emphasis on inheritance and privilege that he would be rejected as he was. I fear we shall lose our minds if we obsess over the whys and the what-ifs of such circumstance."

"How can I not obsess?" Fenton asked, truly hoping she could answer him. "All my life I thought he was dead—yet he was not. Only given away to a servant who would love him as his parents could not."

"I cannot pretend to know your father's mind in this, of course, but equally I cannot question that your mother *did* love him—loves him still."

Fenton thought of his mother and the love she had showered upon *him* all of her life. Had she been giving him a double measure because of the son she did not have? Had Fenton received more than his share because of the loss of Adam? And what of Mrs. Gale's child? She never had a chance for any kind of life, even had she lived. The guilt of his place in the stories of his father's other children made him feel as though he might drown.

"I crashed carriages, drank to excess, and dressed like a fool while Adam fed horses and pulled weeds and my half-sister lay in the ground. There is something so terribly wrong about all of this." He waved the hand not holding Alice's through the air. "And I feel as though I should do something to fix it, to make it right, and yet there is no course for that, is there?" He looked at her. "There is nothing I can do about any of this. It is decided by the fates and I am simply the man who drew the winning hand. Should I simply be glad for it? Should I feel no regret on behalf of the others not so lucky as myself?"

"I don't believe there is nothing you can do," Alice said.

"You would have me present Adam to society as the true heir?" Fenton scoffed. "You would have me tell the world what my parents did? How would that repair what has been done?"

"Sometimes making things right is not about repairing it. Should you attempt either of those courses they would end in greater tragedy. Adam cannot be the next Lord Chariton and to suggest he could is unfair."

Fenton looked back at the ground in front of the log where they sat, still holding her small hand and running his thumb across the back of it. A quick glance to the side showed him Alice's dainty toes, resting on her other foot still encased in her slipper. She continued speaking. "But you can make the right decision now, with the imperfect pieces you've been given."

He looked up at her. "How do you mean? As you said, nothing can change what's been done."

"But you *can* influence what happens next," she said, still holding his eyes. She bit her lip as though gaining confidence before speaking again. "Your mother is not getting better, Charles. I left her to find you only after we summoned the doctor. She is quite unwell."

He made to stand and go to her, but Alice pulled him back down.

"She is resting," Alice said. "But you *must* realize that she came to Foxcroft for a purpose."

It would be impossible for him not to make the connection Alice was so gently leading him too—that his mother had come here so that he would come. So she could tell him the truth before she . . . could not tell him. He tried to blink away the tears.

Alice continued. "I believe your mother came to Foxcroft because she needed to secure those responsibilities she had committed herself to care for until now. She needed to know that Mrs. Gale would have her future settled even with you knowing her past, and she needed to know that Adam would be well cared for throughout the duration of his life. Can you imagine what it has felt like to her all these years not to have both her sons by her side? With a heart as big as hers, can you even bear to think what it took from her to leave him here as another woman's child?"

So why had she done it? Why was that the only course? He thought back to their visits to Foxcroft when Fenton was young and remembered a brown-haired boy bigger than he that he would play with—building mud pies and stick forts. Fenton had been seven years old the last time they visited Foxcroft, and he recalled telling his mother that the boy—that is what he called him, *the boy*—talked funny. He had not thought of that moment in years and years, would not be thinking of it now were it not for the way his mind was racing to pull bits and pieces of memory together as proof of the whole. Adam had been his playmate. His mother had brought Fenton here for the summers so that she might see her sons together. Was it because Fenton had noticed Adam's differences that they never returned? The thought made his throat tight as he realized the probability.

Lady Chariton had to know that at some point the younger son would outgrow the elder, that Charles might one day not find his big playmate so amusing, might even begin to ask questions about him that she could not answer. There was no doubt that the entirety of the situation was painful for her, yet she'd done it. "They could have had him deemed incompetent to inherit and still raised him," Fenton said. "He did not have to be discarded."

"But would he have been happier then?" Alice asked. "I do not mean to say that their decision was the right one—I cannot imagine leaving a child behind—but when your mother admitted to me what had been done, she said that Adam could be safe here. He could be happy. Would he have been safe and happy in London? Could he have found contentment in a society so intolerant of his impairments?"

Fenton stared at the ground, pondering on her words but hating them.

"He does not know who your mother is to him," Alice continued. "He does not know that she gave him life, loved him as long as she could, and then mourned him. Can you imagine how it hurts Lady Chariton's heart to know that? But she *has* cared for him; she has done everything she could within her power to make sure he is happy. And, you know, I do believe he *is* happy. Mrs. Banner loves him as her own, the servants care for him, and he has purpose and work to keep him occupied. It is a bitter consolation, I am sure, but your mother is responsible for Adam's happiness here at Foxcroft—she made it so—and now, with her health declining and her world becoming smaller, she wanted her *children* around her, her sons. She wanted you to know your brother, to be his friend again. She wanted assurance that you would continue her devotion to his care. She also wanted you to forgive Mrs. Gale and see that she was protected from those things that changed her course. Your mother has tried so long to do the right thing, and she needs you to help her continue it now."

Fenton was overwhelmed by all that Alice was saying and what it meant. "She's dying, isn't she?" He spoke in a small voice that sounded like that of a little boy.

He heard Alice sniffle but could not bear to look into her face. She wrapped her other hand about their joined ones. "I hope she will improve, Charles. I hope that very much, but if nothing else I think she chose to share her choices with you now because she needs your help to maintain them. Even if she does recover, one day she will not be here, and she needs to know that you will carry on her charity in her absence. That you have risen so quickly to your responsibilities must have convinced her you were ready to help her with this."

He clenched his eyes closed against the tears but they leaked out all the same. He could not speak, but he did nod his acceptance of this call, this charge to do right by the people who had suffered for the choices of others. He would rise up and be the brother Adam needed him to be, and he would assure Mrs. Gale that she would have a place at Foxcroft for as long as she chose without censure from him. They were heady responsibilities, and he felt the weight of them, but he also felt the lift of his mother's example. She had certainly suffered from all that had happened, and yet she had given charity as best she could.

Alice continued. "And your mother needs you to absolve her of the pain of the past, Charles. Only you can give her that."

He looked at his wife, unashamed of his tears when he saw her own. He reached out a hand and wiped the moisture from her cheek. She smiled at him so softly and tenderly that his chest warmed and his resolve strengthened.

"I cannot do it alone," Fenton said, certain he would fail if this were a path only he embarked upon. He did not have the luxury of bungling an attempt on his way toward doing it right.

Alice smiled. "You do not have to."

CHAPTER 34

On their way back to the house, Alice told Fenton of unlocking the wine cellar and he told her of his realization that he needed to set better limits on himself. "I will not interfere," she said, wanting to be sure he understood her regret for being so high-handed.

"Thank you," he said with a simple nod. It was odd how civilly the argument of the night before was resolved when things of such greater import demanded their attention. "You said you have some remedy?" he asked.

She nodded, but tried to keep her eagerness in check for fear of scaring him away. "Angelica root is known for creating a distaste for liquor," she said. "As well as a tincture of capsicum. Neither can be successful without your own determination, but they can help with the physical reactions and lessen the desire for drink."

He nodded quickly, and she was grateful he was willing to try her recommendations.

Dr. Jeffs had already arrived at the house, and when he finished his assessment he told Alice and Fenton what they already knew: Lady Chariton was getting worse. Fluid had continued to build up in her lungs, and the blockage had not eased—he suspected it was a growth of some kind. He suggested bloodletting to rid the body of the bad blood, and though Fenton was kind about his refusal, he was not interested in that course. Alice remembered that Lady Chariton had suffered greatly from a similar treatment in the past. When the doctor had gone, Fenton entered his mother's bedchamber in order to finish the interview he had fled from a few hours earlier.

Alice did not join him. Not because he didn't ask her to, rather she felt that he and his mother had far more to resolve regarding this situation, and she hoped, if it were just the two of them, that they would reach that resolution sooner. Beyond that, Alice had work of her own to do—her part of a plan she and Charles had developed while they sat beside the stream and let the truth settle into their bones as though it had always been there.

After nearly ten minutes of wandering through the carriage house and stable, trying to avoid the other servants, Alice finally spotted Adam near some cages on the far side of the enclosure. Fortifying her courage, she took a breath and moved in that direction, realizing as she got closer that there were rabbits in the cages. When she was close enough to hear Adam talking to the animals, she felt her fear soften. Though the words were not loud enough for her to hear, the tone was tender.

She stopped a few feet away from him, trying to determine the best way to get his attention, when he straightened and turned in her direction quite on his own. She smiled at him despite her nervousness, and he smiled back.

"Hallow," he said.

"Hello, Adam. Do you remember me?"

He grinned a bit more broadly, then pointed at the cages. "The rabbits are to eat the greens and will be big so we can eat the rabbits."

Alice startled. "Oh, well, yes, I suppose that is the way of things."

"I like rabbits. They do not bite."

"Oh, well, then that is good too." She took another breath to calm herself regarding this strange conversation. His ease in her company was surprising, and she wished she felt at ease herself. "What else do you like, Adam?"

"Frogs and birds and pudding."

"I like frogs and birds and pudding too."

"I do not like greens." He grimaced and wrinkled his nose.

Alice felt a real smile pull at the corners of her mouth. "Then it is a good thing the rabbits like them, isn't it?"

His grimace turned into a wide grin.

"Do you take care of the rabbits, Adam?"

He nodded proudly and then began to talk of the rabbits, and horses, and pigs, and chickens. As he talked, Alice began to see bits of Lady Chariton and Charles in his face—the straight line of his nose, the shape of his jaw—but she thought he favored Lord Chariton. She wondered what the earl would think of all that had happened here, all the secrets that were now known. She felt sure she knew where Lady Chariton's heart lay, but where did Lord Chariton's? Did he miss the son who could not be the heir? Did he push Charles away for the same reasons Lady Chariton clung to him?

It was some time before a groom interrupted the discussion with Adam, apologetic that Alice had found herself in Adam's company again. It was some time longer before Alice could convince the groom that she was not angry or displeased.

"But perhaps you could help me," she said. "Lady Chariton and

Lord Fenton would like Adam to join them for tea. I know he's been told not to cross the hedge, and I do not wish to confuse him by breaking the rules, so I wonder if you could help me set up a table and chairs in an area where he is comfortable so that the four of us might take tea this afternoon."

The groom looked perplexed, but Alice held his eyes until he realized she was both serious and amiable.

"Of course, my lady," he said with a nod.

"Very good," she said. She turned toward the rabbit cages and assessed the ground nearby. "Perhaps here, in fact. I think there is room."

Nearly an hour later Alice was adjusting the cushions on the wicker furniture that had been brought down from the sunroom when she looked up to see Fenton and his mother come around the hedge. It had not seemed possible for Lady Chariton to look frailer than she had this morning, but she seemed barely able to stand, and Alice wondered how much Fenton was having to help her. She *was* walking, however, and had not needed to be carried, which Alice took as a good sign. As she got closer, Alice was heartened by the brightness of her eyes as she scanned the area in search of Adam.

Fenton led Lady Chariton to her seat and helped her to sit, which was more like falling into the chair, she was so exhausted. He adjusted an additional pillow behind his mother, and met Alice's eyes only long enough to share a look that told her he was frightened. Alice smiled with more confidence than she felt.

"Are you comfortable, Mama?" Fenton asked.

"Yes, thank you, my dear," she said, patting his arm.

"Shall I go find Adam?" Alice asked. "He was here but half an hour ago."

Lady Chariton nodded with an eagerness that further warmed Alice's heart as she turned back toward the carriage house.

She found Adam on the front porch of his cottage, laying out leaves on the boards as though making a trail for a fairy to follow. It did not take much for him to agree to join her at the rabbit cages for tarts and biscuits, and she stayed ahead of his more lumbering steps so she could see the look on Lady Chariton's face when they rounded the side of the carriage house.

Lady Chariton's frail chest lifted, and her eyes went wide at the sight of her son. Alice wondered if mother and son had been in such close proximity since the time Lady Chariton last left Foxcroft twenty years ago. Alice's eyes moved to Charles, who looked tense. She gave him a small smile, then stopped in front of Lady Chariton's chair and stepped aside so that Adam could come even with her.

He did not seem to question why he was here and simply looked upon his mother and brother as he would look upon anyone else.

"Hello, Adam," Lady Chariton said, drawing his focus as she smiled up at him. Alice expected to see tears of regret and sorrow, but Lady Chariton seemed nothing but pleased to look upon her firstborn child, all grown up now—a man in every way except his mind.

"Hallow," he replied.

Lady Chariton reached a hand to him and, though he seemed reluctant at first, he took it and gave it a firm shake, as he would with a gentleman. Perhaps a bit too firm, if the slight wince on Lady Chariton's face was any indication. She recovered quickly, however.

"My name is Lady Chariton," she said. "I'm very happy to see you."

"My name is Adam an' I am pleased to meecha, Lady Cherron."

Lady Chariton laughed, a trilling kind of sound. Fenton watched the exchange rather tensely, but at his mother's laugh, his shoulders relaxed and he stepped forward. "Hello, Adam, I am . . ." He paused and Alice watched him work through something in his mind. "You may call me Charles."

"I am pleased to meecha, Challs."

Charles smiled more easily then and put out his hand for Adam to shake, which he did with the same quickness he'd shaken Lady Chariton's.

Alice tried to capture the moment in her mind—brothers shaking hands for the first time, but only one knowing the truth and the significance.

"Would you like some lemonade, Adam?" Alice asked. When she had spoken briefly to Mrs. Banner while the furniture was being arranged, she'd learned that Adam did not like tea. Mrs. Banner had made a tray with all of Adam's favorite things, but declined to join them.

"I knew this time would come," she said, not sad or regretful, just accepting. "And I am loathe to take anything from Lady Chariton within it."

"I like lem-o-nade," he said with careful pronunciation. "It is sweet."

"Yes, it is," Alice said. "Please sit down." She waved to one of the three empty chairs, then met Charles's eye and waved him to another. Adam took his quickly, eager for his treat, and Charles sat in the chair beside him. Alice poured four glasses of lemonade and handed them around before filling the plates with a variety of sweets.

"Adam," Alice said, smiling at the man who took to this impromptu lemonade break as though it happened every day, "Lady Chariton would love to hear about your rabbits."

"I like rabbits," he said with a nod before drinking half his lemonade in one swallow and eyeing the plate Alice was filling. "And frogs and birds."

"I like birds," Lady Chariton said. "But I do not like frogs very much. Tell me what is it you like about frogs, Adam?"

He was happy to do so and began prattling on about the way frogs hop and swim. Lady Chariton was entranced, as was Alice, until she looked up to find Fenton watching *her*, not Adam.

Without making a sound that might interrupt, he mouthed the words, "Thank you." Alice held his eyes and then nodded slightly. The simple acknowledgment filled her up, and she blinked tears away as she went about preparing another plate.

When she had handed around all the plates, she turned her attention back to the conversation, which had moved on to worms, and Alice looked at the three of them—Lady Chariton, Adam, and Fenton—each broken in his or her own way, each perhaps needing the others to be truly content. She wondered at the events that had brought them here. Had Lady Chariton wanted a different course and been bullied into this one, or had she seen the wisdom despite her own pain? At what point was Lord Chariton forbidden to come to Foxcroft? Why did Lady Chariton stop coming herself?

In time, perhaps Alice would learn the answers. For now, it was the very concept of time that concerned her. Fenton had asked Alice if she thought his mother was dying, and Alice had avoided giving a hard answer, not wanting to entertain the worst. As she'd thought of it in the hour since, however, and listened to Dr. Jeffs, she felt the truth of it settle about her like snow on a winter's day. Lady Chariton was in no condition to travel back to Berkshire, and Alice doubted she would regain the level of health that would allow it; she had been declining for longer than they had been at Foxcroft.

As much as Alice wanted to avoid the possibility, she feared Lady Chariton had indeed come to Foxcroft to die. The thought made Alice's heart ache in her chest. She could not imagine her future without Lady Chariton in it and did not see how they would cope, and yet Alice knew that they would. Rather than mourn her already, Alice focused on the singular hope that if these days were in fact Lady Chariton's last, she would die in peace and surrounded by those who loved her most.

CHAPTER 35

Every day for the next week, Lady Chariton had lemonade with Adam near the rabbit cages. Fenton attended each time and felt himself becoming more and more comfortable with the man who was his brother. He also had a stone commissioned for the grave of Mrs. Gale's daughter, and Alice's sketches for the gazebo were given to the carpenter in the village who was at work on an official set of plans. Life took on a kind of tense normalcy at the Foxcroft estate, but no one spoke much of the future. Instead, everyone focused on the present as much as possible.

Adam continued to call Mama "Lady Cherron" and always had some tale to tell of his day, mundane things that he made sound like an adventure. Mrs. Banner joined them now and then, and while Fenton knew it was painful for his mother to see Adam light up when Mrs. Banner rounded the corner, she never said as much.

One night, after Fenton had administered Lady's Chariton's laudanum—which dosage was becoming increasingly heavier to allow her to sleep—Alice asked her mother-in-law about the difficulty of Mrs. Banner's place in Adam's life.

"It is what I hoped for him," Lady Chariton said. She seemed to be growing smaller by the day. Her breath came in gasps, causing her to gulp for air between sentences. "He needed a mother and . . . she gave him everything I could not. Mrs. Banner is an angel . . . I am glad he has had so much love."

After that first week, a day of rain moved the afternoon event indoors, and though the fair skies returned, Lady Chariton's strength did not. A makeshift bed was set up in the drawing room, and Fenton would carry his mother down the stairs every afternoon and pretend his heart was not breaking to feel her wasting away a bit more each day. Adam attended their teas indoors until the day when Lady Chariton was too weak to leave her bed. From that point forward she kept to her room, where she slept longer and her breaths became shorter.

Alice spent some time each day in the garden, transplanting flowers and shrubs from one place to another, instructing Mr. Ambrose on what to order from town and what pruning was to be done. On a day when it was particularly difficult to watch his mother fighting for breath, Fenton found himself in the garden, looking at Alice's accomplishment. His wife was trimming something in another corner and did not see him right away, but when she did, she hurried to him, pulling off her gloves so when she reached him she took hold of his arm without soiling his coat.

"What is wrong? Is she all right?"

"She is all right," Fenton said, though they both knew that was an exaggeration. "But I feel I shall go mad if I don't do something other than pace from her bedside to the stove. Am I a horrid son to leave her side?"

Alice smiled and gave his arm a squeeze. "You are nothing near a horrid son, Charles. We all need our solace."

Fenton looked around, from the pile of new gravel for additional walking paths to the freshly turned ground that would show new foliage next spring, and then back to her face. "Is this solace for you?"

"Yes," she said with a nod. "Since the day someone gave me my very first garden, working with the soil and plants has been my haven."

"Why?" Fenton truly wanted to understand. How could *work* be a haven? Yet he knew it was for her—he could see it in her face when she came inside, could feel it in her words when she spoke of what she'd accomplished or what she would do the next day. He did not understand it, but he believed working in the garden was exactly what she claimed, and he envied that.

Alice inclined her head to the side before she answered. "I suppose I find comfort here because working in the garden gives me a sense of purpose." She looked over the garden, which to Fenton's eyes was all turned up and chaotic. "Without care and attention, a garden becomes wild and overgrown. The weeds move in and choke out the beauty of the place. When the weeds are kept at bay, the glories of God's first life-giving creations are allowed to flourish, bringing health and beauty and even nourishment to the world." She shrugged as though embarrassed for the depth of her words. "Perhaps it is arrogant for me to think it, but when I am at work in the garden I feel that I am working alongside God, bringing forth the best of things and sharing a special kind of joy with the world around me."

Fenton held her eyes for several moments until she ducked her head and turned away. She moved a few steps before Fenton reached out and took her arm. "Show me," he said in a low voice. "You have explained your plans for this garden to me in bits and pieces. Show me." He nodded past her toward the corner of the garden where she'd been working. "Let me see your vision of this place."

A small smile spread across her face, and he wondered if she'd been waiting for him to ask her this very thing. It felt good to have pleased her with the request.

"It will take some time for me to explain it all," she said. "Are you sure you don't mind?"

"Larkson is sitting with Mama, and I can think of no other thing in this moment that I would like more than see this garden through your eyes."

"Then we should start at the eastern entrance," Alice said, still grinning as she turned that direction. "It shall have an arched trellis soon enough, and clematis to cover it in time."

She began moving toward the entrance, but Fenton stopped her and put out his arm. "It would be unseemly for me not to escort you on this tour," he said.

"But I'm filthy, Charles," Alice said, shaking her head.

"Which is why I wear my country dress in the country," he said, using one hand to indicate his charcoal breeches and green coat. "I am not afraid of a little soil."

She laughed and took his arm. "We shall see about that, my lord. Perhaps I will ask you to help me pull out a sunken statue then."

"Let me at it," Fenton said, making an exaggerated display of looking around for the offending statue. "I shall show him who is master here."

She laughed again, and it filled him up as nothing had in the dark and heavy days of the last weeks. What would he do without her here with him? How would he cope? Somehow she had gone from an unwanted bride to his best friend. That alone gave him hope that he could find happiness beyond the lifespan of his mother, which was drawing to a close. He still could not imagine life without her, but somehow he knew that all would be right. As Alice had once said, he did not have to do this alone.

On a Tuesday, three weeks after the revelation of Adam's history, Fenton was keeping vigil at his mother's bedside through the night. He only realized he'd fallen asleep when he woke with a start, and then looked instinctively at the bed where his mother lay when he did not hear the rattled breathing that had begun two days earlier.

"Mama?" he said, still casting sleep from his mind as he blinked quickly. He turned up the lamp on the nightstand and moved from his chair to the side of the bed. Her face was soft, the pain gone from her expression, and her chest, which had toiled for breath these last days, was still. A sob escaped his throat as he fell to his knees and buried his face in the bedclothes.

A hand on his shoulder startled him. He looked up at Alice, tears in her eyes, as she sank onto the rug beside him. She put her arms around his shoulders and he crumpled, giving into the loss that he felt in every ounce of his being.

She was gone.

The woman who had loved him unconditionally would never again kiss his cheek or laugh at his jokes. The woman who had always seen the best in him would never again encourage him to rise to the man she knew he could be. His grief grew from a place low and primal within him until he was howling in pain and heartache. And yet

Alice's arms held him tight. She cried with him, mourned with him, and he found himself clinging to her as though she alone would see him through this dark place. She alone would help him find light in his life once again.

CHAPTER 36

There was not time for family and friends to travel to Devon for the burial. It was a small party, then, that attended Lady Chariton's casket to the family plot on the north end of the estate. She was buried next to a sister who had died young and near her maternal grandparents, who had lived out their lives at Foxcroft. On the far side of the small graveyard was a wooden marker for Mrs. Gale's child which would someday soon have a stone in place.

Alice suggested a memorial service be held for those friends and family who had not been able to attend the burial but who would appreciate the chance to visit her final resting place and say good-bye. Fenton agreed, touched again by Alice's thoughtfulness. A week after Lady Chariton's burial, Foxcroft was filled with guests.

Lord Chariton arrived with his chin high and his eyes dry, receiving the guests' condolences graciously. He said the right words and smiled the right smiles, but Fenton did not give his actions much credibility.

During the last weeks of his mother's life, she had spoken here and there of his father. She explained that before Adam had been born, the earl had not been so unreachable. Adam's disabilities had broken him in a different way than they had her. They had agreed to have children only until a son capable of being the heir were born so as not to risk another simpleminded child. That Fenton had filled that place had been both fortuitous and unlucky as it had ended the marital relationship of Lord and Lady Chariton and solidified their distance, which only grew from year to year.

"I had thought we were protecting ourselves through such an arrangement, but I regret it now," Lady Charition had said, closing her eyes to cover the pain she did not hide so well. "It did not ease our burdens, but only pushed us away from each other all the more. Your father remedied his pain by keeping distance from the people he once loved and taking pleasure from women he would never love." She opened her eyes and gazed at Fenton strongly. "He did not heal as well as I did, Charles. I bear some of that responsibility too."

Fenton did not like the pull of sympathy for his father that such commentary encouraged, but he could not help but wonder at it as he watched his father interact with the other guests. Fenton had a fair understanding of what it had cost his mother to give up her son. What price had it demanded Lord Chariton pay? And what did he think now of that decision? He knew that Fenton knew of Adam, and he must know that Fenton would take over management of Foxcroft. Was he embarrassed that Fenton knew? Was he defensive about the choice made all those years ago, or did he regret it?

When the time for the memorial service arrived, a group of twenty walked to the family plot, where the local vicar gave a sermon on the necessity of death and the continuation of souls. Fenton gave a brief eulogy and, though he looked at Adam, who was watching a blue jay in the trees, he did not introduce him to the group. Lady

Chariton had asked that they keep his identity a secret—not to save themselves embarrassment but for Adam's comfort. She did not want him to be confused. Though the rest of the party must have observed the simpleminded man standing with the teary-eyed cook, no one asked about it and no one who knew offered up the information.

It was a somber group that returned to Foxcroft, which had been outfitted to accommodate a meal for the group before many of them left for their homes. The distance between Foxcroft and London had reduced the number of those able to attend, but those who came truly cared for Fenton's mother, and it was gratifying to feel their sincere condolences.

It was after the meal was complete and people were conversing in small groups that Fenton noticed Lord Chariton was no longer part of the crowd. He extracted himself from the conversation he was having with Alice's parents and, with the aid of a footman, found his father in the earl's bedchamber, directing the packing of his trunks.

"Leaving already?" Fenton asked from the doorway, pushing away the desire to goad his father to anger. He swirled the lemonade in his glass as though it were brandy—of which he'd had none in almost two weeks. He missed it, but with the help of Alice's remedies and his own determination, he had found the strength to resist. However, there was still a strange comfort to be found in having a glass in his hand.

Lord Chariton and his valet both looked up, then Lord Chariton waved his man out of the room. When the door was closed, he turned back to his son. "I left important business undone in London and must return as soon as I can." He did not meet Fenton's eye and instead scanned the room as though looking for something to occupy his attention. "I hope you will be joining me in time for more education. Just because Parliament is not seated does not mean there isn't work to do."

Fenton watched this man—a source of such discord and contention in Fenton's life—and was surprised to feel some of his anger fall away. Yes, his father *had* paid a price—and the accounting had left him hard. It was a shame, really, that a man of such prestige and nobility could be so empty. Not only of compassion and kindness, but of life in general. What did Lord Chariton know of joy? What did he know of love and a gracious heart?

No sooner had the questions passed through Fenton's mind than he wondered how very close he himself had come to being just like his father. Perhaps not in the ways he had always feared, but in matters of making space for others in his life and feeling himself so far above the trivialities of emotions and heart. It humbled him to see it so clearly. But for the grace of God—shown in the love of his mother and the acceptance of his wife—Fenton might very well have been just as shut off as his father was.

Fenton had anticipated a confrontation with his father, a chance to berate and harangue him for all he had done wrong. After everything Fenton had learned these last weeks there was no reason whatsoever for him not to confront his father with the things he now knew. And yet now that the moment was here, Fenton felt that such an expenditure of energy would be a waste. If he wanted to become the man his mother thought him to be, he could not continue to feed the hatred that snarled and snapped each time Fenton was in his father's presence.

"I should like a week, at least, to get things settled here, then I shall come to London," he said calmly.

Lord Chariton eyed his son, wary of the conciliatory tone. "You have been gone four weeks already. That is no way to rise to your responsibility."

Fenton was unsurprised that his father would attempt to start an argument, but he did not show his irritation. Instead he absorbed the words, split them apart to find the truth within them, and reacted only to that portion. "I have been in communication with my secretary and will continue to do so. Feel free to send me any information I need to be apprised of in the meantime, but I very much need a week."

A week to make sure all was well with the household, and with Adam especially. A week to mourn his mother. A week to be with his wife and see her gazebo completed.

Lord Chariton's eyes narrowed, but he simply grunted. Then a smug expression appeared on his face. "I have taken the blame for the conditions your mother presented to you in order for you to avoid being cut off, but they were not all of my own making."

Fenton drew his eyebrows together.

His father seemed to take satisfaction in the reaction and continued. "You have laid all the blame for it at my feet and thought me the cruel and manipulative one, but I did not act alone. Your mother had a hand in it as well. She was not the innocent bystander you believed her to be."

Fenton felt his back stiffen but he kept his tone calm. "And what part did she play, then?"

"That you marry," his father said, almost spitting in eagerness to get the words out. "I cared not if you were saddled with some woman, but she insisted and would not back down. Why, I think that had I not agreed to it, she'd have supported me in the disinheritance." He lifted his chin, proud as could be of his power.

Fenton took a breath and let it out while he processed the information. "I cannot believe I didn't guess it," he said with a chuckle, ignoring the pang of wishing he could talk of it to his mother. But *of course* it had been she who wanted him to marry—she had talked of it for years, had expressed that very wish when he went to her in supplication of her help.

Fenton wondered, not for the first time, if she had known in London that her time was short. Had she pressed him to marry so she would be at his wedding? Had she known she would die at Foxcroft when she insisted on coming here?

"She really was the most shrewd of women," Fenton said. How he missed her.

"And she wanted that Stanbridge girl for you all along," his father added, looking irritated that Fenton was taking things so well. "From the first night she met her, she set you right in the middle of a trap."

"Ah, that she did," Fenton said, replaying in his mind the conversations he had had with his mother. She had been quite particular about Alice, but she'd never pushed him. She hadn't needed to. Fenton trusted her more than he trusted himself and had no hesitations in her choice of his bride. Well, until Alice turned on him, but Fenton understood that better now. While he had kept his heart guarded, she had laid hers open from the start, only to have him be horridly dismissive of her expectation. But they had come together naturally these last weeks. As Lady Chariton slipped away, they had become partners. Sharing the burden. Sharing the time.

"Mama always did understand me better than I understood myself." He met the eyes of his only living parent. "But I shall have to gain my own understanding from this point forward, won't I?" His voice dropped as the sadness set in. "I cannot tell you how very much

I miss her, Father. She was the greatest of women, and, now that I know her part in it, I only wish I could thank her properly for finding me a wife such as Alice. I intend to take full advantage of the good Alice brings into my life. I intend to do well by her and for her and for the family we will one day have."

"You think you are insulting me," Lord Chariton said, his chin still high. "But you are not. I am at peace with the choices I have made. I have no regrets."

Fenton held his father's eyes for several seconds and knew his father was *not* lying. He did not regret the things he had done. But he was also terrified. Terrified that he could have been wrong and that one day he would feel all the things he had determined not to feel. The loss of his firstborn son. The ruin of his wife's confidence. The distance of his heir. Likely, he would seek to distract himself with pleasure, perhaps a new mistress, maybe a new wife. But his choices would haunt him as Fenton believed they had already.

Fenton extended his hand and waited for his father to take it, which Lord Chariton did, though he seemed confused at the gesture.

"I want to thank you for giving my mother a comfortable life. She never wanted for *things* or security, and for that I am grateful."

His father shook his hand once before dropping it.

Fenton took a step backward. "Have a safe journey," he said, then turned on his heel and left the room. It was perhaps the only time in his life that he felt as though he had won an argument with his father, and the success of it filled him as nothing else he had tried before ever did—not ridiculous hats or silly behavior, not yellow coats or red leather boots. It was somewhat shocking to realize that the clothes and the silliness, the confrontations and the dissipation he had thrown in his father's face these years had never once left him feeling as satisfied as the truth had just now. His mind and his heart were clear as they had never been before.

He met Alice at the base of the stairs where she waited for him with a worried expression. "Where did you go? Are you all right?"

"My father is leaving," Fenton said quite calmly, then took the last drink of his lemonade. "I wanted to tell him good-bye."

Alice furrowed her brow, obviously unsure how to react to such a casual comment about the earl.

On a whim, Fenton leaned forward and kissed her on the forehead. "Shall we join the rest of our guests, my dear?"

She still looked confused, but she inclined her head before taking his arm. "Yes, my lord. I believe we should."

CHAPTER 37

Alice wandered through the quiet house. She had thought it joyless and cold when she'd first arrived, and while it was still in need of updates and repairs, there was an atmosphere about it now that was embracing. Lady Chariton's grandfather had built this house, and Lady Chariton had used it as a safe haven. There was something unsettling about the secrets it had kept, to be sure, but there was charity, compassion, and mercy too. It was hard to believe that Lady Chariton was not here, and yet part of her would always be at Foxcroft. In Adam and Charles, of course, but in the spirit of the place, the heart of it.

Lord Chariton had left soon after the service, claiming business in need of his attention. His discomfort at being at Foxcroft had radiated from him, and Alice could not deny she was glad when he finally left.

He did not ask after Adam and did not even look in his direction when Adam and Mrs. Banner had joined the mourning party at the graveside. He did not even react to Mrs. Gale's presence, though Alice had seen him notice her when he arrived and, later at the house, he'd watched her as she'd overseen the dinner, trying to hide her anxiety at his presence. Alice had felt disgust and irritation toward him but mostly she felt regret on his behalf. Despite her burdens, Lady Chariton had found joy in her life—could Lord Chariton say the same?

Assured that the guests staying overnight were settled and the house was still, Alice retired to her bedchamber and some time later slid between the sheets and turned down the lamp beside her bed. It had begun to rain that afternoon and the drops pelted the window, making her bedchamber cozier through its separation from the elements.

She felt her muscles relax as she closed her eyes and let the day wash over her. She would need time to absorb all that had happened, time to accept that she would never read to Lady Chariton again, or feel her nurturing kindness. It seemed that Alice was destined to go through life without a mother, but, oh, what mothers she'd had, if only for a short time each. She was grateful for their influence on her life and for the fact that, despite the sadness of this day, she had felt warm assurance that she had been part of something good these past weeks. She had done all she could to provide comfort to a woman who had changed Alice's world.

And Charles.

Alice sighed in the darkness. As a girl, she'd thought she was in love with him; it seemed silly to have thought *that* was love. During these past weeks, his history and his soul had been laid open at her feet so that she could see him in his brokenness, in his pain, but, somehow, in his wholeness too. He'd trusted her, he'd needed her, and she'd been at his side through the greatest trial of his life—losing his mother, who had loved him so well.

Alice hoped she could love him in such a way that he would never know what it was to live without love. What she felt for him was far more than childhood fancy, and though her mind often wandered to those matters of matrimony they did not yet share, it was not her focus. She believed such things would come in time and not only to produce an heir. One day he would come to her, and she would be ready.

Sleep swirled about her, making her thoughts slippery enough that when Alice first heard the creak in the darkness, she jolted to wakefulness. A moment later, she heard the sound again. Fully awake now, she realized the sound was the hinge of the door connecting her room to that of her husband's. It had remained closed all these weeks, until tonight.

Alice's heart began to race as she heard her husband's feet cross the floor toward the side of the bed he had used on those first nights when he did not have a bed of his own.

"Alice?" he asked in a whisper.

"Charles?" She rolled onto her side to face him, though all she could see was a faint outline in the dark.

"I find my bed most uncomfortable tonight," he said in a nervous voice that made her smile despite her own growing nervousness.

She scooted toward the right side of the bed and pulled back the covers on the left.

He quickly accepted her invitation, but rather than stay on his side as he had before, he moved toward the center. He first touched her shoulder, letting his hand linger there, and then moved his hand down her arm until he took her hand in his and lifted it to his lips. Though his mouth was warm against her skin, she shivered all the same.

"Alice," he said again, with such depth and intimacy that her whole body tingled.

It was all she could do to keep her voice level when she answered. "Yes, Charles."

"I realized something today."

"Yes?"

"I am *not* my father."

Alice felt her throat tighten and quick tears rise to her eyes. "No, you are not."

"Will you help me?" he asked, his voice a whisper once again. "Will you help me become the kind of man that my mother could be proud of?"

Though her whole body felt flushed from his touch, a different type of warmth began in her chest, moving out to her shoulders, hips, arms, and feet. "You *are* that man, Charles. She has every reason to be proud of you already."

She felt his hand on her face then, and as he moved toward her, she rolled onto her back. His face hovered in the air above her, only just illuminated enough to see. He brushed the hair from her forehead before his eyes met hers.

"Every good thing in my life, I owe to my mother, but the greatest of the gifts she gave me is you." He paused, then lowered his face to hers until a mere breath separated them. "I could not have managed these last weeks without you, Alice. I need you so much. I love you."

The words washed over her, and she felt the cracks of her insecurity be filled by the sincerity, by the way she felt the words in her very soul. He *did* need her. He *did* love her.

"You are the best man I have ever known, my lord," she whispered into the space between them. "And I shall love you all the days of my life."

He smiled then, the moonlight revealing a glimpse of the boy who had become a man who had finally come to her. He drew closer, and she lifted her face until their lips touched in the darkness. Within the essence of connection she realized there was purpose in the waiting. They had both grown and because of that, their intent was now pure and their future was bright with possibilities.

Alice savored the moment of understanding that she would never again not belong where she was. She was needed. She was wanted. She was whole.

ACKNOWLEDGMENTS

Thank you to those readers of my prior works who have followed me into this new territory. I am so blessed to have such wonderful support. Thank you to my writing group for helping me brainstorm and piece together Alice and Fenton's story: Nancy Campbell Allen (*My Fair Gentleman*, Shadow Mountain, 2016), Becki Clayson, Jody Durfee (*Hadley, Hadley Benson*, Covenant, 2013), Ronda Hinrichsen (*Betrayed*, Covenant, 2015), and Jennifer Moore (*Meg Finds Her Prince*, Covenant, 2015). Jen also beta read this story last minute, allowing me to work through the roughest parts before I turned it in.

Thank you to the team at Shadow Mountain for making this story shine, and specifically Heidi Taylor and Lisa Mangum for helping make the story just right.

Thank you to all those fabulous historical writers who have documented the time and ambiance of the Regency period so well that writers like myself can see the world too and show it to our readers.

And thank you to my husband who makes it possible for me to write romance and believe in happily ever afters. I am greatly blessed to love what I do and do what I love and return each day to the embrace of my family. Grace and gratitude I give to God for all this and more. May you feel His comforting hand guide you on your journey.

ABOUT THE AUTHOR

Josi is the author of twenty-five novels—including the twelve-book Sadie Hoffmiller Culinary Mystery series—one cookbook, and has been part of several coauthored projects and anthologies. She is a two time Whitney award–winner (*Sheep's Clothing* in 2007 and *Wedding Cake* in 2014) and the Utah Best in State winner for fiction in 2012. She and her husband, Lee, are the parents of four children and live in Utah.

For more information about Josi, you can visit her website at www.josiskilpack.com.

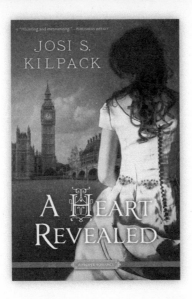

FALL IN LOVE WITH A PROPER ROMANCE

★ "In this haunting and mesmerizing novel, Kilpack weaves an emotional tale of fleeting fame in Regency-era London. . . . Amber's struggle with her new life, her despair, and her hope for a happy future are stirring and real. Kilpack paints an extremely vivid picture of Amber's suffering and reawakening, as well as her initial frivolity and callousness. Exceptionally moving and full of rich period details, this delicate romance is a real winner."
—PUBLISHERS WEEKLY

★ "The unusually well-crafted prose draws the reader along... More literary than other romances....A very compelling read."
—KIRKUS REVIEWS

"Romance fans won't be able to put down this singular and unexpected story." —LIBRARY JOURNAL

Paperback / 336 pages / $15.99
ISBN 978-1-60907-990-1

Learn more at ShadowMountain.com
or josiskilpack.com

SHADOW
MOUNTAIN

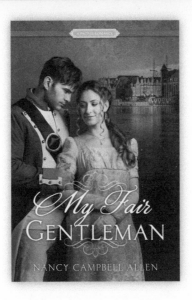

COMING SOON

Jack would rather be at sea than fixing the mistakes of his grand-father, the late Earl of Stansworth. Instead, he finds that inheriting his grandfather's wealth and title—and securing the welfare of his sister and mother—means joining the ranks of high society and living with the aristocracy. Luckily, Ivy Carlisle, the granddaughter of a dear friend of Jack's late grandmother, is willing to teach him etiquette and properly introduce him into society. Jack soon learns that his challenge isn't surviving his new lifestyle but surviving the conspiracies against him—as well as keeping himself from falling madly in love with his new tutor.

Available January 2016

Paperback / 256 pages / $15.99
ISBN 978-1-62972-095-1

Learn more at ShadowMountain.com

SHADOW
MOUNTAIN